THE MCMURDO TRIANGLE

BRADLEY LEJEUNE

Copyright © 2023 by Malcolm Bradley and Martin Lejeune

All rights reserved.

No part of this publication may be reproduced, distributed, or transmitted in any form or by any means, including photocopying, recording, or other electronic or mechanical methods, without the prior written permission of the publisher, except as permitted by U.S. copyright law. For permission requests, contact http://www.BradleyLejeune.com

The story, all names, characters, and incidents portrayed in this production are fictitious. No identification with actual persons (living or deceased), places, buildings, and products is intended or should be inferred.

Book Cover by Martin Lejeune

Also In Series

THE MCMURDO RIFT

THE MCMURDO TRIANGLE

THE MCMURDO WAR

PROLOGUE

I'm saying we call it," came Nelson's voice over comms from the SS *Carol Dearing*. Ben sat in the modified space of the SS *Ellen Austin*'s cockpit and gave a long sigh.

He was in a cramped space, with only room for two seats. A curtain hung across instead of the door that might once have led into it. Ben's wife, Mandy, had tie-dyed the curtain back in more optimistic times. When they had bought the Ellen Austin, where he was now sitting had been a part of something more akin to a bridge, perhaps ten times the floor area. Wasted space that Ben, Mandy and Tariq repurposed to hold equipment vital for their mission.

"Okay," Ben agreed, trying to hide his reluctance. He looked out at the *Carol Dearing*, close enough to appear as a bright spot. Its dull, metallic surface caught a little of the light from the distant radioactive inferno of the large blue star. The star was the only object within almost a billion kilometres of the two ships. It was a very showy star. At a little over a hundred million years old, it was likely already halfway through its life. They had been hoping that there might be another less visible, but more interesting and rarer object to be found out in the cold, featureless expanse of the McMurdo Rift. Then again, they had been hoping for months now with nothing to show for it.

"I was so sure this was the place," Ben added, almost grinding his teeth as he spoke. "All the data, the gravity effects that can't be explained by that blue giant alone, and nothing bloody else for a few light years that could complicate our sums."

"And what with the disappearances," Nelson said, although he sounded a little like he was placating Ben. If he just wanted to move on and be one step closer to putting this whole stupid venture behind them, well, Ben couldn't blame him. Still, points for effort.

There had been great excitement as the two ships, working together to scan for gravitational anomalies, had headed towards this remote part of the McMurdo Rift. A remote part of an already outlying area of the United Terran Colonies. But that was where great discoveries were so often made, on the edge of things. While the *Carol Dearing* focused on the discovery of invisible matter and forces, with the idea of parallel, unseen dimensions even on the table, Ben's crew were just as whacky and "fringe theory." Few disputed the theoretical work behind wormholes was sound. It was just that no one had ever seen one and no one knew how to detect one, if they even existed. Ben, Mandy and Tariq thought maybe they did, and the two ships combined the efforts of their specialist sensor arrays to look for evidence.

The crews of the SS *Ellen Austin* and the SS *Carol Dearing* were all scientists who had given up comfortable lives to prove theories that could have huge repercussions for humankind. If they were true. Success would also guarantee a lifetime on the speaking circuit afterwards.

"Hey, you wanna come over for dinner later?" Nelson asked in his thick Caribbean accent. "Kristin's cooking plantains. We've had them growing just behind the drive cones."

Nelson, as far as Ben was aware—and they went back to university together—had been nowhere near Earth, let alone the Caribbean. Yet he had never adequately explained the almost musical accent he spoke with.

Ben laughed. The *Ellen Austin* was a hotchpotch of a ship, an aging shell repurposed with a narrow budget and a lot of ingenuity by Ben and Mandy. Mostly Mandy, who was three times the engineer that he was. In some parts of the ship, things only seemed to keep running by the use of tape, spare bolts and wishful thinking. Yet, a visit onto the *Carol Dearing* always felt like a journey into chaos.

"I'll check with the boss."

"Is that Mandy or Tariq?" Nelson asked.

Ben leaned forward, even though he had the comms running into a headset and knew there was no one else in the forward part of the ship with him. "He's had enough. I mean, I can't blame him in a way, although no one put a gun to his head and made him come. But he's constantly grumpy and showing the signs of having been out here too long."

Tariq had been a brilliant student when Ben had taught Interstellar Physics at the Mariner Valley University on Mars and had worked in small ways on Ben's theory. He was now, Ben felt, suffering a little buyer's regret.

"It'll be nice to get an evening away from him to be honest, so I'm sure Mandy will be up for it. And we haven't seen Loki in weeks. That young man grows more every time I see him." Eight-year-old Loki, Nelson and Kristin's son, sported a great shock of thick, curly black hair that added almost six inches to his height the last time Ben had seen him. He ran riot in the many spaces of the *Carol Dearing*, which, like the *Ellen Austin*, had been a medium-sized freighter before being turned to its current role. It could have housed a hundred people or more, where now it held only three people and a lot of scientific equipment.

They had turned the very structure of both ships to the sensitive scans that would hopefully pick up the proximity of the wormholes. Effectively, they lived within huge antennas that were, despite their appearance, a marvel of engineering. So far, however, it was all for nothing.

"Okay," Ben said, "let's get going. One more sector to try. We'll prep and jump. You be ready to follow."

Less than five minutes later, the *Ellen Austin* jumped. One moment it was drifting along serenely in space and the next it jerked forward and streaked away at astonishing speed. It went past the vast, hot, distant star that would, in cosmic terms, burn itself out in the blink of an eye.

Unseen, because Mandy had been grabbing some crash time and Tariq had run to grab a drink, a small hit flashed briefly across their records. They wouldn't see it at all until they analysed the data a day and a half later.

The *Carol Dearing*, despite some familiar concerns when it first fired up its drive, was ready to follow a few moments later. Except that it never followed and, several hours later and millions of miles away, the *Ellen Austin* reported it missing.

ONE

Mark Franklin, one time war hero, current time bar owner, stood beside the inner door of the airlock on the SS *Olympic's* starboard side, waiting for an entourage from the SS *Majestic*. The entourage would include the captain of the newest, largest luxury liner from the shipyards of Proxima. Gus, a fitness instructor and Franklin's best friend, stood next to him. Arnold Philby, the *Olympic's* captain and Franklin's former military commander, was a little further down, opposite the airlock.

Compared to Arnold, the other officers and even his friend Gus, Franklin was feeling underdressed. He had planned to wear his white tuxedo until, after a quick run around his cabin, he'd found it crumpled and creased beyond use. If he couldn't go the whole way, Franklin decided just not to bother.

That wasn't quite true, as he had found some black Chino-style trousers and a scarlet shirt. Franklin felt pleased with himself that he wasn't just wearing jeans and a T-shirt. His smugness had evaporated when he arrived in a long line of uniforms. It got worse when he discovered that even Gus was wearing a snazzy suit with a bow tie and an antique-looking waistcoat with a pocket watch underneath. Bloody show off.

"Well, look at you," Franklin said when Gus stopped beside him. The fitness instructor dwarfed Franklin. He was huge and bald, with a black porn-star moustache standing out against his brown skin.

"Good, huh?" Gus replied.

"You look like you robbed your great, great, great, great granddaddy's casket."

Gus beamed, unperturbed by Franklin's acid remark. "Did you see the *Majestic* as she was coming in to dock with us? She's bloody huge. Twice as big as the *Olympic*."

"No, I didn't see her. Ha, *Majestic*. We should rename the *Olympic* the 'SS *Stupendous*' just to piss them off." He wasn't sure that Gus had thought through the implications of having a bigger, more modern and luxurious ship arrive to begin running the route the SS *Olympic* already struggled to make a living on. "I'm don't know why we need to be here," Franklin went on, "the bloody barman and the fitness instructor. What does the snooty-ass captain of the SS *Majestic* need to see us for?"

Gus frowned down at him, finally catching onto the fact that Franklin wasn't as excited as he was. "Arnold wanted you here, of course. You're like the ship's mascot."

"Fuck off," Franklin shot back. He was not the bloody ship's mascot.

In the middle of the line, quite far from where they were, Captain Philby leaned forward and nodded to him. Franklin tried to do his best to hide his body and clothing behind Gus—which, thankfully, wasn't too hard.

His relationship with Arnold in the two months since the events that had led to a Koru cruiser being destroyed had been in a strange place. Although his captain, friend and former military commander had stuck his neck out a long way to help Franklin rescue Gus, Franklin's ex-wife and her Koru first mate, this had only followed a previous attempt by Arnold to stop him leaving the ship. It was also possible that Arnold had tried to take possession of some precious ore that could mean everything to the defence of the UTC.

Afterwards, Arnold had put forward some plausible deniability on that matter, but Franklin's jury was still out.

Lieutenant Stanley now stepped forward and cycled the airlock manually. The airlock didn't require him to operate it. Doing so was a formal gesture between ships of the line to take personal responsibility for opening the airlock. Lieutenant Stanley, formerly a sensor operator on the bridge of the *Olympic*, had been promoted and placed as second-in-command to replace Lieutenant Commander Sneed. The previous XO had been removed from duty following an unfortunate alliance he had made with a former politician during the whole Koru cruiser episode, which had led to a brief mutiny.

Sometimes, Franklin almost felt guilty for doubting his old commander, because Arnold had risked a lot and was even forced to regain control of his own ship to help Franklin rescue his friends. Yet there was that nagging doubt, the sense that Arnold had his own reasons for putting the *Olympic* in harm's way as he had done.

"What's the bet the captain of the *Majestic* has an even more impressive moustache than Arnold?" Franklin whispered to Gus.

"Not taking that bet."

The airlock opened with a slight hiss, as it never balanced correctly with the internal pressure of the ship. It hadn't worked properly for at least the last twenty years.

The first person to step through the opening would be the captain of the SS *Majestic*, who would—along with his crew—spend some time aboard the *Olympic*. Then Arnold and several members of his crew would visit the *Majestic*, most likely so they could have all of its super up-to-date loveliness rubbed in their faces.

"How old must you be to run a ship like the *Majestic*?" Gus whispered.

"If Arnold is anything to go by, then almost dead." Franklin was in a cruel mood today. For one thing, Arnold was only about ten years older than him.

The person who walked through the airlock was certainly not ancient. They did not have a moustache, either.

"Permission to come aboard," the captain of the *Majestic* asked in a rich but feminine voice. She had brown hair tied back into a neat ponytail that she wore beneath the regulation cap. A short-sleeved white shirt came with epaulettes on the shoulder. It was smart, it was regulation, but by comparison Arnold looked likely hot and overdressed.

"Permission granted," Arnold answered. "Welcome aboard, Captain Smith."

"Sounds like a made-up name to me," Franklin whispered to Gus.

"Wish I had taken that bet now," Gus replied.

Gus, his suit jacket and bow tie now removed, but the snazzy waistcoat still hugging his muscular torso, poured a drink from the bottle that Franklin had just put on the bar for him. Franklin hadn't opened up yet as things were quiet, because the whole ship exchange thing was being done during a pause between runs. In fact, the *Olympic* was due in for a few days' maintenance, which would give the *Majestic* a head start on it.

Things had gotten even more quiet since the issues with the Koru a few months before. The news feeds remained vague about things, and there was even some doubt whether a Koru cruiser had been destroyed after all. If it had, the most popular theory, according to a poll on *StellarCast*, was that it was an accident. Perhaps they were testing some new piece of technology and things went wrong. Which was true... sort of.

Still, there had been that footage of the ancient planetary defence emplacement on Regus Mining Station firing into the sky. A test, perhaps... a drill? And the rumours of a significant explosion before that on peaceful Enceladine. Too many worrying, dangerous-sounding events in a supposedly quiet part of space had been affecting the visitor numbers.

Which begged the question why another, even bigger, ship was also being put onto the McMurdo run.

Gus swilled his bourbon whisky around and took an appreciative sip. "You hear about the ship going missing, right out there on our route?"

"No," Franklin replied, his mind still half on passenger numbers and the future of his bar business. Of course, *he* had been in the emplacement... And on the Koru cruiser... And, um... on Enceladine. He needed to stick to being a businessman; there was little profit to be found in fighting shady aliens.

"Yup," Gus went on, almost as if Franklin had asked a question. "The SS *Carol Dearing*. It was travelling in a convoy of two ships. The other one reported it missing. Just plain old disappeared."

"That so?" Franklin said, then sipped his own drink, his eyes narrowing. He thought he knew where it was going. "The *Carol Dearing*?"

Gus leaned forward, confirming that Franklin was playing right into his hands. As he did so, the subtle lighting caught where the deep brown of the skin on his bald head shone slightly. "I looked up the name," he said, almost conspiratorially, "and you wouldn't believe what I found. Turns out that a seagoing ship of the same name vanished in the Bermuda Triangle centuries ago back on Earth."

"Oh, for fuck's sake," Franklin exclaimed. "Not this McMurdo Triangle shit again."

Gus sat back again, spread his arms wide in an "I'm just giving you the facts" gesture. "You can't tell me this isn't weird."

"Space is still a dangerous place," Franklin said, "even in these modern times. Shit happens. Someone slips up on maintenance, a crappy navigator flies you right into a big rock. Who knows, maybe even pirates."

"But the ship they're travelling with knows nothing about it, sees nothing? Tell me that's not weird."

"Could be Koru-related," Franklin said.

Gus frowned at him. Their destruction of a Koru cruiser two months before had put paid, at least for the time being, to the aliens' mining operations on Enceladine. There had been no sign of them since, so maybe he was just letting his prejudices come into it. Not that he had ever felt much prejudice against the Koru people. They had turned the tide of the civil war against Earth, yet he could not hold a grudge. For one thing, he had been responsible for too many Koru deaths himself.

"Shouldn't it be a pyramid?" he added.

"Huh?"

"Technically, it's the 'McMurdo Pyramid,'" Franklin said. "A 3-D triangle, being in space and all. Then again, wouldn't the Bermuda Triangle have been a pyramid? Planes disappeared in that, as well as ships."

Gus grinned. "Surely that was more of a prism. Anyway, there are reports of weird disappearances going back to the first years of humans coming here. Too long ago to just be the Koru."

"Right," Franklin poured himself another bourbon and, with it, saw the chances of him opening the bar any time soon decreasing. He used to be more motivated.

Gus knew Franklin as well as anybody these days and did not miss the tone beneath that one spoken word. "Man, you are no fun. Typical space jockey."

"What?"

"No imagination."

"Harsh."

"And arrogant."

"...Harsher."

"Can't you even conceive of the possibility that there's something more going on here than what you can see?" Gus said. "That the explanation might lie beyond the things you already know about. Where's your wonder? Isn't it possible there're things out there—" he flung out an arm, indicating the vastness beyond the ship, "—right out there, which are beyond your comprehension?"

Franklin grabbed the bottle of bourbon and stood up. "That's enough whisky for you, mister."

Gus laughed, his frown loosening. "I'll make a believer of you yet."

Franklin harrumphed and put the bottle back behind the bar, then got ready to open up. "I hope the next run's a good one and the *Majestic* doesn't fuck with business too much. I swear this McMurdo Rift route is just dying, anyway, and my bank balance is wondering whether buying a bar in the quiet, arse-end of nowhere is the 'set me up for the rest of my life' acquisition I thought it was going to be."

"Don't you be quitting on me, man," Gus said, sounding quite serious about it. "Anyway, what else you going to do if you leave here, go back into the military?"

Franklin scoffed at that. "I think that ship sailed a long time ago." He came out from behind the bar, started taking chairs down from tables; Gus helped. "Although I would like to travel more."

"You live on a starliner."

"That does one little route over and over. I want to see more places." Franklin caught a disparaging look from Gus. "Hey, just now you were asking me where my wonder was."

Gus smirked. "Have you considered being a courier?"

The look Franklin gave to Gus might have frightened a smaller man. "Go fuck yourself."

"I bet Sarah would give you a job," Gus pressed, looking like he was enjoying himself. "Just think of it, working for the ex. Or," he stopped, a chair in each huge hand, his expression letting Franklin know that inspiration had just struck, "you could set up a rival courier firm and there could be all this angry competition between you that ends up with lots of sexual tension. Then you'll have to... you know... consolidate your businesses."

"Her husband's only been dead a couple of months, man," Franklin chided, "have some goddamn respect."

"I didn't hear a 'no' there."

TWO

"The banging and explosions mean that someone is shooting at us." Engee pointed out.

"Thank you!" Sarah replied, thinking how it could sometimes sound like her first mate was being sarcastic, even though it was not supposed to be a Koru trait.

"At least we are due to put the ship in for a service," Engee said.

"They charge more for fixing holes." Sarah gritted her teeth as she pulled the flight controls hard to the right.

"I have them," Engee said, "three ships on our tail... more further back. Might they be pirates?"

"I don't think the *Mutt's Nuts* looks valuable enough," Sarah said. "Someone else really wants our cargo, I think."

"Missile is incoming."

"Or doesn't want our employer to have it."

The *Mutt's Nuts* was heading towards a gas giant, the swirling mass of its atmosphere a dirty orange that was filling up the front view port. When they left one of its satellite moons only minutes before, there had been no sign this was anything other than a normal run.

"Could this be the local authorities?" Engee asked.

Sarah thought of the sealed impact box strapped into the back of the cargo bay. It was the lot of a courier if you ever wanted to do any business. You asked questions, you got signed declarations, but you rarely got eyes on the contents of your package. "Local authorities usually at least give warning before they start shooting."

"You have much experience of this?"

Yes, Engee was learning sarcasm. "Any chance of us making an FTL jump before the drive is blown off?"

"There is a planet in the way."

Sarah pulled a hard, spiralling dive to the left, punching the air from her lungs as the ship's environmental systems failed to compensate. One of the pursuing ships was so close that it overshot, and Sarah could see it through the curving view port. It looked to be short-range, likely not FTL equipped. If the others were the same, then they just needed to jump to get away from them. "No planet now," Sarah replied, "so can we jump, please?"

"We are still in the system," Engee argued. "We could go straight through something."

"There's a lot of space out there, she'll be fine."

"Why, if the ship is named after a male dog's testicles, do you say 'she'?"

"Engee!" Sarah screamed. "Missile coming!" The missile had overshot when Sarah had performed her sharp turn but had been quick to get back onto the tail of its target.

Sarah was sure that she heard her Koru navigator huff right before the FTL engaged and they became quite literal passengers, the Mutt's Nut's navigational system having now taken over a process of what amounted to moving extremely fast in a straight line. The little manoeuvring that took place during FTL flight could not be done by a human. Even a fractionally too-tight turn could break the ship apart or overwhelm the environmental controls and crush everyone on board or otherwise tear them apart.

In-system obstacles were unlikely to be seen in time to be avoided, even by the ship's sensors and systems. Tense moments passed and, happily, they didn't die.

"What we just did was illegal," Engee said.

"Don't care," Sarah replied. "And I've decided that we need some guns. Or a cannon. A great, big, fat, nasty, blow-the-shit-out-of-the-motherfuckers cannon."

The *Mutt's Nuts* touched down on a small patch of land around a kilometre away from the town. It kicked up dust from the dry, hard ground beneath it, much of which settled on the ship in the landing pad next door. "Landing pad" was generous; it was a roped-off piece of field.

Del Rey Starport had somewhat over-advertised itself. Sarah should have realised this when she saw the low cost of the landing rates. Sometimes it was nice to kid yourself that you had got a bargain, that you were a keen, canny operator. Of course, she wasn't sure there were any alternatives, because the pathetic-looking collection of buildings in the distance didn't look like it rated more than one place to park your spaceship.

"So, where is the meeting point?" Engee asked as they stepped down the personnel ramp at the back of the ship. Sarah's husband had not so long ago left the ship by that same ramp and she had never seen him again. Would she ever walk the ramp without thinking of him? Sarah could not decide whether that thought terrified or comforted her.

"Yup," Sarah said, echoing Engee's doubtful tone. "Somewhere here. That's all I have. Still, there's not a lot of town to search."

The ramshackle collection of buildings was even worse close up, made of some—presumably—locally sourced, dark-coloured wood that split as it weathered. The buildings were only one or two storeys high and some of them were part-collapsed. Something that might have passed for a 'Main Street' ran through the middle of the town, identifiable because it was a wide thoroughfare, although it didn't have a true road surface, only mud-covered, compacted gravel.

There was a definite Wild West vibe, which was helped by the fact that the inventively named "Del Rey Hotel" even had saloon doors on one corner, like someone was trying to be ironic. "A good place to start," Engee agreed to the silent question when their eyes met.

Sarah half expected the patrons to stop and look at the two of them as they walked in, especially as one of them was Koru. Engee did sometimes have that effect. Yet no one seemed to notice them, and the bar was busy. The clientele was more diverse than Sarah had expected.

Sarah watched the barman pull something luminous from the pump and, curiosity just about trumping fear for her own health, ordered a pint of it. She had been drinking more than was healthy these last few months, she knew. It was nice to feel other than normal. Engee, pulling a face, ordered just a half and looked at it like she had ordered a glass of radioactive pond water. It amazed Sarah how much she had come to read in those pupilless eyes.

The bar was dimly lit, even though it was the middle of the day outside. Sarah struggled to make out the faces of those more than about five metres away, and no one appeared to be looking out for their arrival. With a shrug, she took out her T-slate and brought up the last message sent from her employer, activating the option to let the client track her slate. Considering the fact that they had been shot at over the package, perhaps it wasn't the most sensible idea. Sarah just wanted the job over and done with.

The man who, moments later, appeared out of the dim recesses of the room, wore a long, brown coat—*proba-*

bly cow hide, Sarah thought with an inward roll of her eyes—and a wide-brimmed hat that was too big for his head. He had to push it up and out of his eyes.

"Dusty," the man said in a high, thin voice. She wondered whether he was passing comment on the state of things outside, or whether he was introducing himself. He was tall and slender close up, towering over Sarah.

"Sarah," she ventured, as Dusty's eyes turned to Engee.

"You're..." he began.

"I am," Engee confirmed.

"That a problem?" Sarah jumped in, her natural protectiveness where her Koru first mate was concerned leaping to the fore.

"Nope," Dusty said matter-of-factly.

"Are we doing the delivery here?" Sarah asked, glancing around the packed bar.

"Here is just fine," Dusty answered.

"Because there were other people who wanted this package too. Or, at least, didn't want it getting to you. I don't know. But I know that they had guns, and they were fine shooting the guns at us."

Dusty smiled an impenetrable smile, letting Sarah know perhaps more than he intended. Sarah felt the risk and fragility of what she was doing for a living. Maybe somewhere in the central systems, working for a big company—because independent couriers did not make money in those central systems—she could have thought of herself as simply a delivery person. A distributor, with only respectable clients. Out here, things weren't always going to be that straightforward. All the same…

Fuck this guy, Sarah thought. Handing her T-slate to Engee, she pulled out the impact box, which was small and easily fitted into the backpack she wore. "Activate the receipt and release the funds. If I stay here any longer, I think I'm going to get a bad case of the yokels."

"Can't do that," Dusty shot straight back.

This brought Sarah up short. She hadn't been expecting that. She considered using the small but heavy and nigh-on unbreakable box to brain Dusty with. There were, however, far too many witnesses.

"You can," Sarah said, "it's easy. You take out that slate that told you we were here, and you press the button that acknowledges delivery." She shook the box in her hand, no longer caring how fragile it might be. "You get this," she went on, "we get paid and nobody called Dusty dies."

Dusty spread his arms wide, the silly cowhide coat coming open, as if he were trying to show that he didn't have any weapons. Sarah wasn't sure that would stop her from killing the bastard, anyway. "No slate," he said, sounding smug.

"Fine," she barked and turned for the door. This guy was just dicking her about. Maybe she looked like she didn't care but there was a sick feeling in her stomach. The overhaul that the *Mutt's Nuts* was due wouldn't happen if she didn't get paid today. In fact, flying and eating would become a lot more difficult.

"I'm not the employer," Dusty quickly added. "He's out the back."

Sarah stopped, hackles raised. *Right, where you kill us and take the box with none of those pesky witnesses.*

"He wants to see you," Dusty went on, that high, reedy voice sounding a little more sinister to Sarah's ears.

Sarah turned back around. Engee, who had been slow to follow her boss' cue, was still by the bar, her hand hovering near the untouched, luminous half-pint, like it might be a weapon. Perhaps it could be. "Get him to authorise the payment and I will be right back there to see him."

Dusty didn't look impressed, so Sarah backed towards the door. "You'll never reach the landing pads," Dusty called after her. It worked; she stopped again.

Sarah glanced at Engee, whose opaque eyes regarded Dusty with what might have been an impassive look, if Sarah hadn't known her better. Her skin, which was now almost always adapted to the browns and dull-metal greys of the inside of the *Mutt's Nuts*, gave her an oddly insubstantial presence in the dimly-lit bar. "Stay here, would you," Sarah said. "If I'm not back in ten minutes, then the *Nuts* is yours. Treat her well."

"She will be a 'him' when I am in charge," Engee called after her.

Sarah followed Dusty through a hallway to the hotel part of the building. A mezzanine level overlooked the reception area and, heading up and onto it, she found a man sat at a round card table, playing solitaire. He had a white suit and hat and, before Sarah even heard him speak, she somehow knew that he was an Earther.

"Ms Carter-Shah," the man said, without looking up from his game.

"Mrs," Sarah corrected him. Hearing the man use her full title, including the maiden name she had kept during her second marriage, somehow caught her off-guard. Of course, it was the name associated with her courier business.

"I apologise," the man said, although he did not sound contrite. Indeed, he had one of the most neutral-sounding voices Sarah had ever heard, and he continued to look at his game.

"That's fine," she said. "Just pay me and we'll call it quits. We have this system where I deliver your package and you give me money."

"Of course," he said, unperturbed by her attitude. He picked up a T-slate and Sarah watched her own device as he confirmed receiving the package. She turned and shoved the box at Dusty.

"See," she told him. "Easy." Dusty's eyes narrowed.

The man looked up at Dusty and, with a dismissive gesture at the box, said, "Get rid of that, would you?"

Sarah raised an eyebrow as Dusty disappeared into a room at the side. "Wasn't that urgent after all, then?"

The man returned to his cards and turned the top one over, then scrutinised what was in front of him. "That?" he said. "There's not even anything in the box."

Sarah bristled. "I almost bloody died for that box of nothing."

"It was a test," the man shot straight back. "Which you passed."

"A test? So the people in those ships at Jenus were not trying to kill me?"

The man pouted in a maybe-maybe gesture. "I left instructions that you were not to be destroyed, but I have a history of hiring overachievers."

"If you're trying to buy me out on behalf of Carey-All—" Sarah began, bringing up the name of the Proxima-based mega distribution service that was perhaps the biggest reason independent couriers could not make a living on the central routes.

The man waved away her objection. "I need you to do a job for me. A real job this time."

"If you can hire a mini fleet to try and kill me, you can hire a faster, bigger courier service than my one," Sarah pointed out.

The man looked and smiled. At least, that's what she thought it meant when the left side of his mouth pulled downward. That, or he was having a stroke. "But I want you."

He picked up his T-slate again and, a moment later, a set of coordinates specifying location in space popped up on her own screen.

"I need you to pick up a package here," the man said. "Then take the package to a location within the McMurdo Rift."

"McMurdo Rift?" Sarah echoed. She had been planning to avoid the McMurdo Rift as much as possible.

"You know the area?" the man asked, his attention now staying on Sarah.

"Well enough," she answered, seeing her opportunity. "Quite a way out, though. It's going to cost."

Not even a beat passed, and her T-slate flashed again. The number wasn't as long as the coordinates she had received, but it wasn't far off, either.

"Will that be enough?" the man asked smugly. She had not been able to stop her eyes from widening. He had a right to be smug.

"It'll do," Sarah squeaked, losing the detached cool she had been trying to cultivate during their encounter. But then a thought came. "Is this danger money? Am I likely to get shot at?"

"Let's say it's 'importance money,'" the man answered. "This package must get to where it's going."

Sarah kept her eyes narrowed. "I've got an overhaul booked in, and some repairs. It can't wait."

"How long?"

"Two or three days."

"Three works well," he said. "Perfectly, in fact. But once the job begins, speed will be of the essence."

Sarah had a heavy feeling in her chest, the sense that this was too good to be true, that she needed to take the smaller payday and leave, get the ship fixed. Of course, she would not be able to afford that cannon she wanted. She glanced down at the slate again. "I'll need some of this up front."

For the first time, the man frowned. "How much?"

How much do cannons cost? "Half now."

"Twenty percent," the man countered.

"Forty."

"You're nowhere near, Mrs Carter-Shah," the man said, a note of warning in his voice.

"Thirty," Sarah said with a roll of her eyes. She needed to get better at this negotiating stuff.

"Twenty-five now," the man replied. "That is plenty for you to fly off with, what with me having nothing but your word that'll you'll do the job. And you'll keep this off your work system. I'll send you the funds directly."

"Then twenty-five percent more at pick-up," Sarah tried, pushing her luck, "and the other half upon delivery." She had the sense that this was highly illegal. Well, highly *something...* The sooner she got her hands on as much of that enormous sum as possible, the better.

After a moment, he nodded. "The first twenty-five percent will be with you by the time you are back on your ship."

She also wondered why an old Earth politician had come all the way out to Del Rey to conduct his business. It had been bugging her since the moment she had seen him. A name still would not come, but the man's face was familiar. She wondered if he knew who she really was, where her history lay, what she was doing during the war and who her deceased husband had been. He had originally called her "Ms" and not "Mrs."

Strange times, Sarah thought to herself. *Strange times.* She felt a sense of dread as she went out to find Engee. There was an inevitability to it. She would soon be returning to the McMurdo Rift.

THREE

Franklin opened the bar but got very little custom for his efforts. It was possible that the tour of the ship for the *Majestic*'s captain and bridge crew had kept everyone else busy and on longer shifts, so they couldn't trickle into the bar as they often might. Arnold could have at least done him a solid and brought them all by for a drink, he mused. In fact, perhaps Arnold had taken them to the *other* bar. Traitorous bastard.

He was closing his afternoon shift half-an-hour early and was considering whether to even bother for the evening, when a voice spoke up from the near the entrance. "Not too late for a drink, am I?"

Franklin turned to see the SS *Majestic*'s captain stood there. She was alone, with no accompanying junior officers of either the *Majestic* or the *Olympic*. Not even Arnold. Her hair was down—a shimmering dark brown that bounded around her shoulders—so maybe she was off duty.

"Of course not, Captain."

"Kate, please," she said, walking across to take a stool at the bar. She looked tired and rubbed at her eyes.

"Captain Kate?" Franklin tried with a mischievous grin. Why had he said that? It sounded like flirting. Sometimes he just had problems with systems of authority now that he wasn't in one. Well... not really. She was an attractive woman up close. Younger than Arnold, likely, but older than Franklin. Her chestnut-coloured eyes were enormous, dark pools that made him wish she was his captain.

Stop it, Franklin.

"If you like." The grin was tired but humoured him. She rubbed her eyes again.

"What will it be? The first is on the house."

A suspicious eye peeked out from between her fingers.

"Yes, it is a bribe," Franklin said. *Stop. Bloody. Flirting.*

The captain put her hands on the bar and squinted at the optics. "Gin? Whatever's good." Franklin reached back and selected something that he hoped would impress. "So why would you be bribing me?"

"So that you will give me a job when the *Majestic* puts the *Olympic* out of business," he waved a hand to encapsulate his little cocktail bar, "and me with it."

She giggled. He liked that a captain could giggle. "Between you and me, I think we're a temporary addition to the McMurdo Rift route, placed here to instill some confidence. I'm not sure why else they would send us out here. No one has actually told me that, so don't take it as written, but I bet we'll be gone in a few months at the most, and hopefully the *Olympic* will be busier again after."

Franklin inclined his head. "Makes sense, I guess. Send the civilian fleet's biggest, smartest new ship, and that tells everyone there's nothing to worry about."

"Yes," Captain Smith said, "the *Majestic* really is something, as your officers are about to see this evening."

The way she spoke the words, it was like she rattling off the company line and letting Franklin know. It endeared her to him.

"If you don't mind me saying so," Franklin said as he placed the drink in front of her, "you are young to be in charge of such a ship."

"I had a command on the SS *Nomadic* before this. But between you and me, I'll confess that I have no idea why they gave me command of such a ship when there were other more qualified captains out there for the *Majestic*. Your own Captain Philby, for one thing."

"I'm not sure Arnold is the type to be jealous," Franklin reassured her. "So I wouldn't be worried on that count."

"Of course. The two of you have quite a history."

"We go back a way," Franklin replied, inclining his head. He was sure that Captain Kate Smith knew who he was, that this was likely why she'd come to his bar. Sometimes he just felt that he should erect some glass and stand behind the bar for everybody everyone to peer at. Might be more profitable than selling booze if he charged entry.

"I have an ulterior motive for coming and sampling your wonderful gin," Captain Kate began.

Oh, here we go, Franklin thought. But what came next was not quite what he'd been expecting.

"I'm hoping to steal you from your captain and from the *Olympic* for a little while. I've got five bars over on the *Majestic* and very little staff. Even fewer of them with any decent experience. And, to top it off, no bar manager or anyone qualified to oversee things on this first trip."

"Technically, Arnold is not my captain. This bar is one-hundred percent mine."

"Of course, I forgot that. But, either way, I could do with your help and... Seeing as the *Olympic* is going to be in dry dock for at least a few days." The way she shrugged was far too alluring for a senior officer. "I'll make it worth your while. Even if you can only spare one run through the McMurdo Rift, it would just get things going for us." She swigged back her gin impressively. "And you'll be top of my list to be hired if the *Olympic* ever goes out of business."

"Tell you what," Franklin said, a wonderful idea occurring to him. "You don't have the room on this run for an extra fitness instructor, too, do you? I know someone who would love to spend a week on your ship."

Walking through the airlock between the two ships was a bit like walking through some sort of magic portal that transported you to a different universe. Although the *Olympic*'s airlock came out on a straightforward corridor, the *Majestic*'s airlock fed into an impressive and almost hall-like reception area. If you've got it, flaunt it. That seemed to be the general idea.

Everything about the *Majestic* was bigger, from the corridors to the doorways and, of course, to the bar. The *Majestic* had five, so Franklin had been told, rather than the two that the *Olympic* had.

Having suffered through the ballroom, the conference centre, the mini aquarium—really, a mini aquarium—and many observation decks, shopping areas, pools, fitness centres, a spa and so on, Franklin sneaked away from Arnold, Captain Smith and the others. They were talking about ship logistics, which was highlighting the difference between the two ships as much as anything, but with Captain Smith trying and failing to be humble about it and Arnold trying just a little too hard not to look bothered. Either way, Franklin was so-o-o not interested, instead heading off to find himself the smallest bar on the ship. Judging by his experiences so far, this would presumably be the closest bar to his in size, and he entered a cosy little cocktail place.

There was a young woman behind the bar, not much over twenty years old, with her strawberry-blonde hair tied back into a ponytail and a silver ring through her nose. She wore a copper-coloured waistcoat over a white blouse, which seemed to be the general uniform for service staff on the *Majestic*. Dark, crimson-coloured decor and amber lighting gave the bar a close, intimate feel that Franklin could appreciate. It was, however, empty.

"I'm surprised you're open," Franklin said as he approached the bar. "Are all the bars on the ship open?"

The young woman gave a thin smile. "Yes. On a regular schedule since we left dock."

"Even though you won't have any passengers until tomorrow?"

"Captain Smith wants the ship operating at full capacity at all times."

"Hmm, not exactly efficient. Is the captain a bit of a slave driver then, is she?" he said with a mischievous grin.

A small smile touched the young woman's eyes, if not her lips. "What can I get you?" He noticed that she didn't answer his question.

"Bourbon, please," It came in a faceted glass that was much nicer than the ones that Franklin had in his bar. "Have you worked on a passenger liner before?"

"First bar job, first passenger liner."

The captain wasn't kidding about the lack of experience in the staff. The more Franklin was thinking about it, the stranger it seemed that they would put out such a ship and not staff it better. He hoped that at least the crew was more experienced. He came back again to how young Captain Smith was, compared to the usual stuffy old farts who commanded the civilian fleet.

This young woman on the bar appeared reluctant to engage in any lengthy conversation, which was something she needed to get better at. For Franklin, a bar person needed to be prepared to provide some company, or at least a willing ear for the customers. He probed gently again. "My name's Mark, and I might join you from the *Olympic*."

She smiled at that but was still turning out to be a bit of a blank slate. Trying not to feel like he was hitting on her, Franklin peered at the shiny, golden pin badge attached to her waistcoat. "Chloe, is it?"

"Yes."

"How did you land this sweet gig with no experience," and, maybe more to the point, he said, "all the way out to here in the McMurdo Rift?"

"I'm working for a year before university, and my uncle got me the job."

"Your uncle?" A penny dropped in Franklin's brain. "Chloe..." he said, adding with a strong, wary question in his voice, "*Little Mouse?*"

The young woman's brow creased, her face darkening. "What?"

"You're Arnold Philby's niece, aren't you?"

Chloe's face reddened.

"I'm Franklin," he said, although this brought no apparent recognition on her part. Franklin remembered a picture—one of very few—in the captain's quarters, which was at least ten years old and of a bright-eyed little blonde girl, shyly looking up at the camera from underneath her brows.

"There you are!" came a roar from behind Franklin, the voice familiar but the tone less so. Franklin looked over his shoulder. "And there you are, too. I noticed you had slipped away, Mr Franklin." Arnold headed around to the side of the bar and beckoned his niece over to him. "Little Mouse!" he exclaimed, his arms enfolding his niece. She didn't flinch the way she had when Franklin had said it.

"Uncle Arnold," she said, and hugged him.

Arnold turned back to Franklin. "Seeing as Captain Smith is stealing you for a run, would you mind keeping an eye on my niece here?"

Although Arnold could not see it, Chloe appeared to bristle at the suggestion. She did not, however, say anything to protest.

"I'm not sure why the captain needs me here," Franklin said, "but she's paying well."

Arnold raised his eyebrows in agreement. "They seem to have enough staff, at least, but there are a lot of passengers who will board tomorrow for their first run. Captain Smith and I were just talking about it. Not a full complement for the *Majestic*, of course, but more than I've ever seen on the *Olympic* at one time." He failed to hide his bitterness over those last few words.

Arnold turned back to Chloe. "I've got time for a scotch before the captain's dinner begins." She smiled eagerly and moved to get him the drink he had asked for as he took a seat next to Franklin.

"I don't have to go to that dinner, do I?" Franklin asked.

"I should think you do," Arnold replied. "You agreed to come over here."

"To help run the bar and because I felt nosey," Franklin said. "Not to attend posh dinners."

"Captain!" came a voice from the doorway and they turned to see Lieutenant Stanley stood there, looking red-faced and out of breath. "I've been looking all over for you. You're not a part of the comm system over here." The second-in-command almost appeared to chastise his captain.

"I know that," Arnold replied good-humouredly, then pointed to the ceiling and the walls. "They do have a comprehensive surveillance suite in all the public areas, however, you could have just asked them to find me. What's the fuss?"

"It's an encoded message for you, Sir," Lieutenant Stanley said, waving a small slate, "straight from the admiralty."

FOUR

Arnold stood in the middle of the captain's office on the *Olympic*, working a thin, light blue plastic dongle between his fingers which bore the insignia of the UTC Navy on it. He sighed, trepidation working its way through his gut—although there was excitement there, too, he couldn't deny that. He had been promised something after the episode with the Koru shield cruiser, although, as with everything else in life, he had needed to be patient about it. Arnold reached forward, pushing the dongle into the desk in front of him.

It was an encrypted communications chip. Whatever discussion he was about to have was to be private; the military didn't send out physical chips very often.

His desk sprung to life and the words "Message connection request in progress..." hung there in the air before him.

It was only about ten seconds before the call connected, even though it seemed like a yawning great chasm of time, and two uniformed men appeared. They were standing one next to the other, almost as if they had known the moment he would make the call. One was in the dark green ground forces uniform, his ruddy, Caucasian face pockmarked, while the other was in the equally dark navy blue of the UTC Navy, which Arnold had briefly worn after the war, and had a distinguished, dark-skinned face, his facial hair showing traces of silver.

He had already made acquaintance with the man in the navy uniform, Admiral Maxwell. Knowing his top military brass, Arnold also recognised the other man.

"General Spencer, Admiral Maxwell. This is an honour."

"Thank you for calling so quickly," Admiral Maxwell said. "My apologies for the cloak and dagger nonsense of the chip."

"Not at all," Arnold replied, although the chip had made him a little nervous.

"We understand you were taking a tour of the *Majestic*," General Spencer said conversationally, with something approximating a warm smile. "Quite some ship, isn't she?"

"She is, General," Arnold agreed. "I've been spending the last few hours holding my envy in check."

"Still not a patch on the best navy ships, though, eh?" Admiral Maxwell said. "Ours are ships built to do a job as efficiently as possible."

Although there was a part of Arnold that enjoyed standing and shooting the shit with top military brass, he wanted them to get to the point.

Perhaps Admiral Maxwell picked up on it. "We—" he indicated the general as well, "well, both the general and I, we were impressed by your report on the Koru activity in the McMurdo Rift area that you dealt with a few months ago, along with their operations on Enceladine and, of course, the reported attack on Regus."

"I'm glad to hear that, Admiral," Arnold said. Nothing appeared to have been done, however, no apparent reaction from the centre of human governance to the blatant Koru disregard for proper behaviour in neutral space. Let alone genuine concern for what they were up to there. "Although I was disappointed by the lack of a UTC response." He knew the admiral would agree with him, but Arnold couldn't help but find himself glancing across at General Spencer. The last time he had spoken with Admiral Maxwell, the man had offered him a job—reenlistment into the armed forces—although with no firm start date. He had heard nothing in the months since and, naturally, had started to doubt it would ever happen.

"Well, that is why we are contacting you, in a manner of speaking..." Admiral Maxwell said. "We would like you to consider joining up again."

Ah. The admiral was pretending in front of General Spencer that he had never made the offer. Whatever politics were at play here, he did not care. That dangled carrot had been agony to deal with these recent months, and on more than one occasion he had thought about reaching out to the admiral.

Still, wise to play along. "I'm honoured."

"That's a yes, then?" It was General Spencer who spoke up, the beady blue eyes that set in the centre of his ruddy face now sharp and intent. He was invested in Arnold joining up again.

He looked over at Admiral Maxwell and, when he spoke, Arnold imparted a tone into his voice that he expected the admiral to pick up on. "Why now?" *When I've been waiting for these long months.*

If Admiral Maxwell caught his light jibe, he did not show it. Instead, the two high-ranking officers shared a telling look. The general then leaned forward and tapped away on the desk in front of him. "I'm sending something over to you."

The projection in front of Arnold now filled up with a holographic representation of two civilian ships, the two military officers still visible behind them.

"These are the SS *Carol Dearing* and the SS *Ellen Austin*," Admiral Maxwell said. "They had chartered a flight plan that took them through the McMurdo Nebula."

"The *Carol Dearing* has now disappeared," General Spencer said. "Sensor records from the *Ellen Austin* do not offer any good explanation. It is there one moment and disappeared the next."

Arnold's eyes narrowed as he peered at the representation of the *Ellen Austin* in front of him, the analytical part of his brain pushing away those mind-fogging and attractive thoughts of his reenlistment. "When you say, 'one moment'...?" he asked.

The general reached forward and tapped again, and now a feed of the sensor data popped up into the bottom corner of the image. Arnold reached out towards it, sweeping a finger sideways in the air. "This must be an older sensor suite on the *Ellen Austin*," he told them, "judging by the low refresh rate."

"That's right," General Spencer confirmed. "You still know your stuff, Captain Philby."

"So, if some sort of missile weapon had hit the ship?" Arnold posited.

"Depending upon the speed they were travelling at—relative velocities and all that—it's possible they could miss it on the *Ellen Austin's* sensors, yes," Admiral Maxwell answered. "But there's no sign of what might have fired such a weapon. That would be harder to miss."

Arnold recalled his conversation with Admiral Maxwell when the initial job offer had come. Talk of phantom ships and unexplained ship disappearances. He had voiced his doubts at the time and the admiral had rebuffed him, but Arnold couldn't stop himself. "We're not thinking the McMurdo Triangle, I hope?"

Quite the opposite of last time, Admiral Maxwell grinned, his thick moustache bobbing up and down as he did so. "Or pyramid."

"No," General Spencer said, all seriousness.

"So, Koru then?" Arnold suggested, getting to the point that the two senior officers had, no doubt, been waiting to make.

"We would like to know for sure," Admiral Maxwell said. "Considering your recent run-ins with them, you'd be a good man to look into this further. And, if it comes to putting a request in front of the council to send a proper military presence out there, that experience might well count for something—add weight to the words, as it were."

So, there it was. He had never expected the job to come without strings attached. Arnold Philby was a realist about these things. He was to be an extra mouthpiece when the time came. He didn't trust the Koru, never had done since they had got involved in what should have been an exclusively human war. The UTC had been too pleased with how the aliens had turned imminent defeat into victory for them, that no one had asked "why" the Koru had become involved when they did. Yet, he was a fair, rational man ready to give anyone and any*thing* the benefit of the doubt.

Either way, his answer here had never been in doubt, as Admiral Maxwell knew. "How soon would you need me?"

"There is a ship that could dock with you by the morning," Admiral Maxwell answered, then grinned. "A fast little gunboat that will make it to Proxima in half the time that anything civilian could."

Arnold blew out a breath. That *was* short notice to leave the *Olympic*, although he knew that these influential military men could smooth the way as much as he needed them to. His new XO, although very capable, was still learning the ropes. "My current XO was my sensor operator only a couple months ago," Arnold said. "I'll be leaving a hole at the top of the command structure here."

"Time is of the essence on this, Captain Philby," General Spencer pressed.

Chloe popped into his head, his beloved, gentle niece. *Little Mouse.* She was now working her first job behind the bar on the SS *Majestic*, which was about to tour the McMurdo Rift where ships were vanishing and the Koru, it seemed, might still be up to no good. A part of him wanted to march back onto the *Majestic* and pull her straight off of it, to bring her back to Proxima with him. But he had no authority to do that, and she would never forgive him for it. What good would he be able to do her from the *Olympic?*

The best way he could protect her and the whole of the sector was to head back to Proxima and ensure that a military presence was sent out to it. "But they will make it work," he told them. "They're well trained and can handle a run or two without me until there is a replacement."

FIVE

Gus and Franklin were making the most of the shiny new facilities on the Majestic by having their first fencing bout for quite some time. Gus was winning convincingly, so that hadn't changed. Sure the fitness instructor was barely breaking a sweat under his mask, Franklin's own vision was becoming blurry when a lighting fast lunge from Gus leaped over his sword and struck him hard in the shoulder.

"That's match," Gus said, the unseen grin somewhere behind the black mesh of the helmet clear to Franklin's ears.

They both stopped and removed their headgear, Franklin working hard to bury his frustration. As a kid, he'd never been the most competitive, always able to take losing well. That was always a little easier when you hardly ever lost at anything, of course. It just felt like swords should be his thing.

"Different ship," Gus jibed, "still kicking your ass."

"Hey, be nice! I thought you were supposed to be a fencing instructor; where's my constructive criticism?"

"You mean, like 'Give up'?"

"Asshole."

Gus seemed pleased with himself. "Anyway, I only give private fencing lessons to someone I'm trying to sleep with."

Franklin shook his head in amazement. "That you're happy to say that out loud makes me wonder why I brought you onto this ship with me."

With a cheeky grin and an upward tilt of his handsome head, making his lack of hair an asset, Franklin's friend looked like he was pondering something. "I wonder if Captain Smith is interested in fencing?"

"Don't you dare!" Franklin said. "Anyway, I thought you were carrying a torch for Engee?"

Franklin knew that would hit a nerve. "I am!" Gus spluttered. "It's just that, you know… it's been a few months. Man has needs."

Franklin arched his eyebrows. "You're a model of restraint, you."

The two of them left the gymnasium and went through to a changing room, pulling out the bags that held their fencing equipment. "To be honest," Gus said, "I feel like a bit of a spare part around here, so stabbing you with a sword and fantasising about women is a welcome distraction."

"Me too... The first bit not the stabbing bit. Or the fantasising bit. Well, the stabbing would be a welcome distraction if I could actually hit you."

"I can understand my boredom. I came aboard the Majestic for a break, but I thought you were being brought on to oversee the bars on the ship. The bars seem busy to me and, although the ship doesn't have a full passenger complement, it can't be that far off."

"And yet," Franklin took up his friend's thought, "all the bars are running just fine and mostly with experienced staff in place. Except for Arnold's niece, but she's in the smallest, quietest bar and good enough at her job. The experienced staff get touchy when I start looking over their shoulder and I can't really blame them, either, because they just don't need me to be telling them anything."

Saying all this out loud, Franklin could feel his own frustration. It felt like they had brought him onto the ship under false pretences, as he was plainly not needed. "I've ended up just helping Chloe when she is on shift for something to do. Sweet kid, by the way."

"It is weird, though," Gus said. "I mean, seeing as Captain Smith is paying good money for you to be here. I'd watch out for an ulterior motive." He shrugged. "Or just take it as a paid holiday and find a jacuzzi to sit in."

They both carried on getting changed until Gus brightened and reached into his sports bag, pulling out a T-slate. "Thinking about it and seeing as you've got the spare time, have a look at what I've been working on. I'd like your opinion."

Franklin watched as the slate projected a 3-D hologram that was familiar to his experienced eyes. He had spent an awful lot of time in the McMurdo Rift, so knew straight away that the star map in front of him was a representation of the overall area, although there were some unfamiliar green dots within it. His internal "Crazy Gus Shit" detector went off. "Oh no, this isn't a McMurdo Triangle thing, is it?"

"This is serious..." Gus complained. Then added, more quietly, "But yes, it's a McMurdo Triangle thing."

Franklin pointed at the hologram. "This is what happens when you have too much time. Or not enough sex. Or both."

"Just hear me out, okay?"

Gus pointed to the green dots that were spread throughout the projection of the star field. "These dots represent the last known position of ships that have gone missing within the rift, right, all of them for the last decade, at least as far as I've been able to find out."

Franklin had long ago stopped being any sort of expert on ships and the amount that might go missing on average. All the same, there seemed to be an awful lot of those green dots spread throughout the projection. Gus reached down and tapped the slate's screen, causing between a fifth and a quarter of the green dots to vanish.

"The ones left now disappeared in the last six months," Gus said.

Shit, that was a lot of disappearances in six months.

Gus tapped again, now leaving around half of the green dots. "And this is the last three months."

"Fuck..." Franklin said, letting go a long, whistling breath, which pleased Gus. "It doesn't mean some hell portal is swallowing them up and transporting them to another dimension, though," Franklin pointed out. "Or whatever you conspiracy theorists think is going on. Weirdoes."

"No-o-o. I mean..." Franklin could tell that Gus wanted to disagree with him about the hell dimension thing. But he had Franklin's attention, so moderated his craziness as he went on. "You're, er... probably right. But then what else is doing this?"

"Pirates? Who knows what the Koru were up to before we blew up their shield cruiser?"

"But the *Carol Dearing*," Gus pointed to one of the multitude of green dots, out towards the one edge, "that was reported as missing less than a week ago. It's still happening." Gus waved his hand to encompass the entire map. "And this is too much for pirates or malfunctions."

"Do you know that?" Franklin pushed. "No offence, Gus, but you're a gym instructor who needs a better hobby. Is this really too much? In all the vastness of space, all the hundreds of thousands, probably millions of ships flying around the UTC and the neutral territories every day?"

If Franklin had expected that to stop his friend, he was to be disappointed. Gus switched the view. "Denebola area. Covers a similar distance as the rift." There were only a smattering of green dots on this one.

"But that's close to Earth and Proxima. Hardly a lawless backwater."

Gus flicked over again. "Jenus and Harman." And again. "Leona." These were a little more spattered with green than Denebola, yet still barely a tenth that of the McMurdo Rift map.

Gus came back to his first projection. It was a lot. Why are we even still doing this run? Franklin wondered. "So, why is no one apart from you talking about it? Why did it take the events of a few months ago to spook people?"

"One word," Gus said. "Koru. They may have helped win the war, but anyone who ever saw pictures of that mothership you destroyed worries about the Koru." Franklin's shoulders tightened at the mention of his famous deed. "You can be the biggest flag-waving UTC nut ever, but you still know that Earth beat the UTC and then the Koru rolled over Earth's forces with ease."

"Earth's much-depleted forces," Franklin felt honour-bound to point out. But Gus had a good point. The UTC had spent its entire existence since the end of the war with a neighbour that had, during that war, been revealed as much more powerful. An alien neighbour who did not do openness and communication, not beyond the pperfunctorypoliteness to maintain some semblance of diplomatic relations. No wonder things on the Olympic had got so quiet. He was suddenly gladder than ever that the *Majestic* was doing the run to build confidence again. As long as it left again once that had happened, as Smith had theorised it would.

"I'm still going with pirates," Franklin said.

"But then people would know it was pirates. Even in somewhere like the rift, so empty and big. These ships are just vanishing."

"Maybe they've got some sort of stealth technology, so no one sees them coming." He was reaching a little.

"You're reaching there."

"No, I'm not." There was something about these "discussions" with Gus that turned Franklin into a twelve-year-old who didn't want to lose any argument.

"If the military doesn't have stealth ships..."

"They do. Low cross-section, sensor-defeating paint and all that."

"And how is something like that going around pirating all these ships? Making them just vanish?"

Franklin pointed a finger, getting into it now. "Or cloaking."

"Piss off!" Gus clearly thought that Franklin was poking fun at him. Another time, maybe he would have been.

"No, I'm serious. Well, kind of. There was a project towards the end of the civil war that was like cloaking a ship. The way it went, the ship sort of half-slides into a parallel dimension and becomes almost invisible in doing so. No sensor signature, and invisible unless you're almost on top of it."

Gus' eyes went wide. "You're kidding me."

"I'm not."

"Parallel dimensions? Right."

"You needed to pay attention in school, Gus. Parallel dimensions are accepted scientific fact."

"Alternate realities and shit?"

"No. These are... thin places, with barely any of the physics of our four-dimensional universe. Pretty useless until someone figured they might be able to temporarily hide a ship in one. Then still pretty useless, as it didn't work.

"I was kinda part of it. A back-up pilot for the prototype. I mean, the whole thing was a bust. The prototype was destroyed in the first live test, people died. But there was a war going on and a lot of people were dying, so there was no fuss about that. They dithered about whether to build another one, then discovered it had a fucking huge flaw. A by-product of tearing the membrane between dimensions which, if you knew what you were looking for, would make it really easy to detect."

"So they canned it?"

"The Koru joined the war and that took the decision out of their hands. Maybe they would have fixed the flaw, but a great big mothership was heading for Earth and the resources were needed elsewhere." Franklin shrugged. "For all I know, the UTC found and continued the work. Enough former officers joined the combined forces after the war. Maybe someone who knew something. Hell, maybe someone went private with the tech. Enough big corporations out there. Over a decade later, maybe someone got it going without the thing atomising the moment it pierced the membrane.

Gus sat down, blown away by what Franklin had told him. It was mad, Franklin guessed, yet until moments ago it had been just another forgotten bit of his past. Gus looked up at him. "Could it be that?"

"It's far-fetched. But then what explanation for all your little green dots isn't?"

"Pirates with cloaking technology. I'd love to know if that was the case. You said there was a flaw?"

Franklin nodded. "Devastating, if you know what you're looking for." His forehead creased as the name came back to him from well over a decade before. "Phase-field particles. They resonate at a very specific frequency. Easy enough to pick up. Shit, I could probably put something together if you gave me the right stuff.

Gus stood up, drawing himself to his full, towering height and raised his well-shaped eyebrows at his friend.

"No," Franklin said.

"Aw, c'mon. You said you were bored. Imagine if we got to the bottom of this."

"We won't. For one thing, even if I built it, we would have to send it through the ship's sensors to get anything like a decent range."

Gus pushed him playfully in the shoulder, the same one he had struck earlier.

"Ow!"

"Let's build it first, worry about the rest later."

About ten minutes later, Franklin and Gus walked into the ship's smallest bar—which, amusingly, was called "Franks"—to find Arnold's niece working behind the bar and only three of the tables occupied by drinkers.

Franklin walked straight up to the bar. "Morning Chloe," he said, "two bourbons please."

"Bit early, isn't it?" Chloe said with a slight grin. She was, as Arnold had described, quiet as a mouse, but Franklin discovered she had a sense of humour. Chloe was opening up and making the occasional cheeky comment, although always in her own understated way. It was, however, a work in progress, and she looked horrified by her own comment, glancing over at the customers at their tables, perhaps worrying that they might have overheard and taken some offence. It was all very Chloe.

"We need some thinking juice," Franklin replied.

"Franklin has figured out how someone is blowing up ships all over the sector without being discovered." Gus said, far too loudly.

Chloe went pale. "What?"

Franklin shoved Gus. "No, that's not..." Several patrons were now looking over them with worried expressions. "I've just got to..." Franklin drifted towards the end of the bar, "do some stock ordering. Chloe, can you pass me the admin slate?"

Chloe turned and grabbed the bar's admin T-slate for Franklin and handed it to him, while he continued to edge away from the customers. "I think we're good for stock. It's not been busy enough in here to get through it."

Franklin smiled awkwardly at her and backed away further.

"Be a week before we'll need to do an order from the stores," she added, her eyes narrowing.

Franklin grabbed Gus' arm and pulled him over towards the other side of the room, hissing at his friend as he went. "What's the matter with you? You'll scare half the ship to death; and this is all still just theorising, you know. A bit of fun. I'm only doing this to keep you from propositioning the ship's captain or something. And we won't find anything."

Gus just shrugged, like he didn't understand quite what the issue was.

"And then there's the fact that this could get me into quite a lot of trouble," Franklin added. "So let's not draw more attention than necessary, eh?"

Gus leaned forward as they sat down at a table. "Nice. Do tell."

"Although the ordering system is set up to offer only what each department needs," Franklin explained, gesturing with the slate, "the stores is all one place. Theoretically, I can order what I want and see if anyone bothers to check if it's really needed in a bar. Bet they don't."

"What are you going to order?" Gus asked.

"The parts to build a radio wave detector." Franklin rolled his eyes. "One that will pick up the right frequency for the phase-field particles. I mean, I'll have to look up how to do it, but I've got a general idea of the sort of stuff I need. Didn't you ever build a receiver when you were a kid?"

Gus shook his head. "I think you'll find that most kids were playing games and chasing whoever they were into chasing. For me, it was Jenny Hurst. Then Ariana. Then there was Christi. No wonder you're still pining over one woman."

Franklin glanced across from the slate. "Do you want me to do it?"

Gus grinned. "You want to do it, too, admit it."

Franklin moved his head back and forth. "Okay, I want to do it. I'm not sure if I *can*. It's been years since I've messed with anything more complicated than a beer pump. Plus, like I said, to scan past about a couple of hundred miles, we'd still have to connect it to the ship's sensors without being found out."

Franklin looked up to see that Chloe had just arrived with their drinks. "I don't want to know," she told him and hurried off back to the bar.

SIX

They were coming to the end of a boring few days. Sarah and Engee were in a hotel room, facing each other across a small table, next to a window that looked out in the shipyard. Although the hotel room was air-conditioned and had gravity, the vast shipyard existed in a vacuum and without gravity. It was a large, lattice-like framework of metal girders that contained at least a dozen ships throughout its structure and was only a little over two-thirds full. A mix of machines, people and piloted vehicles moved around the structure, working on the ships.

In the comfort of the hotel room, Engee and Sarah sat quietly. Sarah was working away on her slate, keeping up with overdue admin for her courier business. Across the table from her, Engee had been using a 3-D projection slate to watch television programmes with the sound off. Sarah had suggested that Engee either turn the sound up or put in an earpiece, yet she appeared content with just watching the pictures.

"And none of this is real?" Engee asked Sarah, pointing to the projection.

Sarah looked up, trying not to get distracted from her admin. She had almost finished, having initially put it off rather than getting on with it while she had time to kill. "Well, some is, I guess," she replied. "But it's mostly made up... Yeah."

Engee took in Sarah's vague reply for a few moments, staring at the images, and Sarah tried to remember where she had been on the spreadsheet.

"Why?" Engee asked, interrupting again just as Sarah found her place.

Sarah sighed and put the slate down. "I guess you had to be there."

"Where?"

Sarah pointed at the images of a centuries-old TV programme Engee had dug up from the online archives. "Well, in this case, I think it's the late twentieth-century."

"There is no television like this in the UTC today?" Engee asked.

"Well... I'm sure there is somewhere, but... I dunno, maybe the universe got interesting enough without us having to make up stuff. And big enough too. Newsfeeds are what everyone cares about now."

Just then, Sarah's slate chimed an alert. She picked it up, seeing the message she had been waiting for. She looked to Engee. "She's ready!"

Engee put her own slate down. "I am eager to see the modifications."

Sarah stood up, but paused, glancing back at the slate. "Are you sure you are okay with the life of a courier?"

Engee looked curiously at her. On a Koru, the expression more closely resembled wide-eyed surprise. Or, perhaps that was just Engee. "I am not sure I understand, friend Sarah."

"You were a rebel leader on Home Nest. Someone who mattered. Months have passed since we found each other. Perhaps it might be safe to reach out to your group again, The Unbound." She indicated the slate. "Rather than sitting around and watching old television programmes. I don't want to be... holding you back."

Engee's expression was serious. "I have thought on this, friend Sarah. And, although I believe I have most of my memories back, it would not be right for me to approach them until I find a way to do so safely."

Sarah nodded and they walked, although Sarah stopped after a few paces. Engee stopped and turned back, the surprised, curious look flickering across her features again, which had taken on some of the earthy tones of the hotel room. "What is it?"

"It's okay to say you are scared, you know," Sarah said. "After what was done to you."

"I am scared." Engee said. "I am scared that The Unbound are no longer out there. That all my friends are gone. That it might be my fault."

It was one of the rare moments when Sarah found it hard to meet Engee's gaze, even though those opaque eyes did not seem to radiate any of the fear and hurt in her words. "But you are right," Engee went on. "I will try to reach out once this contract is over."

Sarah and Engee exited the airlock in their spacesuits, accompanied by the engineer, Ralph, who waited for them just inside the facility. They made their way towards the *Mutt's Nuts*, which was suspended in the framework above them.

"You planning to go to war at all?" Ralph asked over comms, pointing to the several small turrets dotted around the hull. They amounted to more than most ships would have for protection from space debris.

"A person doesn't usually plan to need point defence," Sarah said, "and it's a shitty thing not to have it when you need it. Let's just say there's been one or two times recently that it would have been nice."

It was plain from the exterior of the ship that they had made significant alterations to the cargo section. It was an amazing amount of structural change in a short time. The rear was a lot bigger, and it made the *Mutt's Nuts* look like it had gained a beer belly.

"The cargo section is now split-level," Ralph told them. "Let's go in and have a proper look."

The cargo section was open and exposed to the vacuum of space as they climbed the steps.

"Although it is split-level," he went on, "you can fold back some of the top level in the middle there." Ralph used a control on his T-slate to make a large, central portion of the floor above them at peel back in parts. The slate was a bulky, vacuum-proof work slate and, for the duration of the work, had access to the ship's controls. The folded-back floor created a new gantry around the outside, halfway up what was now a two-storey space.

Sarah was impressed. "Yes, this will do nicely."

Ralph was in his element and hadn't finished wowing them yet. "Come with me," he said. "You're going to love this next bit."

They went up two flights of stairs and through a small airlock section, before arriving in the pressurised galley. Beyond that, they passed through a small corridor, off which lay the sleeping quarters, and arrived in the cockpit. "We'll fire up the primary systems," Ralph said, tapping away on his slate. It felt strange to Sarah, seeing someone other than her or Engee doing such a familiar thing to her ship. She felt a little violated on the ship's behalf.

Following several more gestures on Ralph's slate, red lights flashed somewhere within the steel framework beyond the cockpit window, and a dark slab of metal around fifty feet across slid down in front of the ship. An alarm was sounding in their helmets, although, being in the vacuum of space, was not actually sounding outside of the ship.

Floating just their side of the cockpit glass in front of them, a target sight came up, and Ralph reached forward and pressed a trigger on the console, causing a bright-red compressed energy beam to come from somewhere at the front of the ship and hit the metal slab. The window reacted and dimmed instantaneously, protecting their eyes from the brilliant flare of light, before receding to show that a dark, smoking smear had appeared on the metal slab.

"More than just point defence, that one," Ralph said with a smile. "You asked for something to shoot back with, but..." His eyes narrowed, even if the smile stayed. "Is the courier business getting more dangerous these days, Mrs Shah?"

Sarah just grinned, feeling happy with what she was getting.

Ralph lifted his hands up. "Hey, credits are good, so it's all fine with me. Must have come into some money to afford all of this in one go, though."

"Big job," Sarah replied. Then, a little less brightly, "But I've got a bad feeling about it."

Ralph handed her his slate so that she could complete the final payment. "Hence the..." he made a shooting gesture towards the dark metal slab beyond the window, "...weaponry."

Sarah handed Ralph his slate back, and he turned to leave. "Much obliged," he said as he left the cockpit.

Sarah turned to Engee once he was gone. "Shall we take her for a spin once Ralph is clear?"

"If you mean we should check how the *Mutt's Nuts* flies with the modified cargo section, then yes, I think that is a good idea."

Sarah watched the external feed to make sure Ralph was well clear of the ship before she delivered any actual power and heat to the drive cones. "This is *Mutt's Nuts*," she said over comms, "requesting permission to leave."

"I have your clearance coming through now, *Mutt's Nuts*," the controller replied, having got the go-ahead from Ralph. A moment later, a metallic clang somewhere above and below them showed that the docking clamps were releasing. Sarah manoeuvred away from the yard and, once clear of the facility, accelerated hard to test how the new, less-stream-lined *Mutt's Nuts* handled.

"Feels good," she whispered, while searching the sensor in front of her. She found what she was looking for. "Ah, that's what we need."

Sarah flew the ship towards a group of asteroids that were, in space terms, close to the shipyard. She found one that was several metres across and brought up the floating target, before turning to Engee. "Here we go," she said, wearing a manic grin. The compressed energy beam hit the rock explosively, only a short blast being required to crack the thing into three distinct parts.

"I am not an expert," Engee said, "but I think that is impressive for something mounted on a small ship like the *Mutt's Nuts*."

Sarah was checking a readout in front of her. "It is, but we will have to watch out for the power drain. On a bigger ship, a military one, there might be a separate reactor powering the larger energy weapons..." She tapped the console. "But we have only one little reactor, so that laser is drawing power from the same place that gives us thrust. Firing it for more than a moment or two at a time is going to cost us elsewhere if we're in a fight."

"That is a problem," Engee said, her subtle expression shifting into a worried one.

Sarah spun the ship around and brought up the targeting for the point defence lasers. "Not so much. If someone is chasing us, then these little beauties will matter more, and they use a lot less power, so we won't have to sacrifice much speed." The much thinner beams of point defence weapons scored marks onto the smaller targets that Sarah was selecting for them. "Want to have a go?"

Engee took over the point defence targeting, and Sarah was both impressed and a little jealous to see how quickly her Koru first mate picked up the method of efficiently identifying targets.

Engee kept blasting away with the PDWs, enjoying herself. "What is it you say...? I could do this all day."

"Yes, you're scarily good at it. We had better, however, get on with the job that is paying for these upgrades, eh? You want to plot the FTL?"

"Aye, captain."

Sarah laughed at that. She hadn't laughed a lot in the last few months, yet Engee was so uncomplicated to be around. Her innocence was still sometimes childlike, and it was the only balm she had to soothe the gaping wound left by the absence of her dead husband.

Sarah awoke, pulled from sleep by the sound of the FTL. She was sweating and shivering from a familiar dream that was retreating into the recesses of her mind the more fully she came towards consciousness, so that it felt strange and disconnected from her again by the time she spun her legs around to get out of bed. Not bothering to wash—who the hell was she trying to impress these days, anyway?—Sarah pulled on her flight suit and headed up to the cockpit, her long, red hair half caught in the collar. There, the familiar whine of the FTL engine was more comforting than it had been in her quarters.

Sarah looked at the jump readout. "Are we almost at the exit point?"

"One minute," Engee replied. "Did you sleep?"

"Sort of. Not as restful as I would have liked."

"You are still missing him, Mr Vikram Shah?" Engee asked, with none of the caution or sensitivity a human being might have employed.

Sarah raised an irritated eyebrow. "Sometimes, pointing out the obvious isn't the best thing, you know."

Engee seemed to think on this for a moment before replying. "Koru do not wonder if it is best to say something, we just say it."

Sarah shrugged a sort of reluctant agreement. "Well, I guess you must have a very honest society."

"Unless we do not want someone to know something. And then we lie."

"The funny thing is," Sarah said after a few moments, not realising that she had wanted to talk about it until Engee had brought it up, "I was used to not seeing him, especially after I started the courier work. But it's knowing that I *can't* see him, that's the hardest thing. I wish I'd seen him more in those last few months."

"Death does not knock." Engee said, and Sarah looked up at her, puzzled. "It is the best translation I have for a Koru saying. An old saying, as we are not these days encouraged to think of ourselves as individual with our own relationship to mortality. It means that we never know when death will come—for us, for those we are close to. So, we should leave nothing unsaid or undone this day that we would wish to say or do tomorrow. Just in case death turns up without warning."

"That's a little depressing," Sarah said.

"I always thought of it as rather beautiful. In fact, I thought of it on the day I started my insurrectionist movement."

A brief moment of silence fell upon them, broken as the alarm sounded to warn that the FTL was about to disengage. The ship exited into an empty area of space. Space was, of course, mostly empty, yet the places where people tended to head to or meet up at were usually the busier parts of it.

Sarah looked in confusion at the navigation and sensor readouts. "... Nothing here."

"We are a long way, even to the next planet," Engee concurred. "And that does not look like much of a planet to me."

"Our rendezvous point is in a big bit of empty space, it would seem." Sarah heard the worry in her own voice.

"So, what do we do?" Engee asked. "Just stay here and wait?"

"The thought of that makes me nervous. Let's do some flying around; we'll stay nearby and see if we can spot anyone coming. You know, be prepared."

"Well, the nearest large body looks to be that cold, rocky planet I mentioned."

"That'll do," Sarah said. "Let's head for that."

They kept to a sub-light speed but still pushed the *Mutt's Nuts* hard, not wanting to make themselves an easy target for all that nasty nothingness out there.

"There's nothing down there," Sarah said as the *Mutt's Nuts*' sensors fed her a bunch of not very interesting information about the planet. "You want to fire the lasers again?"

"Very much," Engee replied a little too eagerly.

Before they even had a chance to power the weapon up, a communication alert flashed in front of Engee. She glanced over at Sarah, who nodded her ascent, and Engee opened the channel.

"Greetings, *Mutt's Nuts*," came an accented male voice over the comms. "Please stand by to receive your landing coordinates."

"Took their sweet time," Sarah said to Engee. "Wonder how long they've been watching us for." She then switched over to transmit her reply. "Copy, standing by."

Sarah peered at the coordinates as they came through, matching them to the scans of the system that the *Mutt's Nuts* had been taking. "It's in a small asteroid belt. So narrow and spread out that I didn't initially register it was there. And I'm still not getting any sort of construction or industrial readings from it." She shrugged, feeling a little better either way. "Let's take a closer look then."

They pulled a smooth turn and headed towards one particular section of the belt—a thin smattering of asteroids that were not visible until they were close up.

"Would now be a good time to power up the weapons?" Engee asked.

"Calm down, warmonger. We have the point defence active, but if they've got any sort of military grade sensor package, or even one of the decent civilian ones, they'll probably pick us up when we prep the laser, and that will look a little... *threatening*."

The asteroid that the coordinates had them homing in on was small, even among the insignificant collection of rocks that it called home. However, once they got close, Sarah could see that there was a tunnel bored into it, which was why there had been no external construction or industrial readings. Landing lights lined the tunnel and were dotted around its entrance, like an invitation to head on in.

As they did so, Sarah saw that there were open bay doors at the other end of the tunnel. Once the *Mutt's Nuts* had landed inside, the doors closed behind her and there was the distinctive sound of the bay re-pressurising.

"Welcome aboard, *Mutt's Nuts*," said the comms voice. "Please stand by."

"Copy," Sarah replied officiously, trying not to show that she felt nervous again. The bay was empty, and the *Mutt's Nuts* seemed exposed to anyone who wanted to do it harm. She resisted powering up the laser, although it would, now that they were *inside* the asteroid, provide a likely deterrent to anyone inside the asteroid wanting to do them harm.

And then they just sat there.

Half-an-hour passed, and Sarah began to lose her patience. "This is ridiculous. Why are they keeping us so long?"

"Yes," Engee agreed, although she did not sound impatient to Sarah. "It has been thirty minutes. Perhaps it would be wise to contact the controller. They may have forgotten about us."

Sarah doubted that; they were the only ship in the bay. She stood up, full of nervous energy. "I'll go out into the bay and wave at them." It sounded silly when she said it out loud, yet she felt the need to follow through and started towards the door. "Of course, they could easily poison the atmosphere out there," Sarah added, halting in front of the door. "Or blow the doors once I'm out there. Would it be weird if I went out in a suit?"

"Why would they kill you?" Engee said. "Then we would not deliver their package for them."

"That would teach them, eh?" She turned back to Engee. "The problem with being dead is you don't even get the courtesy of an explanation."

They exited the ship together and headed straight for the back of the bay. Sarah could tell that the bay was carved out of the rock in quite a rough-and-ready fashion. Arriving at the door that looked most likely to head further into the rock and, she guessed, the rest of the station, Sarah pushed the button next to it and was relieved to find that it wasn't security locked. It opened on a corridor that was, like the bay, roughly hewn from the rock. The whole place had the sense of something made in a rush. Not poorly, but sacrificing speed over appearance.

At the other end of the corridor was another closed door, although, unlike the first door, this one had a small porthole in it and Sarah peered through it, seeing the back of a large man who was speaking with two other people.

"Bastard!" Sarah barked.

"What do you see?"

"Motherfucker."

"What…?" Engee insisted more urgently.

"Fucking Nigel. I do not fucking believe it."

"You are swearing even more than usual."

Sarah turned back to her first mate. "It looks like they hired another bloody courier."

"Why would they do that?" Engee replied. "They have already paid us a lot of money."

"I don't know," Sarah said, "but I'm going to find out." She reached, pressed the button and marched straight through the door as it slid open, Engee hurrying after her.

"What the hell is going on here?" Sarah demanded of the two people opposite the large man. "I thought we had a deal."

Nigel was opposite a man and the woman, both of whom were short and thin. They wore overalls as a sort of uniform, although there was no insignia or wording. They looked worried, and it was the woman who eventually cleared her throat and spoke.

"My name is Aida Halstrom," she said with a Scandinavian accent. "I am the commander here. There, er... seems to have been a misunderstanding."

"I can clear that up," Sarah said, moving forward one more step and throwing a thumb over her shoulder. "Fuck off, Nigel."

Nigel, tall with pockmarked skin and small, round glasses, glared at Sarah. "Too slow, as usual, Shah."

Sarah turned to the two station staff. "I'm here right when I said I would be here."

Aida Halstrom knitted her fingers together. "It appears that someone has employed Mister, erm..."

"Dick-face," Sarah put in.

"Martens," Nigel corrected."

"...Martens, too."

"And the package is being loaded onto the *Montezuma's Revenge* as we speak," Nigel put in.

Sarah suspected Nigel had no idea what the name he had given to his ship, the *"Montezuma's Revenge,"* referred to, and would have loved to let him know right there and then. Instead, she turned her anger on poor Aida, whose companion twitched a little as Sarah did so and, for the first time, she noticed he had a small CEW pistol attached to his side.

Sarah pointed at it and then nodded back towards Engee. "Reach for that and she'll rip your throat out with her teeth before you even have it off your waist. Engee looked as worried about that idea as he did, but Sarah ignored that and turned to Aida, placing only a few inches between their two faces. "We had an agreement, and either I'm leaving here with that package or the money I was promised."

"We don't have authorisation-"

"Well, why don't you hop on your comm system and get it? We'll wait, won't we Nigel?"

Nigel rolled his eyes and huffed, while Aida squirmed. "That's not possible right now," she answered. "And we cannot transfer you the credit. We're... off-grid here."

Sarah could believe that. They had been hard to find, and she would never have known where in the system they had not contacted her first. She couldn't help but wonder why such a level of secrecy was necessary, that an entire base—small as it was—should be hidden out here. They were evidently lightly staffed, though, as she had seen no one else since arriving and, if possible, she guessed they would have more people in the room right now, stopping her being threatening.

Yep, it was all very odd, and maybe she should just let Nigel walk away with whatever the hell the package was, but the remaining money was just too much to let go of. Plus, there was the principle of it. And, more than that, it was *Nigel.*

"Look," Nigel said in that superior voice of his as he backed towards the door, "I have my package." He held up a T-slate. "And I have the delivery point. You can sort the rest out between yourselves."

Sarah turned back to Aida, who shrank back. The man, however, put a hand on Aida's shoulder and—although nearly swallowing his Adam's Apple in the process—he stepped between Sarah and his supposed boss. "I have an idea," he said under his breath as Nigel disappeared through the door, raising his voice again once the other courier was gone. Sarah noted that his voice was the same one she had heard over the comms system earlier. Was it really only these two people on the entire station? "Why don't we just give you the delivery coordinates, too? As long as the package gets there, in one piece, somebody gets paid. You figure out how that happens."

SEVEN

Franklin had soon reverted to type during his time on the *Majestic*, just hanging out and working in the cocktail lounge, the appropriately named "Franks," that was almost exclusively otherwise staffed by Arnold's niece, Chloe. Right at that moment, Franklin was standing behind the bar watching their only customer leave, while Chloe collected his glass and returned to the bar.

"You don't have to be here, you know," Chloe said. She looked around at the empty bar. "It's quiet enough for me to handle things."

"Are you trying to get rid of me?" Franklin joked.

"It's just..." Chloe looked awkward. "I appreciate you looking out for me and all that, but I know what I'm doing now."

"Ah, how fast they grow up."

"And you get your money either way. You can take it easy, enjoy yourself. You're not being paid by the hour like me."

"I'm on a strange ship," Franklin said, "but being here, working in a bar, feels comfortable... Familiar."

"Missing your own bar, eh?" Chloe teased.

Franklin's lack of a reply spoke volumes, so he changed the subject. "So, why the *Majestic*? Why the McMurdo Rift?"

"My uncle..."

"That's all? Arnold could have asked me or..." he made a face, "got you in at the other bar on the *Olympic*. The rubbish one. Or, I'm sure he could pull some strings somewhere to get you a job closer to, you know... civilisation."

Chloe gave him a lopsided, searching look. "You don't like it out here, do you?"

"It's not that," Franklin said. "But I came out here to get away from things. The McMurdo Rift, the *Olympic*... they're good places to disappear to. You're... too young for all that, though."

"How do you know?" Chloe said, and Franklin saw a coy smile that had likely driven some boy or girl crazy at some point. "How do you know that I'm not interesting enough to be running from something?"

"Bad break-up?"

Chloe's face fell, horrified. "W-what? No! W-well, it's just that... I've never seen the rift. I'm looking forward to that. And being able to say you've worked on the *Majestic* on her maiden voyage, that's got to be worth something."

"What's their name?"

"No, it's not–"

Just then, a junior officer who Franklin didn't recognise walked into the bar and straight up to the two of them. It was untimely, and Franklin made a mental note to pick this conversation up again at some point. "Captain Smith would like to see you," the officer told Franklin in an officious tone.

"She does realise we have internal communications on the ship, right?" Franklin asked. He did not like the snotty young officer's tone. "All the latest post-nineteenth-century technology. Why did she send you all the way down here? Slow day on the bridge?"

The junior officer's grim expression didn't waver. "She's in her office."

Franklin relented. People who didn't rise to sarcasm were no fun. "Okay, I'll just finish up here," he said. Snatching up the glass that Chloe had placed down.

"Now would be good," the officer pressed.

Nope, Franklin did not like this young man's attitude, and the rebellious part of him wanted to tell the guy where to go. He was, however, a paid guest on the *Majestic*. A little diplomacy was necessary, especially as they might have just caught him doing something naughty... probably illegal.

"Am I in trouble?" Franklin asked.

"I don't know," replied the officer. "Have you done something?" His look must have hardened, as the officer backed down a little. "The captain just asked me to fetch you, didn't tell me why." He glanced around the empty bar. "Sometimes doing so in person is a little more discreet."

Franklin walked into Captain Smith's office which, unlike on the *Olympic*, wasn't just off the bridge but was instead a brief ride in a lift, then down a corridor, left and... Well, the ship *was* a lot bigger than the *Olympic*.

Away from Franks, the rest of the ship seemed busier. Not its full complement yet, but still over a thousand people mingling in their finery or stood by the ship's many large exterior windows and gazing out at the beautiful vastness. The clientèle on this first run for the newly built SS *Majestic* seemed, on the whole, a cut above the usual mix on the *Olympic*, which could be described as "a mixed bunch." The *Olympic* had a lot of septuagenarians ticking off an item on their bucket list and youthful adventurers passing through on their trip around the known galaxy. These were mixed in with others, travelling for business or even to see family, using the *Olympic* simply to get from A to B.

The *Majestic's* current complement of passengers, on the other hand, had come as much to be on the *Majestic* as to tour the McMurdo Rift, Franklin felt. To eat fine food, take spa sessions and otherwise be a part of the first journey of the civilian fleet's newest ship.

When Franklin stepped into her office, the captain was sitting behind her desk and wearing glasses, which was at the same time amusingly old-fashioned and also attractive, in a "school marm" way.

Behave yourself, Franklin.

She looked to be going over an inventory or ship's logs of some sort and glanced up only to indicate that he should take a seat. Yes, he was feeling like he had been sent to see the headmistress.

"Captain Kate," Franklin said once he was seated.

"Captain will do," she answered, without looking up.

I am definitely in trouble. This was classic, the way she was carrying on with her work and letting him sit and sweat, just because she could. It seemed like a cheap trick, and Franklin felt himself losing respect for her as the moments passed. He guessed that she wouldn't care, especially if she was about to throw the book at him about the stock he had appropriated for his and Gus' science experiment. Franklin stretched his neck a little, trying to see what was on the shiny projection screen on the surface of her desk, but to no avail.

Captain Smith stopped what she was doing and leaned back in her chair a little, fixing Franklin with a stern look. *Phew*, she was quite good at that. "A certain supplies order for the cocktail lounge where you appear to be spending all of your time has come to my attention."

He was going to try to appear innocent, he had already decided, even if it was useless; it was probably what she expected of him, and he didn't want to disappoint. "Really?" he answered, sounding as relaxed as possible. "You are a very hands-on captain, aren't you? I assumed you just let the quartermaster's department deal with that sort of thing."

"Evidently. This supplies request contains several—well, more than several—items that I can't imagine you making use of in the cocktail lounge."

Franklin shifted in his seat, as if about to stand up. "If this is about Franks, you want to talk to Chloe, Philby's niece. She essentially runs—"

"Sit down, Mr Franklin!"

Captain Smith was very authoritative, and Franklin felt compelled to obey.

"Are you really going to try to pin this on the niece of your old captain and friend?" she asked. "A teenager? That's low."

"Of course not. I was just making the point that I'm not needed to run anything here, even for one of the most inexperienced members of staff, as Chloe is. There are more than enough bar staff and managers. "It leaves me wondering whether you brought me here under false pretences."

"Pretences?"

Franklin looked Captain Smith in the eye, trying to decide if it was her turn to play the innocent. She did not, however, seem too fazed. "You know, like I've been deceived."

"I know what false pretences means," Captain Smith said. "But, either way, does it justify making some sort of joke order to the cocktail lounge stockroom? I expected more from a war hero."

"It's not a jo..."

Captain Smith raised an eyebrow, as if warning him to measure his words and speak only the truth.

"It's not a joke order," Franklin pressed on. "I need that stuff."

Captain Smith brought the order up on her desk and started flicking through it, listing items he had requested back to him. "Three rolls of foil composite... five metres of shielded wiring... a whole bunch of nano chipsets, most of which I have no idea what they even do.

"What are you doing, Mr Franklin, building some sort of replacement for the bar staff? Auto bar security, perhaps?" Captain Smith let her sarcasm hang in the air for a few moments as Franklin continued to sweat. He realised he had to tell the truth, as ridiculous as it sounded.

"I need it to make a receiver for detecting phase field particle emissions."

Captain Smith looked at him for a moment, blinking once or twice, probably trying to decide if he just made that phrase up on the spot. "What?"

"Phase field particle emissions. They are a by-product of a phase field generator. Surprisingly easy to detect with relatively straightforward equipment."

"Mr Franklin," Captain Smith said. "Let me just stop you there with a 'What the fuck?' Are you making this up just to mess with me? I don't care what you've done in the past, you do not want to mess with me on my ship."

"It's a real thing," Franklin said. "Believe me, Captain. Whether there are any in existence in the universe right now, or even anything capable of creating them, that's a different matter, I'll admit."

"So, this is some sort of science experiment. You want to use my resources to prove a scientific theory? Is that it? Because you're bored or something?"

"Well... put a certain way, that's exactly it."

Somehow, her eyes narrowed even further.

"Put another way, if we're right, we could save lives. We could even save this ship."

There was a long, reluctance pause. Eventually, with a visible sigh, she bit. "I'm listening."

Franklin couldn't believe what he was going to say next, yet it was the easiest way to start. "Have you ever heard of the McMurdo Triangle?"

A vein throbbed on the captain's temple.

"I don't believe in it either," Franklin cut back in. "But something is causing a lot of ships to disappear without trace in the McMurdo Rift. A ship called the *Carol Dearing* just last week."

Captain Smith relaxed just a fraction. "Go on."

"We... Gus and I-" The captain interrupted with a roll of her eyes, but Franklin pressed on. "We have a theory that someone is doing this undetected. They may be using a type of stealth technology. And, if they are, they may not be aware that it has a fatal weakness that can be detected with what is essentially a modified radio device."

"Radio?"

"Yes. Pretty basic technology, but that's why it might get overlooked."

Captain Smith rubbed her chin. "McMurdo Triangle, eh? Surely, if you're in space-"

"Pyramid, I know."

"I was going to say 'prism'."

Franklin inclined his head appreciatively.

She was quiet for a moment. "So, who do you think it is? Pirates? Some sort of separatist movement?"

Franklin had other possibles, but he kept those to himself for the moment. "Whoever it is, it would be nice to see them coming, wouldn't it?"

She chewed her lip, a gesture which suited her, if not the captain of a star liner. "And you can build this thing with the parts on this order?"

Franklin winced. "Maybe. I'm not an engineer, more of a hobbyist when I was a kid. Plus, it would need to be patched into the ship's sensor array to have any actual effective range."

Her eyebrows went up at that. "And how were you planning to do that undetected?" She held up a hand. "Actually, I don't want to know.

"But, as big as we are, no ship is infallible to attack, especially an unarmed civilian ship. If there's any chance we could see something coming... How much chaos will this cause?"

"We could set it up in Franks. It's the quietest bar in the ship, anyway, and," he glanced away and mumbled the last bit, "I believe there's access to the sensor array nearby."

Captain Smith smiled at that. "Okay, you can have the parts and I'll even find an actual engineer to help you. As much to make sure you don't damage my ship as anything else."

Franklin nodded. "Someone who knows what they are doing would be very helpful."

"But I need a favour in return."

Franklin's head tilted. "Yes?"

"Remember how you were saying about false pretences?"

EIGHT

United Military High Command occupied a large, round building in Proxima City. The slow easing into this unfamiliar environment that Arnold had hoped for was not going to happen. Instead, he would meet with the UTC Council as an "expert" witness on the developing situation with the Koru in the McMurdo Rift.

They had found him a room to prepare in as he waited—a small, three-metre square room in the huge, maze-like structure that surrounded the central hall, made even more claustrophobic by the presence of both General Spencer and Admiral Maxwell, who were hovering about behind him as he adjusted the tie on his new uniform in the mirror. It looked good on him. Even if it was not the uniform of Earth's military, being in it felt like coming home. Like he was once again where he belonged.

"Now, just go in there and tell them what you've told us," General Spencer said.

"Really, Ralph," Admiral Maxwell said from a couple of steps further back. "That's the best advice you've got?"

The two men had been bickering like this almost constantly. Maxwell did not sound as edgy as Spencer did, yet Arnold could still sense his tension. The way he had been recruited had felt clandestine, with his initial unofficial work reporting to Maxwell during the recent encounters with the Koru. But now here he was, a rear-admiral. He nodded his confidence to them.

"Seriously, though," Maxwell added, "make it sing. You are our best shot at getting them to listen in good time. The threat posed by the Koru is a clear and present danger. If the council will not act..."

Maxwell didn't finish the thought and Spencer cut in. "One thing at a time. There will be other avenues if this doesn't work. But, for now at least, action by the council would be preferable."

Arnold wasn't sure what Spencer meant by that. Still, Arnold didn't mind the pressure that the two men were putting on him. He knew what he wanted to say and felt the courage of his convictions, which were strongly held. The UTC could not trust the Koru and needed to a military presence in the areas where their interests might conflict. Such as in the McMurdo Rift.

A staff officer knocked on the door and poked her head in. "They are ready for you now."

Maxwell and Spencer accompanied Arnold as far as the chamber doors and then, with nods of encouragement, scooted off to find another entrance that would take them to where they could observe the proceedings.

The council chamber was a large auditorium with a visitor and observation gallery. A huge, round table sat in the middle—dwarfed in the vast space, as big as it was—and the twelve councillors sat around it. Arnold could see that the table was made from a type of dark wood which, most likely, could only have come from Earth. He wondered if anyone sat around the table saw any irony in that. This was the UTC's civilian government at its highest level.

"Good afternoon, Rear Admiral Philby," Councillor Hawthorne, the current chairman of the council, which rotated around the table to a new chairman every year, said as he welcomed Arnold. The title still sent a tingle through him.

"Good afternoon, Councillor Hawthorne," he took in the table, "councillors. Thank you for inviting me."

"I believe you have a presentation for us?" Hawthorne asked. *No preamble*, Arnold thought. Could be good, could be bad.

"I have."

"In your own time, then," Councillor Hawthorne said, stroking a neatly trimmed, slightly pointy, white beard as he spoke.

Arnold activated the holographic display, the controls familiar enough. It seemed that the facilities in the UTC

Council chamber were almost as old as those on the *Olympic*.

He made eye contact with as many of the councillors as he could before he began. "You are, of course, familiar with the fact that there is a Koru-held planet close to the McMurdo Rift," he began. "Last month, while captaining the civilian liner SS *Olympic*, I observed an attempt by the Koru to occupy a neutral planet within the rift."

"Rear Admiral," Councillor Hawthorne cut in, "you were an officer serving within Earth's navy during the civil war, were you not?"

"Yes."

"And, until this moment, you have chosen a civilian role aboard the *Olympic*, rather than serving in the UTC military, as you would have been able to do with more chance of advancement and a better rate of pay?"

"I... Well, yes."

"You see how this might appear, Rear Admiral?" Councillor Hawthorne said. "Here you are, brought in with an advanced rank after all these years," he glanced up towards where Maxwell and Spencer sat in the gallery, "a person who may have plenty of reason to resent the Koru involvement in the war."

So, Hawthorne was far from stupid, although Arnold did not enjoy the inferences about his newly acquired commission. Still, he bit his tongue and took a moment to craft a suitable reply. "I have no feelings of unfinished business with the Koru. We all suffered in the war, and that was a long time ago.

"In fact," he went on, finding his flow, "I would say that my experiences there make me more likely than many to be reluctant to see us rush into another war, especially with an enemy as capable as the Koru. That said, if their recent actions in the McMurdo Rift suggest they were in any way preparing for conflict, the sooner we knew and reacted to it, the better."

The chairman's eyes narrowed for a moment, then he appeared to relax. "Let's see this evidence you have, then."

Arnold brought up the planet that had caused so much recent fuss on the holo display. In some ways so familiar to him, although he had hardly ever ventured down to it while captaining the *Olympic*. Indeed, he had almost never left the ship while he served there. A navy man through-and-through, he had been most at home on his ship, moving through the expanse of space.

"This is the planet Enceladine," Arnold said. "It is in the McMurdo Rift, with a small native population, industrialised primarily within the last one-hundred years. The UTC—and Earth before that—has traded with them, provided some non-military technologies, and there is a small but significant tourist trade there associated with a starkly beautiful natural landscape and its position on the route through the rift." He smiled. "The Enceladines have a natural gift for producing, how shall I put it...?

Tourist trash. Knick-knacks that visitors buy as if they are acquiring important cultural artifacts for a bargain price.

"However, it was recently discovered that the Koru had set up a mine on the planet, without seeking any official approval or permission from the locals."

"Approval?" a councillor across the table asked.

"Well, it is a sparsely populated planet, so ownership of territory outside of the major settlements is often a moot point. All the same, for an alien authority to come in—"

"Have the Enceladines requested assistance in the matter?" Chairman Hawthorne asked.

"Not formally," Arnold answered. He moved on, determined not to be kept from the main point of his presentation. "This is the ore they were extracting at the illegal mine."

He clicked through to a high-resolution picture of the small piece of ore Franklin had retrieved from the mine, so that it appeared huge in front of the gathered councillors. Chemical analysis figures popped up next. "The Koru are able to use it to produce an effective energy shield around a ship. I am aware of an attempt to replicate this energy shield on base ore that only produced a minimal effect, but we believe they are refining it and using a high-powered process on the refined product that creates a highly effective shield."

"How effective?" It was the chairman. Arnold appeared to have his full attention now.

"Both compressed energy and kinetic weapons were stopped. The report I received from the same man who obtained the sample of the ore was that the shield appeared to become overloaded over time. So, it likely does not make a ship so much invulnerable as able to take a lot more of an enemy ship's firepower before becoming damaged. All the same…"

"A significant advantage," one councillor said.

"And imagine one of those mother ships with a system like this," another put in.

No one had ever seen another of the Koru motherships that Franklin had destroyed during the battle for Earth, yet if they could build one there was little reason to assume they could not build another.

"Could we replicate the technology?" Councillor Hawthorne asked.

"Perhaps, given time. The only source of the mineral we know of is on Enceladine, which isn't necessarily a problem. They would likely trade for it. Generating the required power is, as is forming a cohesive layer in the vacuum outside of the ship. Either way, we're not there yet."

"Unfortunate."

"And time may not be on our side. Coupling this and their recent aggression, which included firing at the Regus mining facility, an independent but UTC-related base, and firing upon an independent courier ship, can we afford not to be prepared? To show our strength? I would recommend the council send a fleet detachment to the McMurdo Rift."

"Would not sending such a force appear as provocation?" said a woman whose name escaped Arnold, although he seemed to remember that she was a deputy to Hawthorne's position.

Arnold tried not to sound condescending when he replied, although it was hard. "The idea of provocation merely by the presence of military assets is a known fallacy, councillor. Military power is always, first and foremost, a deterrent. At worst, it is planning ahead."

A tiny smile played across Councillor Hawthorne's lips at that. He was silent for a long time, regarding Arnold. It seemed like the rest of the chamber was holding its breath until he spoke. "Thank you, Rear Admiral. You have given us a lot to think about. We will need time to consider."

Arnold saluted and walked back out to the reception room where Spencer and Maxwell were waiting.

"How do you think it went?" Maxwell asked.

"A little resistance at first, especially from Councillor Hawthorne, but I think they came around."

"Rubbish," Spencer said, drawing a look from the other two men. "You did your best, Philby, but Hawthorne runs that council—he did even before he headed it and likely will afterwards. And he never takes time to consider anything he wants to say 'yes' to."

Maxwell huffed. "Come on, Ralph."

"I'm serious."

The three of them were out of the building and in an armoured car before any of them spoke again. "I think we might have to take matters into our own hands if they don't act," Spencer said once the screen separating the three officers from their driver was in place and the car was moving.

"Don't be so dramatic," Maxwell chided the general, although Arnold detected a note of warning in the words.

"Our own hands?" Arnold repeated, before thinking about what he had said. He felt uncomfortable under the eyes of the other two men, but, seeing as he had started the thought, he felt that finishing it might be the best way to clear the air. "The military cannot act without the authority of the executive."

"Of course," Maxwell agreed. Although it did not sound to Arnold like Admiral Maxwell was agreeing with him at all.

NINE

Torres had taken the straightforward concept of Franklin's phase field detector and created something that had wires strung across at least half of the cocktail lounge. He had pictured something that would fit on top of a single table and had assumed that an engineer borrowed from the ship's experienced crew would simplify and miniaturise his design. Instead, Amelia Torres—who, in her easy confidence and gung-ho manner, reminded Franklin a little of a pilot he had once flown with—had a created a monster.

Torres hadn't been shy in telling a man she had only just met that his design was inadequate and could be much more effective. She had ordered lots more parts from the stores, safe from repercussions from the captain. This was partly because the patch into the sensor array was a lot more complicated than Franklin guessed it would be. Then again, the sensors he was most familiar with belonged to the Olympic, a fifty-year-old ship.

In short, Torres was a god-send who almost completely took over and made a piece of kit which, although it looked haphazard, was far superior to anything Franklin could have slapped together.

Along with Gus, Franklin had been relegated to "a pair of helping hands." It was now, however, time for the exciting switch on.

"Are we good?" Torres called out from where she had removed a panel that Franklin hadn't even noticed on the far wall by the storeroom.

"No signal coming through," Franklin answered, trying not to sound smug. Even Torres wasn't infallible.

"Did you turn the modulation dial like I said?" she asked. "It's on zero if it's all the way to the left."

Franklin was glad that she couldn't see him flushing as he turned the dial.

"No, he didn't!" Gus called out helpfully. Asshole. "We've got signal!" Gus added with excitement, as a line of red lights sprang to life. Behind him, two customers walked into the cocktail lounge, saw the mess that was taking up half of it and turned on their heel, leaving again.

"You couldn't have done this anywhere else?" Chloe complained, not for the first time. "I like having customers."

Franklin ignored her and crossed his fingers as he activated the holographic display that would show a representation of the space around the ship for millions of miles and would hopefully pick up phase-field particles if they were present.

Torres came to join them, and her face fell a bit. "We can increase that range."

"It's longer than I thought we would get," Franklin admitted.

"No," Torres said. "We're piggybacking for now, but I'll figure a way to free up a channel for us. Let me speak to comms on the bridge. We can reconfigure our own channel and that will boost the range. Maybe even double it."

"It's awesome," was all that Gus could say.

"It's green," was Chloe's input as she came to stand behind Franklin, her hands on her hips. She was right; the holographic display was green.

"Well," Franklin said, "let's see if we can get anything. I hope we do. I agreed to give a speech at the captain's dinner tonight for this."

It was several hours later when Captain Smith walked into the bar to find Franklin and Gus hunched forward, staring slack-jawed at the hologram. She glanced over at Chloe.

"They've been like that since Torres finished it," Chloe said. It sounded like what it was, a complaint.

"How were you ever planning to hide all this from me?" she asked Franklin.

Franklin chuckled. "It's... um, bigger than I planned. But it is working... Well, as far as we know."

"As far as you know?"

"We'll know for sure if we get a hit. If something's out there, that is."

The captain put a palm to her forehead. "I can't believe I agreed to this." She turned to Chloe. "How many patrons have stayed for a drink since this..." she gave an encapsulating wave of the arm, "health and safety nightmare took over half of the bar?"

"I have at least been able to start a deep clean, Captain," Chloe replied, answering the question by not answering.

"We've had passengers on board for less than a week," Smith said. "How much deep cleaning is there to do?" She turned back to Franklin. "I must be mad. I should at least have made you do this somewhere where there are no passengers. If this gets back to Proxima..." She trailed off, her eyes narrowing. "Well, Mr Franklin, time to keep to your end of the bargain. I've got a dress uniform I think will fit you. I'm guessing you don't have your own?

Franklin blanched. "Dress..."

Gus guffawed. "She's dressing you up and putting you on show."

"I'm not!" Captain Smith protested but ruined it by grinning. "Now, come on. It'll be fine. Over before you know it. You might even enjoy yourself."

Franklin's look as he came with her suggested he didn't think he would.

Despite her reaction to the sight of the detector, Captain Smith seemed remarkable at ease as they strode back together to her office, where she had the dress suit waiting for him. "Did you really get me on this ship so I could speak at a dinner?" Franklin asked.

"I hoped you would," Smith admitted. "The detector thing just gave me an excuse to..."

"Make me," Franklin finished for her.

She shrugged, unrepentant. Franklin felt her glance at him, as if considering her next words. "It will be nice to have you sitting next to me at dinner. Being the captain of a ship like the Majestic is ten percent commanding a ship, forty percent administrating and fifty percent PR, and I only really enjoy the first part."

"In that case," Franklin said, feeling a strong desire to flirt with the woman, "you should have just asked me if you wanted to have dinner with me."

They reached the office and went inside. "I do find you intriguing. Even to the die-hard UTC faithful, you're a legend for what you did."

"Might have been different if it had been a UTC ship I destroyed that day," Franklin replied.

His short tone didn't appear to put Smith off. "And you're not what I thought you would be. Not full of yourself."

Franklin grinned.

"At least not in the ways I expected."

"Funny."

She indicated a bathroom to one side of the office. "The suit's in there. I think I sized that up correctly, at least. You should be quick. Dinner started three minutes ago."

Franklin felt like a penguin. The trousers even made him waddle slightly, and sitting down in them made everything around the middle of his body feel tight and restricted.

Captain Smith sat to Franklin's right on the huge, round table at the front of the banquet hall. There was a man with a square jaw and stubble who was at least ten years older than Franklin to his left. A newscaster or reporter, or something, who had won an award reporting during the civil war. He was very interested in Franklin, while the captain's attention was being monopolised by the woman on the other side of her.

Franklin found his mind wandering as he looked over at the captain. Kate, as she had insisted he call her when she was trying to lure him onto her ship. He smiled at that.

"I know," the man said next to Franklin, "It is quite funny, isn't it?"

Franklin hadn't the faintest idea what the man had been talking about, realising that his attention might have wandered quite some time ago. He smiled wider and nodded. "Yes."

The hall was quite something, chandeliers hanging overhead and so much wood panelling that Franklin guessed the interior of the hall was worth more than he would earn in a lifetime. All the same, he wasn't thinking about that. He was thinking about emerging from the bathroom in the captain's office earlier on to find Smith hastily buttoning up a fresh shirt, her hair down, the top of her bra showing. It had been an oddly arresting moment. He was a big boy now, had seen lots more than that before; and yet, in an almost Victorian sense—like a hiked skirt and an exposed ankle—it had stuck with him.

He hadn't wanted it to. His ex-not-wife had rolled into his life again several months ago and upended years of suppressed feelings. Then her husband had died an arms-length too far away from him. Sarah had vanished again, as only she could after all that, and Franklin had felt in limbo ever since. He didn't want limbo, either.

Smith caught his eye, laughing at something the woman had said, a glass of wine halfway to her mouth. The laugh straightened into a smile that was just between them for a moment, then she was back in her conversation and Franklin was back to being just as lost in his.

"Speaking of Mr Mark Franklin," Captain Smith called out only moments later, "who would like to hear our honoured guest make a speech?"

Oh. Franklin obviously hadn't read that smile quite right. There was a round of applause and, Franklin realised with dismay, the whole of the banquet hall had quieted their conversation. A waiter appeared and pushed a button mic onto his suit. Franklin's own heavy breathing could be heard throughout the hall, then there was a sudden cacophony as he cleared his throat.

"Um..." *Why didn't I think of what I was going to say, rather than keep thinking about the top of Smith's bra?* "My name is Mark Franklin... And I'm an alcoholic."

A few gasps and murmurs sounded around the banquet hall.

"Kidding, kidding. Although I do own a bar. It's over on the SS Olympic. Other liners are available."

Next to him, Smith cringed a little. Ha, ha, regretting our decisions now, aren't we?

"But seriously... It's wonderful to be on a beautiful new ship. A testament to the UTC's civilian fleet. And so big. Big, big, big. Yup." Franklin picked up his own glass of wine and drained half of what remained in it.

"And yet, standing here, I'm somehow reminded that the big things don't matter so much as the small things. The little moments you'll enjoy here on the Majestic. The memories of a family holiday. The new people you might meet. Treasure those moments; they're far more important than the moments that end up defining you. For one thing, you don't even get to choose those. They just kinda happen."

Smith caught his eye again, an "are you okay?" raised eyebrow. He looked away.

"A toast then," Franklin said, noting more than a few bemused looks around him. Then he noticed a connection request in his slate, which was on the table beside his plate. It was Chloe. He held up a hand and picked up the slate, almost grinning when he saw the look of exasperation that Smith now wore. "Just got to get this...

"Chloe?"

"Are you in the banquet still?" came the voice of Arnold's niece on the other end of the connection.

"Yup."

"Have you got me on speaker?"

"Yup. And I'm on a mic. Everyone can hear you. Say 'hi' to everyone."

"Oh... hi," she squeaked.

Franklin held up the slate to the gathering in the banqueting hall, that numbered a few hundred at least. "Hi Chloe!" a few of the more enthusiastic diners called out, including the guy next to Franklin.

"Look," Chloe hissed, trying to lower her voice but still heard all around the hall. "You and the captain should come to Franks now. There's a... you know. The thing. It did a thing. Gus is having kittens."

TEN

The ship rocked to the right as they dodged another of the asteroids. Ahead, Nigel's ship was still moving faster than they were.

"Stay with him, stay with him!" Sarah told herself. Engee sat at the sensor station behind her, trying to warn Sarah about approaching space rocks, most of which could kill them. The little point defence CEWs were working overtime.

"He is pulling away from us." Engee said.

"No shit."

Engee was becoming quite accustomed to Sarah's sarcasm by now and was even known to throw a little humour back. "Scanning for faecal matter, just to be sure."

"Not now! Now is not humour time."

"Just so you know, the targeting systems that came with our weapons upgrade are working well."

"Again, that's nice but—"

"For instance, I have acquired a weapons lock on the *Montezuma's Revenge.*"

"We can't shoot Nigel, can we?" Sarah asked, feeling a strange mixture of horror and exhilaration at the thought. Nigel had been a persistent rival to Sarah's couricr business ever since she had been operating in the outer systems. He had an uncanny knack of outbidding her on jobs, so she had been furious to find him waiting in the out-of-the-way asteroid rendezvous. Sarah had assumed the entirety of this very well-paid job was hers. Apparently not.

"A well-placed compressed energy shot from the point defence weapons might only damage his drive cones enough to slow him down a bit."

"Or they might blow him to bits, and the package with it. Either way, it's all a bit extreme, isn't it?"

"May I remind you we have already been shot at on this job ourselves." Engee had a point. And *geez*, she was also quite scary when she wanted to be. "What is the point of all those weapons if we do not—"

"Okay! But don't kill him. Maim, maybe, but no killing. And do not destroy the package, whatever you do."

Almost immediately, a bright red streak appeared at the front of the ship, but the *Montezuma's Revenge* jinked deftly out of the way. A moment later, there was an incoming comms request, which Sarah accepted.

"Are you fucking shooting at me?" said Nigel's nasally voice over the crackling transmission.

"We, er, slipped," Sarah answered.

"Look, I turned up first. The job's mine. Give it up, Shah."

"They hired me first, you bastard!"

"And yet they didn't trust you enough not to hire me too."

The poor base commander at the little asteroid where Sarah and Engee had turned up to collect the package had been as confused as they were about the situation. Someone had fucked this up and, tempting though the thought was, she did not want to kill Nigel, or even damage his stupid ship, even if it was named after a case of the squits.

"How about we go halves?" she said with a heavy, sick feeling in her stomach.

"Seeing as I'm leaving your paunchy ship for dust, I don't see—"

Nigel didn't get any further, as another fierce CEW shot had just lanced out from the *Mutt's Nuts* and struck the very edge of an asteroid that the *Montezuma's Revenge* was about to fly around. Large splinters of rock had exploded off it, and they showered Nigel's ship, which was passing it at high velocity.

"Oops," Engee said behind Sarah. It wasn't a very convincing "oops."

A second later, the *Mutt's Nuts* was also flying through the debris, the little pieces of asteroid making horrible noises against the hull that made Sarah wince at the thought of what they were doing to the outside of her ship. She had to pull to port to avoid the *Montezuma's Revenge*, which was slowing and starting to spin.

"Bollocks, what the...?" Sarah slowed the ship and waited to match speed with the other, now out-of-control, ship. "Nigel, you big sack of package-stealing shit, you're not dead, are you?"

There was no answer. The feeling that she was presenting her backside to a sneak attack from Nigel gave way to a different sort of worry as the ship drew closer on her rear camera view.

"Oops," Engee said again, although she sounded a little more contrite this time. There were quite a few dents and even some holes in the front of the *Montezuma's Revenge*. It was—or had been—a much sleeker-looking ship than the *Mutt's Nuts*, Sarah had to admit. It was painted black, although in the vastness of space, that sort of colouring gave little to no advantage in stealth over other ships. Unless you were too close for comfort, in which case, ninety-nine-point-nine percent of all ships in existence would pick you up on some sort of sensor system. And why would a courier want to be stealthy, anyway? It was good for people to know when you were delivering their package.

"That damage in the nose could have taken out his comms," Sarah said.

"And maybe Nigel."

Sarah did not want to think about that. "Let's just get in there. Suits on; there's probably an atmosphere breach."

The ship's environmental systems were kaput, which meant no gravity, as well as no atmosphere. The lights were doing that thing that Sarah didn't think actually happened in real ship accidents—she was still trying to think of this as an "accident"—where they blink intermittently while those discovering the wreck explore it, adding to the grim atmosphere. Although, aside from the fact that things were floating around, the interior of the *Montezuma's Revenge* was not looking too bad. Of course, they were not at the front of the ship yet, having entered through a side airlock into a corridor. The external airlock on the *Mutt's Nuts* was just behind the cockpit and was barely used, as they came and went via the cargo bay, depressurizing it if they were coming and going in vacuum, as there was an airlock between the bay and the galley.

At the end of the corridor was the entrance into the cockpit, which was a sliding door currently in the open position, allowing them to see through into an almost bridge-sized space—much larger than at the front of the *Nuts*. As she went in, Sarah could tell that it must double as living quarters. Seeing as this was a smaller ship than the *Mutt's Nuts*, the rest of it had to be just cargo bay and engine. There was, indeed, a hole in the front of the ship. They could not see all the way out, but things were mangled towards the bottom of the console just to the left of the pilot's chair, and it didn't seem likely that had happened from the inside.

"I will be less impulsive in the future," Engee said, sounding mortified by the results of what she had done.

"Where's Nigel?" Sarah wondered out loud. The pilot's chair—there was only one, the co-pilot's seat having been ripped out—was empty. It didn't look damaged. "In fact," Sarah turned back to the door that they had come through into the cockpit-cum-living area, "why did he open the door?"

The door between the corridor and the cockpit was a sealing bulkhead door. Leaving it open had spread the vacuum issues caused by the hole at the front to the rest of the corridor, perhaps to much of the rest of the ship.

"Maybe his suit was not in the cockpit," Engee said.

That didn't sound likely. Most ships of this size had multiple suits in varying places, usually in the bay and the cockpit at least, often in other rooms, too. Suits were basic safety equipment. Nigel was not the type to only have one suit and, if he did, it would have been in the place that served as his living space and his main workspace—the place where he flew the ship from.

Sarah squinted back along the corridor, which was mostly in darkness now, only illuminated by the sparse, brief flashes of light. "Is there...?"

"What?"

Sarah could hear that her friend was on edge, still freaked out by the results of her eagerness to use the ship's new weaponry. "...Someone out there?" Sarah drew the small B-17 "Black Arrow" pistol that Franklin had used against the Koru during their adventures on Enceladine and strode towards the corridor. Just as she did so, the light flickered brighter and for a little longer, exposing a figure frozen mid-step with a large box in his hand.

Nigel.

He was crossing from a corridor that presumably led to the cargo bay and across to the airlock, and, noticing that he had been spotted, went from sneaking to rushing, which was awkward with the large impact box in his arms.

"Shit!" Sarah exclaimed, instinctively pointing the weapon in his direction but knowing that there was no way she was going to fire it at him, even if he looked about to steal her ship.

"What?" Engee said again, more urgently, having not seen what Sarah just had.

"Fucking Nigel! He's after our *Nuts*!" Sarah was suddenly glad that Engee's understanding of humour had not yet spread to innuendo.

They rushed down to the corridor as quickly as they could in the awkwardness of their suits but, even though they were not carrying a heavy box, Nigel had enough of a head start and the airlock was closed when they got there. Perhaps he wasn't familiar with the controls on the *Nuts* side of the airlock connection, as the lock hadn't been cycled and they could step into it. He had, however, locked it behind him.

"Shit," Sarah said, "what do we do?"

Engee pulled out her T-Slate. "I cloned most of the ship ops onto my slate at the shipyard; Ralph showed me how."

"Well, that's not too secure," Sarah said. "But, right now, a lifesaver."

Engee began tapping away. "I will just unlock-"

"Wait," Sarah interrupted. "I have a better idea. Hand it over." Engee did so. "You've got engine start-up, everything?"

"Most things."

Sarah could hear that Nigel was starting the engine. "Wanker's going to fly off with us in the airlock," she observed, lifting the slate. "Except he's not." With a tap, the engine powered down again.

A few moments later, Nigel tried to power up for a second time. Sarah gave him a few more seconds this time, then cut it again. A moment later, a comms request came in from the cockpit of the *Mutt's Nuts*. "Har-de-fucking-har," came Nigel's voice as she accepted it. "You've got remote access."

"We've got remote access, dumb ass. You were going to fucking fly away and leave us after we just came on here to rescue your sleazy behind."

"You came on to loot the package."

"That too."

"We are sorry we broke your ship," Engee said.

"Engee's sorry," Sarah corrected, although she wasn't sure whether she was pointing out that Engee was the one who had done the breaking or whether she, herself, was not sorry. Perhaps both.

There was a moment's pause on the other end of the connection. "You can make it right by cutting me in on the delivery."

Sarah huffed. "Does that mean you're coming along? On *my ship?*"

"Too fucking right it does."

ELEVEN

"Admiral? What time is it?"

Lying in bed in the darkness of his bedroom, Arnold looked bleary-eyed at the face of Admiral Maxwell, over a metre high and suspended above his bed. Fortunately, he knew the admiral could not see him. He glimpsed the dark green of General Spencer's jacket at the side of the image. The two men were inseparable, like some kind of double act.

"Early, I know," Maxwell said, without quite answering Arnold's question, but we need to talk to you, and we couldn't do it in the office.

"I'll let you in," Arnold said, gesturing to extend a virtual control panel down towards him from the base of the image, the fuzziness clearing from his brain. "Please make yourselves at home and I will be with you in just a moment."

He heard the two men enter his luxurious, hi-tech apartment as he got out of bed. It was brand new, or near as dammit, with all the upgraded appliances and features, and he was still getting used to its level of automation. In truth, he missed his captain's quarters on the Olympic, although he expected those feelings to dissipate with time. Arnold was where he needed to be. So far, he felt a little more politician than a Rear Admiral, but he could live with that. For now, at least.

Maxwell and Spencer turning up at his apartment at—he peeked at the time—four-thirty in the morning; well, that was at least a little concerning. What did they have to speak to him about that they could not discuss at High Command?

"Morning, gentlemen," Arnold said as he entered, attired in his uniform, just in case, but having rushed too much to appear at his immaculate best. "Can I get you something to drink?"

The two men were sitting down, although Spencer seemed full of energy like he wanted to get up and pace around, and he waved away the polite offer. "We don't have time for that."

As Arnold took a seat opposite them, Maxwell cast an eye at his friend and fellow officer, his expression reading to Arnold as if Spencer was, perhaps, being a little dramatic. "We've got someone on the council. I won't say who at this stage, but this councillor and General Spencer go back a way and, well, this person gives us an insight into what is going on in the council's closed sessions.

"A heads-up," Spencer said, "on the way things are going."

"And the councillor has told us they will not even consider the requests we put to them yesterday."

Arnold deflated a little, feeling a little air pass out of his chest. "Well, that is disappointing."

Spencer made a strange noise, like he thought Arnold's words were an understatement. Perhaps they were, although, so new to things in the capital, Arnold had not known what to expect when he put his proposal forward. "Perhaps we could try again? Look to gather more evidence." He thought of Mark Franklin. "I have a friend who might help in that regard."

Maxwell got to his feet. "I'm not sure you understand, Philby. From what we've heard, they were never going to do anything. They heard you out to humour us."

"We've been aware of a benign policy towards the Koru," Spencer said, "but we hoped recent events might at least shake that somewhat."

"But this is genuine policy," Maxwell took over, "if one that is held secretly within the council. It would take outright invasion from the Koru for them to act, and even then their action would likely be one of rolling over and exposing their bellies." For the first time since he had started speaking with Admiral Maxwell, Arnold saw genuine anger there, the sort of passion that more usually came from General Spencer. "It's almost as if there is a Koru agent or influencer within their midst."

"Really?" Arnold said, incredulous at the thought.

"Well, we don't know that," Maxwell said, a more pragmatic tone returning. "Even our councillor friend could not give us that insight. Either way, the pro-Koru sentiment on the council, especially in the council's lead, Hawthorne, is apparently unshakable."

"And that," Spencer added, "is a dangerous thing."

Arnold could not help but agree. It seemed bloody-minded. He understood the sense of gratitude that the ruling elite of the UTC might feel towards the Koru; in a way, they owed them their existence. Add to that the fear of what the Koru military mobilised en masse could do, especially if they had another mothership in their fleet. Yet there was never any security to be had in only hoping your more powerful neighbour did not one day decide they wanted to rule you. Or, worse, exterminate you.

"I am appalled," Arnold said. "Yet what can we do but keep gathering evidence? Perhaps go around them as much as we can, garner popular support? The media, perhaps?"

"A good idea," Maxwell agreed, "but too long-winded. If the danger is more immediate, the UTC will be caught with its proverbial pants down."

"Underwear around the ankles," Spencer said, a surreal sort of agreement.

"So what do you suggest?" Arnold perhaps understood why the two officers, senior though they were, had not wanted to hold this discussion at High Command, but he was still a little confused why they had felt such urgency. He needed coffee.

Ah. The looks that flashed across the faces of the two men in front of him—the same look, really—told Arnold that they had come to the real reason for their visit. The next words would matter more than any of the others.

Maxwell spoke. As forthright as Spencer often seemed, the naval officer appeared to be the senior member of their miniature cabal. "Between Spencer and myself, and several other junior officers who feel the same way that we do, we could command the vast majority of the military."

Which was the way military structures worked. Although the military always enacted political policy.

After several silent moments on Arnold's part, Maxwell spoke again. "Should I go any further?"

Arnold swallowed before he spoke, different emotions warring within him. Maxwell's insinuations angered him; It offended him that they were being spoken in his living room. And also, he wasn't. "I was a loyal officer of Earth. To the last, Admiral. There were years when I could not have served in the UTC military. And yet, so soon after I have joined it, you ask me to... what?"

"I ask nothing of you," Maxwell said. "Not now. But there may be a time, sooner than any of us would like, that for the security not just of the UTC, but for the whole of humanity, you might have to make a choice. I would like to know whether we can count on you when that time comes."

Arnold held the other man's gaze, steel in his own, then let it drift across to Spencer in the same way. "I will do what is best for the UTC. I can say no more than that."

Spencer look displeased with the answer, but Maxwell clapped his hands together and, with it, a little of the tension lifted. "We can ask no more of you than that. But ask yourself, Rear Admiral Philby, what was in your heart when we asked you first to report to us several months ago. Remember those feelings that made you agree, then I think you will do what is right."

TWELVE

"It's not anywhere near us, is it?" Captain Smith asked Franklin, peering at the holographic display that dominated the rear half of the cocktail lounge. Now that it had a hit to show, even in the moment's excitement, Franklin allowed himself a sliver of pride at how well his crazy machine had worked. Well, Torres' machine, in truth. The engineer was not with them, and Franklin wondered if someone should contact her.

"It's right at the edge of our range. Or what I thought was our range. The strength of the signal makes me think we could push it a way further if needed." A red blip moved near the furthest extent of the green, grid-latticed sphere—a see-through, ball-shaped Russian doll of sphere nestled within sphere—that was casting a glow back across all of their faces. He looked to Gus. "They're definitely using phase-field. It's glowing on the detector like a bloody beacon. I'm guessing they aren't aware of the emissions—or expected no one else to be."

"Is it coming towards us?" Chloe asked. Maybe the most pertinent question that could have been asked. Nervous though she appeared, however, she had still found time to chew Franklin out for letting the whole of the banquet hall hear their call. Even with the captain there, she had used a few choice words when to describe Franklin when the two of them walked into the cocktail lounge.

Gus, who usually had the technical know-how of a carrot, worked controls as he tried to discern that. "They've been hovering at the edge of the range since we spotted them. I'm not sure what they are up to."

Franklin turned to Captain Smith. The decision about how to react to this was hers. "What do you think?"

"Well then, I guess they are going the same way that we are. My instinct is to run in the other direction. I do not mind admitting that. But who knows if doing so will only cause them to come after us?"

"Better to know what it is doing," Franklin agreed. "Keep to our predetermined route and not act like we're following it or running from it. Hang on," he added, having a thought. He turned a thick dial with a loud click and the red spot disappeared. Instead, a more traditional 3D sensor picture took its place.

"Impressive," Smith said. "How did you...?"

"Torres. You need to give that woman a promotion."

Smith smiled. "She's patched the actual sensor feed, too. Would have been nice if she had informed me, but..."

They were passing through a pretty empty bit of space and there was very little to see on the sensor feed, except for a distinctive blue spot with tiny writing beneath it that would need to be magnified to be read.

"What is that?" Chloe asked.

Gus did the honours again, tapping to zoom in on it. "The *Laughing Zebra*. A small cargo ship."

"And probably their next victim." Franklin said. He looked at Smith. "We need to warn them. Hail them on comms."

"Conventional comms will take a while to reach them," Smith replied, "and I doubt a small cargo vessel has a quantum receiver. Conventional comms are also likely to be picked up by your green dot there, if it is another ship with malign intent."

She had a point. The *Majestic* had nothing to defend itself with. Yet he could not sit and watch these pirates or Koru, or whoever the hell they were, kill the occupants of another innocent ship. "I would wager they have no idea that we're here right now. A stealth ship that cruises along sending out a strong sensor signal all the time is no stealth ship at all. Whatever they have will be short range, low power and used sparingly.

"If we could take a shuttle, run a curving path towards the *Laughing Zebra*, then maybe they wouldn't ever spot the *Majestic*."

"We?" Captain Smith asked, sounding alarmed.

"He means 'him and me,'" Gus cut in. "I'm the one who does stupid, dangerous shit with him."

Even the *Majestic's* shuttle craft were better. If it was possible for a ship to feel like it was cutting through a vacuum, then that's what was happening right now. For Franklin, sitting at the controls almost felt dirty. Like the way he enjoyed flying it was being unfaithful to every other ship he had flown before. Well, every other civilian ship, at least. There was nothing like flying a military fighter.

Franklin was skirting the line between urgency and stealth. Which was maybe a little ironic, given that they were chasing after a stealth ship. Having started out on one curving path, he had reversed things after a little while to curve back the other way, therefore hiding the direction he had come from. It was frustrating when you were rushing to save lives, but the cargo ship would have only a small crew on it. They mattered—he was here putting himself in harm's way, wasn't he?—but they could not risk putting the thousands of lives on the *Majestic* in danger, which could be the case if he gave away his position too soon or took a path that could lead the Koru stealth ship back to the *Majestic*. They would expect that the little shuttle craft had launched from a larger ship.

Left far behind them, the *Majestic* was slowing, having decided to turn around, which meant that this was a potential one-way trip, especially if the *Laughing Zebra* went down to the stealth ship. And that made Gus' presence behind him mean a lot. He didn't *need* Gus to be there. He could fly the shuttle fine on his own and had tried to tell Gus that. His friend hadn't taken offence, only chastised him for wasting time.

Franklin understood the captain's decision. Heading towards where they knew a stealth ship suspected of being responsible for a high number of unexplained ship disappearances in the sector—even if doing so would only have been continuing their current route—was irresponsible. Not to say that he wouldn't have done so, but, then again, no one would catch him taking responsibility for a whole starliner. No, thank you. He was too stupid and impulsive.

Case in point.

"When can we hail the *Laughing Zebra*?" Gus asked.

They were burning the shuttle craft hard and, despite the curving path, and should be catching up. He would straighten up in a moment, close the distance a little quicker. They were blind as far as the stealth ship was concerned, not even able to take updates via comms from the retreating *Majestic*. Neither were they close enough for the less powerful sensor on the shuttle to see the Zebra yet. Assuming that the cargo ship had taken no big turns, they should be soon. He would turn on the sensor just before they hailed. And then hope not to die.

"Will they have to appear to attack?" Gus asked. "Will they be visible to our sensor when that happens?"

"My guess is they'll have to drop the phase field," Franklin said. "But only briefly. I'm sure they'll have everything to minimise their appearance on sensor, too."

He heard Gus let out a long breath behind him. "Are your buttocks clenched as hard as mine are?"

Franklin smiled at that. "Getting ready to switch on the sensor and hail." His hand stopped part way to the control. There was an incoming comms request. "What the...?" It was from the *Majestic*.

"What's that?"

"*Majestic*'s hailing. Are they *trying* to get themselves killed?" He accepted. What else could he do? "Shuttle 3."

It was Captain Smith's voice. "Franklin?"

"Smith?"

"I'm still in the bar, watching your machine. That little red dot."

"You're still in range? It should have vanished over ten minutes ago."

"Okay, well..." *Why the hell are you calling me and lighting us both fucking up like targets?*

"It appeared again. It's coming after us."

THIRTEEN

There were nine of them crammed into the slim, cramped vessel, a small sample of the glorious Koru people on a righteous mission. GH-456 sat in the command chair and stared at the void on the primary display.

This was his first command in the Koru Navy. He had not enjoyed the opportunity to serve in the previous conflict with the humans and was determined now to make a name for himself and the ship's crew, who were, to him, like a craftsman's tools. *And a fine tool set they are*, he thought.

Compared to most ships, there were only a handful of crew, and they worked within touching distance of each other, something which made for a camaraderie and closeness that, GH-456 supposed, most captains would struggle to foster. Their ship was designed for stealth, surviving almost entirely on its ability to go undetected.

The technology to achieve this was recent—the ability to remain invisible to the enemy—and also timely. GH-456 had the double honour of not only being among the first to make use of it in the field but also to be the only novice commander in a stealth strike ship.

It was dangerous work and the ship's ability to go undetected centred around a drive that could open a temporary tear between dimensions. It had gone terribly wrong during development on more than one occasion. Lives had been lost, brave warriors vanished or so utterly destroyed as to have been barely detectable as matter. A certain sort of craziness came with being where they were, but also a stronger sense of duty, of desire to do something special. They had not yet been able to hit anything big, but perhaps soon...

This area had recently become important to the Koru. The humans called it the McMurdo Rift, while the Koru still referred to as Iktook-Shar. That was a name so old that it predated the formation of the single nest society and the naming conventions that saw almost everything except Home Nest given a formalised designation. Any self-respecting military, even the humans, GH-456 supposed, would understand the significance of energy shields on a warship.

The Koru had been content to let the humans settle it for themselves many decades ago, even though no one claimed it and no treaty between the different species acknowledged anybody's true ownership. Ownership, territory, profit... these things in and of themselves seemed a significant driving force for the humans and the sector had not been of interest to the Koru back then. In time, the humans had taken what they had wanted and, mostly, had left again. Such was their way.

But now the Koru wanted Iktook-Shar for themselves. GH-456 did not know if this was about the shield ore or something more. For all he cared, the greater glory of his people, their mere right by strength and power, were all the justification needed. But they did not want a war with the humans—not yet, at least. And that was where GH-456's stealth strike ship came in. Better they were scared away. This was an area that had already lost much of its value to the humans. Now, if they lost confidence in their ability to navigate the area safely...

GH456 stared at the blank consoles, waiting for them to come back after they had cancelled the dispersion field and entered normal space again. The cabin lights bloomed back up to full luminosity and frantic activity began among his trusted crew, as they sent out a scan and made sure that no one was about to shoot at them. Before they had started the mission, a representative from Military Reconnaissance Division had personally assured him that there was little to no activity, as far as human military ships in the area. That said, the longer their mission ran, the more GH456 expected that they would draw attention. They had to.

"Can you detect anything?" he asked the sensor operator, TS187.

"Affirmative, Captain. As expected, we have closed on the merchant ship we picked up at the extent of sensor range earlier on. Shall I send over coordinates to targeting?"

The temptation to fire and vanish again, as they had been doing, was strong. It was the safest thing to do. However, their mission brief had been to escalate targeting over time if not recalled, and the ship before them was no bigger than their last target, or the target before that. They were in the middle of nowhere and perhaps could risk a broader, more powerful sensor sweep, as there was almost no chance that the small freighter would have the means to detect it.

Of course, if it did, then the ship would have a very good chance of seeing them coming—or at least to send out some sort of SOS or make note of their presence. All the care they had taken so far could be undone. Their last target had been two ships travelling together, but one had jumped away as they fired on the other and the crew of the stealth ship had worried that they had been discovered. GH-456 had expected military ships to show up, and they had lied low for a time. Yet no military ships had shown up, as yet, and these were the risks they took. GH-456 had faith in his crew, confidence that they would execute all duties as well as was possible, even if they were to become the hunted.

"Hold that," GH456 said to the sensor operator. "Let's risk a wider sweep, see if we can find ourselves a better target. If not, then proceed as planned."

"Captain," TS-187 agreed. A full, quantum sensor sweep would pick up everything within the system, perhaps even make contacts between this star and the next. They could use their sensors only rarely, but the ship was fitted with the best available, with a considerable power source available in their dispersion field generator. Waiting for the result was like experiencing an odd mixture of excitement and dread. He wanted a better target, but he also knew that the better targets were more likely to see them coming. Or maybe, finally, they would even turn out to be a military ship. Would he run then? To destroy a military ship would be a glorious prize but was not a part of their brief. They were to escalate ship disappearances and to make the McMurdo Rift a place that UTC shipping did not want to go. That was all.

"Two more contacts, Captain," TS-187 said, urgency changing the pitch of his voice.

"Two?" he couldn't hide his surprise. This was the busiest piece of space that they had yet operated in. The McMurdo Rift was quiet at the best of times, he understood, and they had kept their operations away from its few population centres.

"One is smaller. Looks like a shuttle craft heading towards us—or to the merchant ship. It is hard to tell. The other is much bigger and further away. In fact, it looks like it is completing a turn and heading away from us. By its size, it could be some sort of freighter again, but it is more likely a passenger liner."

"Military?"

"Nothing to suggest so."

This was odd. Some sort of personnel transfer from a passenger ship to the freighter, perhaps? Although the freighter did not appear to have turned itself to accept the shuttle. And the other ship seemed to be in a hurry to leave. Something illegal, maybe, instead?

The other ship, the bigger one, was too much of an opportunity to miss, however. More than that, if they could pull off the kill without either of the other two ships seeing them—only the death throes of the big ship—then they would return with a terrifying tale to tell of the big ship that inexplicably exploded in space.

This could be the best opportunity they would get to fulfil the remit of their mission.

"Men, this is the moment all our training and field experience has been leading to," GH-456 told his crew, speaking quickly but giving the moment the necessary gravitas. "We must go on-field again and make a turn to set pursuit of the larger vessel. We're going to aim to come back off-field behind it and launch three torpedoes. Then we need to disappear again and do all of this while leaving the other two ships only to see the end result."

"But captain," cut in TS-257, the ship's dispersion field operator, "we have only recently come off-field and these quick successive operations are a risk."

GH-456 had expected this protest. In fact, he was pleased to hear it. "I know, and this is noted TS-257, but this is our moment. We must take the risk to obtain glory. Proceed everyone."

Several moments later, the ship was on-field again, and they were again working with a sensor range that was not much better than visual range. They flew uncomfortably close to the shuttle but felt sure it could not see them. A couple of minutes later, they came off-field again and fired their weapons. It was a perfect execution.

Gerard Dupont was stood by one of the Majestic's full length exterior windows. He had been doing so quite a lot during the journey around the McMurdo Rift.

There had been little to see much of the time, except for the vast expanse of stars, which ended up looking much the same after a while. The colours of the rift itself had proved diverting while the ship had been in the best place to view them, but Gerard had found himself more and more looking forward to the mealtimes in the vast banquet hall. He watched news feeds, he swam, he had even started to read a book—something he had not done in a long time.

Yes, he thought as he stared out of the long window, the stars dim in comparison with the interior lighting in the corridor where he now stood, I will be glad to finish the cruise and head home again to Mars.

Gerard had been about to turn away when something caught his eye. Three bright points grouped close together flared brighter than any of the stars. He did not know what this phenomenon was, but they were beautiful, glowing with a faint blue tinge, and seeming to grow brighter by the moment. "Hey!" he called back to his wife, who was stuck to her slate, as usual. "Vanessa, some and look at this. It's..."

She didn't look up from her slate. "It's what?" she answered, equal parts irritated and disinterested.

"Oh, shit. It's coming straight for us!"

"On-field!" GH-456 called out as the last command of the operation. They would vanish and be away and, even if the larger ship sent out an SOS of some sort, the cause of their demise would be a mystery and the legend of the McMurdo Triangle would continue to grow. "On-field, TS-257!" he called out again, sharper this time. It was not the moment to let a silly slip expose them. They needed to be away as quickly as possible.

"I'm trying, Captain," TS-257 replied. "But I'm getting no response."

"Try again!"

"But, Captain," TS-257 replied, "if I push it too far..."

GH-456 knew the risks of pushing the dispersion field too far. There had been many experimental stealth ships before the one they now rode in had been perfected. And "perfected" was stretching things. They were riding in a glorified prototype. He sighed. "Fine. Keep course, power low. We will coast and hope they do not notice us, then try again as soon as it is safe to do so."

FOURTEEN

Three perfect, bright spots had appeared one after the other, evenly placed along the line of the retreating *SS Majestic* as they sped towards it. They were small, even in the enhanced view port in the shuttle that contained Gus and Franklin. Franklin had turned the ship as soon as he got the communication from the *Majestic's* captain. There was nothing he could do to stop what was about to happen, however. Franklin was a man who had almost always been able to do *something*, so the feeling inside him had been a sickening one as he waited to see if the stealth ship was going to—as expected—attack the *Majestic*. They didn't have to wait too long.

Now that the attack had happened, that sickness was mixing with a trembling rage, a feeling so sharp and hot. He had been a much younger man when he had last felt this way.

"*Majestic, Majestic*, report!" he called over the comms. "This is Shuttle 3, please be advised that we are in-coming." In the moments before it had been struck, he had called for them to jump away—screaming it over comms, as if this would not have been Smith's first thought—but they had not done so. The *Majestic* was of the latest design in passenger liners, yet something of its size, even something so recently built, would not have been able to jump away so quickly. Only military ships carried the redundancy of a separate, short-range drive that could be fired up quickly enough to get them out of trouble. Such things were expensive and, on passenger ships, unnecessary. Except for right now.

As the shuttle drew closer, the occasional flare within the ship showed the progress of the damage caused by the three strikes, even though there was little evidence on the outside, because of the vacuum's tendency to extinguish fires without the oxygen to keep them going. For a ship the size of the *Majestic*, this gave it a little more chance of some sort of survival, of not being torn into so many pieces, of retaining pockets of functioning atmosphere. Franklin had to hope.

One of the strikes had hit around the drive cones and the ship had lost its thrust. The explosions within the *Majestic* were so forceful that they could already overcome some of its momentum, and the enormous ship was slowly pitching forward.

"The *Laughing Zebra*," Gus said behind him.

Franklin looked at the readout on his console. "It's still there," he replied, assuming Gus was telling him that the Koru stealth ship had turned and now the freighter had met the same fate as the *Majestic*. Maybe even they would be next.

"I know," Gus said, "and if they haven't seen this," he gestured towards the unfolding fate of the *Majestic* through the enhanced view port, "then we need to get them over to help, there are people that need to get off the *Majestic*."

The sick, angry feeling in his stomach was growing ever colder. "But what if we bring them over to their death as well?" Something in the top corner of the enhanced picture caught his eye. It was a blur—a smudge, really—and he zoomed in just a little further, trying to get the shuttle's optics to clean up the image as much as possible. At best, he got the impression of a small ship moving away from them. "Scratch that," he said. "I think that's the bastards hightailing it away."

Every instinct within Franklin wanted to race after them and somehow take them out. Which was absurd, because he and Gus were in a defenceless shuttle. What was he going to do, ram them? Anyway, Gus was right. They needed all hands to enact any sort of rescue. The *Majestic* had escape pods—he had seen some of them when he first came on board, although the name "pod" was a little misleading, as each fitted twelve people in it. However, given how widespread the damage was, who knew how many were functioning and how accessible they were? The designers would not have worked with the idea of multiple torpedo strikes in mind.

"Come in, *Laughing Zebra*." It was Gus, who had accessed the comms from his position in the rear. "This is *Majestic* Shuttle 3, requesting emergency assistance."

Silence stretched on for several moments, and the two men looked at each other.

"Read you *Majestic* Shuttle 3," came the static-filled reply, the voice full of a regional accent Franklin recognised as coming from the Hatha region, on the other side of Proxima from the capital city. A farm girl far from home. "What that come up on sweep?"

"That *Majestic*," Gus answered, and Franklin noted how he had slipped into the same regional dialect, even catching some of the accent, as if he had been used to speaking it in the past.

"She in trouble?"

"She came under attack."

"Same thing been taking other ships?"

Franklin and Gus exchanged a look; Franklin nodded. "Same thing."

"Then good luck. We not wait to die."

Franklin balled his fists. "Wankers."

"*Majestic* save your lives," Gus said. "Ship after you 'til it find bigger target."

A pause on the other end. "It still here?"

"Gone. We saw it leave." *Probably.* The other ship had been only a shadow on the shuttle's sensors, but they had seen it for a moment. In his gut, Franklin now felt more than ever that it was a Koru ship, yet why they were waging a clandestine war in this way was beyond him.

"We come round, Shuttle 3. Meet you there."

Franklin breathed a sigh of relief. There was room for maybe twenty in the shuttle if they packed in uncomfortably tight, although the environmental system might have something to say about that. Plus, the shuttle wasn't interstellar capable. Although *The Laughing Zebra* would take nowhere near the number of people that were on the *Majestic*, but it might just make up for the destroyed or malfunctioning pods. Even a small freighter could jam in a couple of hundred people for a short time, at least. Of course, over a thousand people were on the *Majestic*, although Franklin did not how many would still be alive.

"*Majestic*," Gus said, having switched to hailing the stricken starliner. "This is Shuttle 3, please let us know your status." Nothing came back. "The freighter *Laughing Zebra* is en route to assist with rescue."

"No pods yet," Franklin said.

"It's not been long," Gus countered. "Can you land on it when it's spinning like that?"

The spin had picked up slightly. If the environmental systems on the *Majestic* were struggling or giving up, the ship would be becoming a very unpleasant place to be. The spin was also more likely to end up breaking it apart.

"Sure," Franklin lied. It was going to be terrible to land on, but not impossible. "Let's get on there now, though, before that spin gets any worse."

He approached the *Majestic* as quickly as he dared to, expecting at any moment for several pods to come careening towards him. They would, of course, have an automated collision avoidance system, but the closer he got, the better it would have to be to avoid him. Using the manoeuvring thrusters, he matched speed. Locating the closest bay, he tried to decide if its atmospheric shield was up.

The *Olympic* was too old to have an atmospheric shield, a piece of technology that was only around twenty years old, so had to go through a lengthy depressurizing process for the whole bay. Even that, to be fair, was an outmoded way of doing it. Franklin could see that the blue atmospheric shield was intact as he got closer to the bay, and he knew that shield would cling to his ship as he passed through—*if* he got the landing right—like the way objects can sometimes pass through the surface of a soapy bubble, the bubble reforming again behind them. He did not drift diagonally towards it but rather in little stages, like the shuttle was climbing invisible steps. *Up-and-forward, up-and-forward, up-and...*

With an ungainly jolt on the stick, the shuttle lurched forward into the bay, and straight into trouble.

FIFTEEN

"Our delivery destination is moving." Engee was sitting in the co-pilot's seat of the *Mutt's Nuts*, Sarah at the helm. Nigel was in the seat behind them, which was different, as he had spent most of the journey with his feet up on the table in the galley, eating his way through their stores. Engee had been looking at the small tracking slate that they had received on the asteroid. Nigel had one, too, and had occasionally made a point of checking it right in front of Sarah, as if he didn't trust them to go to the right place. Asshole.

"It's because we're getting closer," he said. Sarah did not see Nigel wave off-handedly behind her, but assumed he had, as it was the perfect accompaniment to the superior voice he was using. It didn't bother Sarah so much when he spoke that way to her, but, when he took that tone with Engee, she got all protective and ragey.

"Closer?" Engee queried.

"To the planet," he said slowly, like talking to an idiot. "Which moves relative to everything else."

"She's not talking about the coordinates, dumbass," Sarah said to Nigel. "She's looking at the slate. You know, the one you've been making *way* too big a point of looking at for the whole journey." *Man,* she could not wait for this to be over and to be rid of him.

"The point's relative position in space is moving," Engee confirmed, Nigel's sarcasm not affecting her.

Sarah heard Nigel sit up a little behind her, probably checking his own slate. "Shit, you're right. That means it's a ship. They didn't mention that."

"More than that," Sarah said, "it means they knew its flight path. But now it's changed. Wonder what they've had us tracking all this time and why it's not going where they thought it was going."

"Whatever it is, it is not moving quickly," Engee said. "At least we will not have to chase our delivery destination all over the McMurdo Rift."

"We're nearly on it, aren't we?" Sarah said.

"Hand control to me," Engee said. "I will slow and adjust course as we will be in-system in just over a minute."

Engee loved flying the *Nuts* and, mostly, Sarah did not begrudge her that, but her Koru first mate had an unnerving talent for using the ship's weaponry, despite professing inexperience with and a dislike of weapons in general. Considering the unpredictable way this string of related jobs had been going, Sarah wanted to be ready for trouble. "Hand me the slate, I'll take care of that. You bring up fire control."

Behind her, Nigel perked up a little at that. "That nasty CEW you tried to kill me with?"

"If Engee had meant to kill you, she would have," Sarah replied with a sideways grin.

"Can I have a go?"

"No!" both Sarah and Engee replied at once.

Nigel huffed and sat back in his seat again.

"They're not toys, you know," Sarah said, like she was speaking to an over-inquisitive child.

"Maybe he could manage the point defence?" Engee suggested, sounding like she was mediating between them.

Sarah sighed. "Fine, I'll send control of the PDW suite back to you. Don't let us die, okay?"

Nigel brightened again. Looking at the slate, Sarah laid in a course correction, executing a slow turn as the ship decelerated, though it was still travelling well in excess of light speed. She wanted to come out of the jump a little sooner than the computer would choose to. If she didn't like what she was seeing, then the *Mutt's Nuts* would be out of there again as soon as it could.

"Are we ready?" she asked a few moments later and got a positive reply from the other two. "Okay, I'm going to jump out manually on three, two..."

"Manually?" Nigel squawked in panic.

"one..."

Sarah cut the light speed engine and, had someone been floating around nearby, they would have seen the

Mutt's Nuts appear almost from nowhere, like space had suddenly vomited them into existence.

"Manually!" Nigel said again, more of an enraged squeal this time. "Are you try to fucking kill us?"

Even on their sub-light engines, they were still moving at quite some clip, although the surrounding space was empty. There were no ships, no rocky or even icy bodies of any sort. "Where's that ship we're looking for?" Sarah asked Engee, ignoring Nigel's protests and smiling a little inside.

"Directly ahead. Still moving slowly."

Sarah used the enhanced view port to zoom in. Still nothing. Even though the ship was coming towards them, they still might have expected to at least get some sense of a drive plume. "Can't see it. Don't like it," she said, preparing to jump away.

"We have another contact." It was Nigel.

Next to Sarah, Engee squinted at her own display. Then she rubbed at the screen, as if checking to see whether what she was looking at was a mark or a smear on the surface of it. "We do. So faint. Some sort of phantom reading? A comet?"

"That's a ship," Nigel stated. "It's on a route to pass us, though. It's..."

"What?" Sarah demanded, on the verge of bringing up the sensor screen herself, rather than have to listen to Engee and Nigel's confusing babbling.

"It's gone," he said. "Vanished."

"It has," Engee said. "See, a phantom."

"Are we staying?" Nigel asked after a few more moments. Sarah could hear the tension in his voice. Almost fear. Something was wrong here; he knew it, she knew it. Maybe it was a need to get this damned job done that stayed her from jumping away as she had promised herself she would, yet she feared it was something darker within herself. A sort of morbid curiosity that didn't just want to stare into the face of danger but also wanted to stick its head in danger's mouth.

"Let's get a little closer to the delivery point," she said. "But you be ready on those PDWs, Nige."

"Don't call me 'Nige.'"

Even in a tense moment, there was always time to wind their unwanted partner up. Sarah continued the way they had been going, keeping the enhanced view in front of her.

"We could signal them on comms?" Engee suggested after about half-a-minute of quiet tenseness in the cockpit. "Wait," she added, before Sarah could tell her first mate that announcing their presence in such a way would be a terrible idea. "I've got another contact approaching the first one."

Just as Engee said that, a tiny but distinct dot made itself clear on the enhanced view port. Sarah squinted myopically at the display. "That's our delivery point. That's a big ship, larger than the cargo vessels that usually run around out here."

"Military?" Nigel suggested.

"Again, military and 'that big' don't tend to be a combination around The Rift."

"You sound like you know it well."

Sarah and Engee exchanged a glance. Without ever agreeing about it, neither of them had shared any of their recent history with The McMurdo Rift with Nigel and, although he was likely aware of the death of Vik, Sarah's husband, he had made no mention of it since stepping aboard the *Mutt's Nuts*. Probably a good thing, as almost anything that Nigel said on that subject would have caused Sarah to hit him.

"A starliner?" Engee suggested. "The *SS Olympic*." Something within Sarah twinged at the way Engee said it. Almost a longing, although Sarah did not know if that was for the place or a certain fitness instructor that her first mate had been rather friendly with during their time in the area. Thinking about it, maybe that twinging feeling inside was all her own, the name of *Olympic* casting its own spell over her.

"What the...?" Sarah said, as she continued to watch the enhanced view.

"I saw it too," Engee added next to her.

"Saw what?" Nigel asked.

"It... glowed for a moment," Sarah said, trying to make sense of what she saw.

"Glowed?"

"Only a little," Engee said. "Small. There and then gone."

"Like a pulsar," Sarah said, airing her thought out loud. Then it happened again. The dot that was the ship they were heading towards glowed and dimmed again. The second ship heading towards it could now be glimpsed in the enhanced view. A greyish dot barely distinguishable from the surrounding darkness.

A moment after she could see the second ship, a comms request came from it. Sarah accepted the request. They may have been spotted, but comms were not guns or torpedoes, and they were still far enough away to turn tail and run.

"Unidentified ship," came an accented voice. "This is *Laughing Zebra*. Tell me your purpose."

Tell me your purpose. Shit, but they sounded scared. "This is *Mutt's Nuts*." Sarah paused, considering her next words. "Our purpose is our own. Is... er, everything okay with you?" Perhaps another time she would have cringed at the awkwardness of her comms message, but not right now.

"*Mutt's Nuts*, please be aware hostile ship in vicinity," the accented voice told her. "We are on way to aid *SS Majestic*, struck by multiple torpedoes."

Sarah glanced across at Engee, who mouthed the word "Phantom" back.

"Please assist."

"That's our delivery point, isn't it?" Nigel asked from behind her. "The *Majestic?*"

Yes, and someone just blew it up. Sarah remembered seeing that the brand-new SS *Majestic* was coming out to do the run through the McMurdo Rift. It had seemed odd to her and, of course, she had thought of Mark and Gus and Arnold Philby, those she knew on the SS *Olympic*, which might be put out of business by a bigger, more luxurious ship doing the run. She had privately wished the *Majestic* misfortune, but not *this.*

"There goes the light again," Engee said. Then she added, showing uncharacteristic trepidation as she spoke the words. "Could the light be explosions, do you think?"

"I doubt it," Nigel answered, no hint of his previous sarcasm present. "From here, a light that bright could only be a drive plume."

"So why—" Engee began, but Sarah's horror cut her off.

"Is it doing that?" Sarah finished as the light flared and vanished again in the distant image on the view port. "Because the ship is spinning, Engee. It's spinning way too fast. It will be a wonder if it isn't in pieces already."

SIXTEEN

The rate of spin of the vast ship was increasing and, although the atmospheric shield that kept space outside of the bay and a breathable, controlled environment inside of it was intact, things were still dangerous inside the bay. A magnetic system kept most things in place should, for any reason, the shield fail; but these magnets were not, apparently, strong enough to hold everything in place against the g-forces being created by the spinning ship. Ironically, perhaps, things might have been better if the environmental systems had given up the ghost or if vacuum reigned within the bay.

The shuttle shifted sideways, seeming to make its own "oof" sound as some sort of large storage box hit it in the side. At the controls, Franklin desperately corrected as he tried to land the craft while, at the same time, not wanting to land it on its nose or roof.

"How the hell are we going to get anyone out of this?" Gus asked. "If we can even survive the docking bay, that is."

Franklin frowned with concentration as he unsuccessfully chased the floor for the third time in succession. "Engines," he said. "We've got to get to the engines."

Something else struck them, another shuttle this time, glancing off and passing almost surreally in front of the view port before disappearing through the atmospheric field and out of the bay. Alarms started blaring, and either something went wrong with the controls or Franklin over-corrected, because in the next moment he was hurtling towards the back of the bay. The shuttle landed too heavily and toppled to one side, sliding across the floor of the bay and coming to a stop with a thump and, disoriented, Franklin cut thrust before he ended up shooting them back across the bay again at shuttle-wrecking speed.

As their reality turned, he waited for the shuttle to begin sliding, ready to up the power again and stop it from finding another brief resting point somewhere. But that didn't happen. Franklin and Gus looked at each other for a long moment before, the world continuing to turn, Franklin finally dared to say what was on both of their minds.

"I think we might be embedded in a wall or wedged somewhere."

"Who knew that would ever be a positive?" Gus said. "Maybe I should take up flying, 'cos I could have done that."

Franklin reached over and popped a small hatch to his right, revealing a small equipment cupboard. He took out two round, grey objects, each just over a hand span in width and with an almost half-circle handle attached to the top of it, handing one of them back to Gus.

"Breach magnets," he said in answer to his friend's questioning look. "For blocking hull breaches by micro meteorites and, well, anything else that might go puncturing the hull of a ship." Grabbing the handle of one of them, he twisted it so the handle moved to the left about thirty degrees, causing it to emit a small, momentary whine. "There's a powerful, charged magnet in each of these that helps to make sure it stays where it's needed. We're going to use these to get through the ship and reach the engines."

Gus indicated the spinning ship that the shuttle had become a part of. "Stop this."

Franklin nodded. "Obviously the bridge can't; some sort of severing of command and control, I guess. I don't know why they haven't sorted it in engineering, but we've got to try, or almost everyone on this ship is going to die."

Gus looked doubtfully at the breach magnet in his hand.

"Just turn it on when you need to stick to something," Franklin said. "All the walls have enough metal in them, I'm sure. And, you know... just don't let go."

"Man, this is a bad idea," Gus said, although he turned the breach magnet as Franklin had shown him and made to undo his straps.

"We survived my last bad idea, didn't we?" Franklin was referring to the time just a few months ago when he had made Gus jump out of a moving ship in vacuum.

Gus launched out of his seat towards the door. "I'm not sure that's the reassurance I was looking for."

"Careful!" Franklin said as Gus opened the door and made to poke his head out of the shuttle as it lay on its side. A cylindrical metal object that Franklin didn't know the purpose of glanced off the side of the shuttle with a nasty thump. It was an almost perfect illustration of the point he had been about to make. It was more than a metre from the door but looked and sounded heavy enough to break any head that it did land on. "A lot of shit flying around out there. Make sure it's clear before you do and get straight over the top of the shuttle and into cover."

Gus may not have had the head that Franklin did for these sorts of moments, but he did have the body. He slipped lithely through the door and out of sight in one swift movement. On Franklin's turn, however, the turning gravity had him hanging onto the doorway and thumping the breach magnet hard against the exterior of the shuttle to keep him in place. He had a moment to glance about him and along the bay, to comprehend the amount of chaos in just this one small part of the ship as so many objects tumbled through the middle of it at one time.

He hugged close to the exterior of the shuttle, expecting at any moment to be knocked and lose his grip on the magnet or to have his last moment be the sight of something enormous tumbling towards him. But the moment of suspension passed and then he was turning off the magnet and scrambling in an ungainly fashion down toward Gus.

"Took your time," Gus said, and Franklin couldn't quite tell if he was serious or joking.

Either way, it seemed it deserved the same reply. "Go fuck yourself."

The similarity of the layout to the *Olympic* was what enabled Franklin to know that they only had to take one turn on the journey toward the *Majestic's* engineering section. *Know* was a strong way to put it. It was more that he hoped the picture he had in his head was more or less accurate and, fortunately, it was.

After the turn, they faced the long corridor towards the back of the ship, and this gave them the greatest problem, quickly going from something they could run along to a lengthy slide, then to a thirty-plus metre drop and back again. Although at least they did not have to navigate any stairs. There was nobody in the corridor as they moved along it—doing so agonisingly slowly while waiting for the ship to come apart around them or an explosion to rip through the wall that they were clinging to at any moment. What they did hear were the sound of distant screams and a multitude of creaks, groans and thumps, both near and far.

Then, as they neared the end of the corridor and the "No Unauthorised Personnel" sign that marked the entrance to engineering, they heard a mighty roar, a sound like angry, blustery wind that did not intend to let up for even a moment.

"Are those the engines?" Gus called out to him, raising his voice to be heard over it.

Did you ever even go to the rear end of the ship on the Olympic? Franklin thought to himself. Although, to be fair, when was the last time that he had? He had turned into one of those people who just let the ship take him wherever and didn't worry too much about the "how" of it.

"No," he said. "That's the reason we're still spinning. If anyone was alive in there, they've already fled." He opened the first set of doors between the rest of the ship and one of the entrances to the engineering section. It opened into a small space about the size of an airlock. Closing the door behind them, as the ship slowly shifted, it was a little easier to move around and stay with it.

The roaring sound was twice as loud now that there was only one door between them and the engineering section, and they could feel heat radiating through the doors and the wall beyond it. Franklin pulled two suits from a locker in the wall. "We'll need these on," he told Gus as he threw one at him.

Gus looked at the vacuum-rated suit he had been given. "Is there no atmosphere in there?"

Franklin pointed towards the sound beyond the doors. "Something is helping that fire burn, so the environment in there must be intact. But I'm betting it is damned hot and hard to breathe in there either way."

In the slowly shifting room, the two men moved to straddle the corner between the floor and the door they had entered through. "Are we just going to open the door and get roasted?" Gus asked.

"We'll be fine." Even in his own head, Franklin did not sound very convincing. "First one to get changed without falling over goes through the doorway last," he added to get his friend moving. Both of them fell over several times before they had their suits on, so Franklin did the decent thing and offered to go first. If Gus was right about the roasting thing, it wouldn't matter either way.

The doors were not as hot as he worried they might be, and the inner—sealed—portal that led through into the engineering section of the *SS Majestic* opened without creating any sort of catastrophic back draft. The sight that greeted them once they had stepped through, however, did little to fill them with confidence. Although a maze of steps, gantries and platforms, it was here and there possible to see just about all the way up in the vast space that they now stood in. The lights were out and whatever secondary systems there should have been seemed to have failed them too, so they should not have been able to see that far, but flames that occupied much of the far wall and extended across the distant ceiling provided their own illumination.

There were no signs of other people, save for a booted foot extending from a platform a couple of storeys above their heads. The angle of it suggested that they were not conscious and, if that was the case, Franklin wondered how they had remained in that position as the ship turned. Although Franklin wanted to head up towards them and see if there was anything he could do, he knew that he had to assume the worst for now and get on with what he had come to do. The first part was quite wide and open and, the longer they spent in it, the more chance they would end up dangling from the floor.

Gus stepped as if to head towards the owner of the booted feet, and Franklin had to reach out and stop him. "No time. We'll check on the way back." Through the helmet, it momentarily looked like Gus might disagree, but in the end he simply nodded and they started towards the other side of the vast engineering section.

"What are we going to do?" Gus asked as they reached a natural corridor heading deeper into the section, towards the engines, which was formed mostly by a mixture of pipes and what looked like a long bank of instruments that Franklin was not one hundred percent on the purpose of. He knew what he was looking for, but not exactly what it would look like.

"The top cones are firing," Franklin said. "That is why we are spinning. I'm going to cut them and, if possible, fire the bottom cones or some manoeuvring thrusters. Anything that will slow the spin, and hopefully bring it under the control of the environmental systems. So..." He slammed his breach magnet against one of the large pipes as if for illustration, while the floor fell away from them yet again. "We can stop this shit and evacuate to the *Olympic.*"

"Can you do that?" Gus asked, finding a point for his own magnet and shifting his body as he found a point in which to wedge it.

Franklin's answer grin held little mirth in it. "We'll see, eh?"

SEVENTEEN

"Say again, *Laughing Zebra.*"

"We collected three pods so far. Is all. Less than thirty survivors."

Sarah blew out her cheeks in despair and flopped back in her seat. She looked out of the view port at the vast, slowly tumbling ship for a moment, then glanced over at Engee. "Less than thirty," she repeated. "Out of what? A few thousand between the crew and the passengers?"

"This is the McMurdo Rift," Engee said, her voice tinged with a sort of doubtful hope. "It might have been operating at well below capacity."

"Mark said that the *Olympic* rarely runs with less than a thousand." Sarah threw up a hand towards the view port. "And this." This was the *SS Majestic*, so much grander and surely much busier. The crew member on the *Laughing Zebra* had confirmed which stricken ship they were looking at, although Sarah had already worked it out. She had seen about the *Majestic* being assigned to the McMurdo route—remembered being both dumbfounded at such an assignment and also worried for Franklin and Gus and for the business of the *Olympic* in general—and, once she was sure that it wasn't the *Olympic* in pieces before her, came to the logical conclusion about which ship it had to be.

A small tinge of relief had run through her when she had realised that it wasn't the *Olympic*, followed by a wave of guilt for thinking that way. Mark, Gus, Arnold, even Mark's cat, Geoff, who had taken as much of a liking to Engee during their brief stay on the *Olympic* as Gus evidently had, she had feared for all of them when she saw the stricken passenger liner. And yet, now that she was here before the thing, hearing of less than thirty souls saved so far, the horror, the fear, was filling her up again. She could not sit where she was while all those people died.

The centre of the *Majestic* appeared to be buckling; so there was the hope that it might give entirely. That was a grim thing to be hoping for, but at least that separated section, free of the thrusters, might prove a little easier to approach; a chance to save more people than there was right now.

"Shuttle entered bay at rear," the voice from the *Laughing Zebra* informed her. She hadn't even realised the channel was still open.

"Which shuttle?"

"From *Majestic*. Came to warn us. Went back to stop ship spinning."

So, some crazy bastard had flown back into the ship after it had been hit. That knowledge made Sarah even more desperate to get back in there, too. But what could they do? Now and then she saw evidence of an explosion or fire flaring behind a view port. In between those moments, the ship just kept on shedding bits, pieces falling from it like a comet shedding ice particles. Her brain felt stuck, caught between the desire to act and the sheer foolishness of doing so. Even if she went in by herself, she had a responsibility not to die in there and leave poor Engee alone with Nigel, who Sarah still did not trust in the slightest.

"Tracker's switched." It was Nigel who spoke from behind her, pulling her mind from its uncomfortable quandary.

Both Sarah and Engee turned back to look at Nigel, but it was Sarah who spoke. "What?"

"The tracker has switched; it's no longer tracking the *Majestic*."

"Then what the fuck is it tracking?" Sarah had had enough. She had been more messed around on this job than she ever cared to be again. She had been shot at, sent to the middle of nowhere, seen her commission handed over to bloody Nigel and now led to the horrible sight of the stricken *Majestic*. If they were being fucked about with again, then she was just going to give Nigel the tracker and the box and drop him off at the nearest planet with a spaceport. He could have the damned fortune the job came with.

"A person, I guess. Look for yourself." He pushed it across to her own screen and she could see what he meant. The delivery location was *on* the *Majestic*, and it appeared to have life signs. Their heart rate was elevated, unsurprisingly, but they were alive and heading towards where Sarah guessed the bridge would be.

"Well... shit."

Nigel stood up in a sudden, dramatic movement. "You've got powered EVA suits on this rust bucket?"

Sarah half-stood in response, ignoring the jibe—there had been many. "Don't tell me you're feeling heroic?"

Nigel laughed so sharply that he coughed. "You're funny sometimes, Shah. I'm going to deliver my package. You know, 'cos I'm a courier."

Sarah pointed out of the view port. "On that?"

Nigel snorted. "No wonder I'm always beating you to the decent contracts. You haven't got what it takes to be the best."

"I'm going to pretend you didn't just cheese all over my cockpit."

"Half a job, that's you."

Out of the corner of her eye, Sarah could see Engee's gaze bouncing between the two of them, like a child watching mom and dad hurling insults at each other. She shuddered at that unpleasant image.

"If I make delivery on my own, the money's mine," Nigel said and turned to leave.

"Not if we leave you to die on there," Sarah replied. She winced when she heard Engee gasp. "Alright, for fucksake," she went on, getting to her feet. "Engee, you good with the *Nuts* until we get back? First sign of danger you prioritise yourself and the ship, okay?"

As soon as Sarah left the cockpit and followed Nigel down the crew quarters corridor towards the galley, she felt a great weight was gone from her shoulders—her spirits lifting despite the horrendous danger that lay ahead if they went inside the crippled starliner. Whether or not he knew it, Nigel had helped her make the choice she wanted to make.

The best powered EVA suits were in the cargo bay and the two of them were silent as they changed, the lanky Nigel almost too tall for the biggest suit. Sarah realised she was glad that he fit into it. She still did not trust Nigel, but she also did not want to go into the *Majestic* alone. In fact, every time she thought of doing so, Sarah found she did not want to go into it at all. Curious though we she was about the delivery and who this recipient on the dying ship was, self-preservation was a stronger motivator. It gave her a small, warm feeling that the thought of saving lives was stronger. Her husband had died on a stricken spaceship not too long ago.

Indeed, the lack of escape pods coming from the *Majestic* brought to mind for Sarah the shield-equipped

Koru cruiser that she and her friends had played a part in destroying. Most particularly, she remembered Mark's description of the escape pods that would not operate, the look of confusion and fear on the faces of those inside. Was this, the destruction of the *SS Majestic*, the work of the Koru military too? When she considered the regard for life that they had shown their own kind, and the attack on the Regus mining station, then thousands of passengers on a starliner were not much of a leap at all.

Sarah glanced behind them to the impact box that was still strapped against the wall and made a decision. "We should open the box."

"No," Nigel said. Just that. Almost as if he had been reading her mind. Or, perhaps, having similar thoughts.

Sarah became petulant. "It's my fucking ship."

"It goes against everything we stand for."

Sarah rolled her eyes. "Oh my, you take this courier business very seriously, don't you?"

Nigel's eyes flicked up towards her as he checked the seals on his suit, but he didn't answer. It irritated her.

"Man, you're long overdue getting laid," she huffed.

"I expect you are now, too."

If Sarah had been holding a gun at that point, she would have shot him and gone alone to the *Majestic* after all. A small flicker across Nigel's face, gone almost before Sarah noticed it, told her he knew he had crossed a line.

"Yes," he said through gritted teeth, "I have nothing much else but the job and my ship. It's who I am, and I haven't even got my ship right now. Least I can do is do this right."

It was the most honest, unguarded thing she had heard him say, but she couldn't let it win the argument. "What if what's in there is the size of a piece of fruit?" She indicated the impact box, which would have to be handled between the two of them. "Taking that through a collapsing ship is stupid."

"We could locate the recipient and bring them out," Nigel said. It was a reasonable argument.

Sarah stepped towards him, her eyes searching his face. "Come on; it must have occurred to you that our delivery might have something to do with all of this."

"If it's a bomb, then it's a little late to the party."

Sarah laughed at that, even though it was an inappropriate thing to say. "You're right, we'll rescue the recipient and anyone else we can along the way."

"If you say so," Nigel said, implying the last part of that was not his idea. He locked his helmet in place and turned towards the back of the bay.

Sarah waited for him to take several steps and opened an equipment cupboard that was just a couple of metres away from the impact box. She pulled out a compressed energy cutter and turned it on before Nigel even realised that anything was happening. He stopped and looked back in time to see Sarah cutting into the lock at the front of the impact box.

Nigel made no move to stop her, even though he likely had enough time to wrestle her away from the box before she got through the lock. What Sarah did feel was the weight of his disapproving look, before comms inside her suit crackled into life. "Careful!" Nigel snapped. "You're getting sparks all over your EVA suit. *Ah,* it was almost like he cared.

Sarah stepped back to see the mangled results of her hasty handiwork. The impact box's useful life was over. Nigel stepped up beside her. "We still don't have to, you know."

Sarah grinned inside her helmet. If Nigel was so above all of this, he would have stayed on the other side of the bay, and there would have been no "we" about it. She pulled up the lid and found, encased within a lot of protective packaging, a gunmetal grey object, cube-shaped and a little less than a metre across.

"Could still be a bomb," Nigel said.

Sarah was not an explosive's expert, but she had seen enough pictures to think that Nigel might be right. Looking a little closer, she could see, on one side, some dials and switches, perhaps a read out of some sort. Then she noticed, of all things, a slip of paper tucked down the side between the object and the packaging. She reached out and grabbed it and heard Nigel suck in a breath as she did so.

It was a printed note - how quaint and extravagant - which read:

Dear Captain Smith, I hope this finds you well. I apologise for the clandestine theatrics, but I cannot reveal my identity to you via what may not be a secure method of communication. Think of me as 'H' for now.

It is my sincere belief that you and everyone on the SS Majestic is in grave danger. If my information is correct, they have sent you to the McMurdo Rift to die in a specific manner, killed by a ship or ships you will never see coming. Lambs to the slaughter. These are Koru ships, and there are those in positions of power who are aware that these stealth ships exist, and that they are already operating in the rift. They hope that your destruction will give them an excuse for war with the Koru, and perhaps much more besides.

Enclosed you will find a one-of-a-kind piece of secret military equipment that may just keep you alive. It is a type of sensor called a 'Phase Field Particle Detector.' The name is not important. What matters is that if you can connect it to the Majestic's sensor system, then it MAY BE capable of detecting one of these ships before they can get close enough to fire on you.

I realise that this may be a lot, Captain, and must look like some elaborate hoax or worse, but I am deadly serious. We are working to remedy your situation but, until then, stay alive. It is just possible that the stable future of the UTC depends on it.

Your friend,
H.

Sarah finished reading and looked up at Nigel, who had been reading the note over her shoulder. Saying nothing more to each other, they turned and headed for the back of the bay.

EIGHTEEN

The good news was that the flames that had been flowing almost like liquid up the wall, and even across the ceiling several storeys up, had ceased. Franklin had watched the last moments of it retreating towards a pair of previously obscured bulkhead doors, revealing a small crack in the wall right next to the doors. He glanced around, looking for evidence of whatever could have punched a hole through the bulkhead between engineering and the engines themselves, the thickest in the ship.

"Do we need to get into there?" Gus asked, pointing at the doors.

The station they had left behind just around the corner, the one that Franklin had planned to operate the engines from, but which had appeared to have no power going to it, meant that *yes*, now they did. Franklin held up the metal bar he had found along the way in answer. Aside from the body they had seen lying on the stairs, they had spotted no one else in the engineering section as they moved through it. That should have been a clue that he could not shut off or fire the engines from in there. Surely someone would have tried to do so before fleeing. What they might not have tried is the crazy step of manually operating them from beyond those doors... where all that fire had been coming from.

Franklin stepped forward to begin his efforts to jimmy open the bulkhead door and noticed something... his feet were starting to lift off the floor. Only this time it was not the turning ship changing gravity on him.

"What the...?" Gus began.

"The environmental system is finally giving up the ghost."

"Great."

"No, this is a good thing." Franklin got some purchase with the thin end of the bar but could not move the doors so much as an inch. "Except it doesn't help with getting these open."

Gus shoved him aside and placed his breach magnet to floor, pushing his foot against it. "This is the one thing I *can* do," he said, "so let me be useful." He worked the bar furiously, turning a crack into a gap, then into something wide enough to get the bar through, before he levered it open. This all happened in seconds, but Franklin's elation became horror when he saw what lay beyond.

Gus did not notice at first, as he had his head and shoulder down, forcing himself into the gap, widening it enough so that Franklin could pass. "Come on," he gasped when Franklin failed to move, then he followed his gaze. In the engine section, detritus filled the space; ruined, twisted parts of the ship floating around in it.

And there were bodies, too. And parts of them. Gus almost slipped and let the doors shut. "Fuck." He just about recovered, his quivering arms holding it in place.

Beyond the detritus, Franklin could see that part of the back of the ship was open to space, the glow of engine plumes evident somewhere beyond. "Stay here," he said, ducking under Gus' arms as gracefully as possible, given the circumstances, then launching himself across the space in the steadily disappearing gravity.

Gus gave a wheezing laugh in answer. "As long as I can, buddy. As long as I can."

Franklin did his best to focus in on the point he was aiming for, concentrating on having tunnel vision so that he did not have to look at the horrors of what the torpedo attack had done. Perhaps a little oddly, he thought of the bogus supplies order he had placed so that he could make his stealth ship detector. Little good any of it had done them. With horrible timing, a familiar body floated in front of him, her face frozen in a terrifying death scream. "Torres," Franklin said, remembering how much pleasure the engineer had taken in teasing him about his own limited talents. He had tried not to feel offended at first, then found himself ribbing her back, at the same time realising just how much she brought to his unworkable design. "I'm sorry."

"What," Gus wheezed in his ears. Franklin had left the channel open.

"Nothing." Gus didn't need the news right now. He had liked Torres, too.

Franklin reached an access ladder and climbed it. Manually firing or cutting an engine meant doing exactly that. He needed first to cut the upper engines, some or all of which were still firing and causing the ship to spin in a way that was not only preventing rescue of the passengers and crew, but most likely putting too much g-force on people in some parts of the ship. Franklin had felt severe g-force in his life, and he knew that having your organs and bones crushed by it would not be a great way to go. Fortunately, the manual shut-off was not subtle, and Franklin saw the first one coming up as his helmet light fell across it. A great big handle in the "up" position, he yanked it downwards without hesitation and moved on along the gangway.

He was about halfway to the next engine's cut-off when the effects of stopping the first one started to be felt. The only gravity now was the spinning of the ship itself, a gentler gravity than the one the environmental system had imposed, which had caused the world to keeping moving on them as the ship's spinning had overwhelmed it. Franklin had to assume that the other two engines were still firing, feeling with senses he had honed through years of flying smaller ships, not yet dulled by all that time on a starliner, as the angle of the spin shifted.

Keep going. Two more to cut up here, and then let's hope something on the bottom will fire for us.

Franklin reached the second engine and cut it. Moving along the gangway in zero gravity with the ship turning about him was slow, but it was still a lot easier than it would have been with the environmental system still functioning. He moved onwards, time and even the gangway itself seeming to stretch away from him.

He felt and saw the explosion at the same time, both blinded and thumped across the whole of the front of his body at once. The lack of gravity meant that he went tumbling backwards, spinning feet-over-head, expecting at any moment to feel pain exploding in his back as he hit some part of the structure or got impaled on something pointy. Instead, Franklin's gloved hands reached out and found a railing. His left shoulder was wrenched, a sensation like it was about to be pulled from its socket. However, his fingers held on just long enough for his other hand to find the railing.

"There's a lot of fire up there, you know," Gus said over the suit-to-suit comms.

"I know, I know," Franklin gasped back, pulling into a crouched position as debris whizzed and spun over his head.

"You okay?"

"That's, um... an... evolving situation. Good news, though."

"Yeah?"

"The last of the upper engines just shut itself off."

"Should we go? This door's really heavy."

Franklin almost laughed as he finally dared to straighten again. "Nearly done," he said, then realised that the gantry was peeling away from the bulkhead that it was attached to.

"Oh, oh, I see you! You're... dangling?"

"I know, I know!" Franklin pushed himself away from the railing in the direction of the level below. He landed with an "oomph" and a feeling that his knees, as well as his shoulders, were getting too old for this. Turning, it seemed like this rear section of the ship was disintegrating, and Franklin was feeling more and more like he and Gus were becoming just two squishy little things among so much flying death. There was a hole in the back of the ship big enough that he could have flown the shuttle through it. That would have been quicker, if he had only known. Franklin again had to ask himself the question about whether any of those engines were likely to fire, anyway. And, if they did, whether they were as likely to explode and kill him as they were to provide the countering thrust that he was looking for.

Yet the dying hulk of the SS *Majestic* was still spinning at a rate that would make the rescue of those left alive on board near impossible, so he bounded and pulled and swung himself to where he could manually fire the thrusters. The first station was missing, so Franklin hurried onto the next one. The engine was exposed to space and part of the drive cone was gone, meaning that nothing happened when Franklin pulled the lever. Hardly surprising.

The meshed metal walkway below his feet shook and Gus came in on the comms again, tension and urgency back in his voice, all traces of his earlier levity gone. "Everything's coming apart, Franklin. Give it up. I don't even know if you'll get back to me."

"Just one more to go," Franklin said but, looking through to where the manual operation for that final engine would be located, he could see could occasional flares of light that did not fill him with confidence. Indeed, a part of the structure had collapsed so that a huge, bent metal girder partially obstructed his view. "I can do this," he added, forgetting that the comms channel was open.

"I know you can, buddy," Gus said. "Just... soon, okay?"

Franklin started moving, ducking and turning to the side as the thick girder buckled a little more. It seemed impossible that some metal as thick as that should be able to buckle at all.

Just as he was straightening, there was a sudden, violent shudder that had him floating through the air for a few moments, his arms flailing for something to grab a hold of. The only thing he found was a thick, insulated cable that sparked at one end and came terrifyingly close to his midsection before he got it under control. Then Franklin was moving again and the manual operation for the last of the lower engines was in front of him.

Even as a former pilot, Franklin never thought on a day-to-day basis about how big ships like the *Olympic* and the *Majestic* worked. They were, in essence, six large and powerful fusion reactors, "strapped" to the back of a structure. The cut-off lever was on, as expected, and the manual fire button was comically red and round. A cartoon version that surely did not belong in the real world, let alone amongst the horrors of this dying ship. Franklin pressed it and, for a moment that seemed like an eternity but was actually only a second, nothing happened. Then it seemed like the force of a fusion reactor was going right through him.

NINETEEN

Even through the protection of the EVA suit, Sarah felt like she was covered in bumps and bruises. Entering the *Majestic* had not been as hard as expected. They had abandoned the initial idea of heading through one of the spacecraft bays as a stupid one, after looking into the closest bay to the front of the ship and finding it full of flying debris, such as ships, crates and impact boxes.

An external airlock was not an option, as all such airlocks would either have needed to be operated from inside or through an authorised connection to the ship's probably now-screwed systems. Luckily, sort of, Sarah and Nigel found the handy ingress point of an open part of the ship that had either been sheared off or blown away. *That'll do*, she had thought grimly. There was little debris as they entered, perhaps because the *Majestic* had, by then, been spiralling through space for some time, and the contents of this part of the ship—presumably including some passengers and crew—were already many miles distant.

Sarah had not been prepared for just how much of a relief this lack of dead bodies and horror would be. As they made their way onto the least collapsed of the corridors on the exposed part of the ship, she looked down to see one of her gloved hands shaking. Even with the manoeuvring thrusters of the EVA suits, navigating the corridors was without bumping into the side of them was almost impossible, as the perspective of the ship continued to alter around them. The first bit of both good and bad news came when she and Nigel reached a sealed bulkhead door.

"Ah, shit, how do we get past this, then?" Nigel asked, frustration clear in his voice.

"No, this is good news," Sarah said. "It means there might be people still alive through there."

"If we can get to them."

"Ye of little faith," Sarah said with a self-satisfied grin that Nigel wouldn't even be able to see. She took out an object that she had grabbed from the cargo bay of the *Mutt's Nuts* on her way out of the door. It was hexagonally shaped and made of a smooth, dark, plastic-like material, the size of a side plate, although several times thicker.

"What's that you've got there?"

"A bit of specialist rescue equipment. I've only got the one of these, so let's hope it works. Took it as part payment for a job a year back. Felt like a dumb, soft idiot at the time and never knew if I would get the chance to use it." Nigel snorted at that. "Now..."

Sarah took a couple of steps away from the door and held the object out in front of her, feeling a liquid that was free of the vacuum in which she now stood sloshing about inside it. Orienting an arrow on the device upwards towards the ceiling, which was difficult with the spinning of the ship, Sarah pressed the operation button. Two small, metallic struts extended from the top and the bottom, with rubbery-looking ends that kept going until they found the ceiling and the floor. A light flashed and Sarah withdrew her hands, while the object adjusted so that it was sitting exactly halfway between the ceiling and floor. Four more struts extended, one from each side, and continued to anchor the object in place. Once all the rubber feet were set, a membranous material began to flow from the central part, forming a semi-transparent film that filled all the spaces between the struts and the outside of the corridor. It became a layer separating them and the bulkhead from the rest of the corridor that they had just come along. As Sarah watched, the material hardened further, becoming almost opaque, and the flashing light went out.

"Nice," Nigel said.

"If it holds and if we can get through that bulkhead."

Nigel pulled out some rather lower-tech equipment. "Leave that to me," he said.

Sarah watched as Nigel took his screwdriver and forced his way into a panel near the bulkhead door. It was mildly impressive, how quickly he got it open. He was full of surprises, she had to admit. He had also likely been a criminal at some point.

Sarah turned to look at her device, waiting for the thing to give. She had long ago forgotten what it was called, and the thing did not have its name printed anywhere on its surface, so she willed it to stay in place with the inner mantra: *Come on, weird corridor thing. Come on, weird corridor thing.* She only had to say it twice before she decided that the device was holding, barely even quivering in place, although the thing looked flimsy.

"Let's keep going and then," Sarah said, and stepped forward. As she passed through the bulkhead, there was a violent shudder. Sarah braced herself, expecting the ship to come apart around her or for the walls to come closing quickly in, bringing with them a swift and hopefully not too painful death. That did not happen, however, and instead the spinning of the ship slowed a little.

"Environment's still intact," Nigel noted as they took a right and then left, heading towards the front of the ship.

"Wonder why the spinning is stopping."

"Don't care. Let's just finish our delivery and, you know, save some people if you want." Nigel had a way of making their current heroic actions sound not very heroic at all.

The next corridor widened, becoming an entrance to the grand banquet hall. As they approached the ornate double doors, which were shimmering and pearlescent, covered in ornate raised patterns inlaid with gold to give a bevelled, 3-D effect, one door burst open and a square-jawed, stubbly man in his late forties or early fifties staggered towards them. He in fine clothes—a tuxedo and a shirt now torn open at the neck.

"Thank God," he said as he saw the two EVA-suited figures walking towards him, "are you our rescuers?"

"We are... here to help," was all Sarah could manage for reassurance.

"Where is the captain?" Nigel asked, cutting straight to the chase as far as he saw it.

"I don't know," the man said, coughing and clutching his chest as he spoke. "She was at dinner—I was at the captain's table, you know—but she was called away in very public fashion." He coughed out a wry laugh. "I was annoyed, as this was my one dinner with the captain during our cruise, I paid extra for the privilege, but... Well, now it doesn't seem like such a big deal, eh?" He turned and looked back towards the ballroom as the door closed behind him. Sarah followed his eyes, could see the haunted look in them. "It's bad in there," the man added, before she could give voice to the question on her lips.

"You should get to the life pods," Sarah said. "The *Majestic* is a ruin and we don't know how long the environmental systems will hold." She glanced towards the doors. "Did you have anyone in there?"

The man shook his head. "So many people hurt. It is three-storeys high in there and the environ systems did not hold things in place. The captain's table itself broke apart on the ceiling, taking the chandelier with it.

Sarah Nigel looked at each other as the man followed the escape lines on the floor towards the nearest life pod station. She didn't want to go in there, didn't want to see the human mess she knew would be waiting for her, and was almost glad of the distraction when she noticed movement some way to her right. Several people in uniform were coming from an adjoining corridor.

"Captain," both Nigel—who was looking at his slate—and the woman at the head of the approaching group said the word at the same time, although she finished with, "Smith." Her eyes rose in surprise, but then she continued. "Are you two a part of the rescue effort?"

"We *are* the rescue effort," Sarah said. Adding, "I'm sorry."

Captain Smith was a handsome woman approaching middle age, who was managing to look important and in charge, despite having blood and what might have been grease or soot smeared across her face. Her uniform shirt was dirty and slightly torn, her shoulder-length hair in disarray. "Understood," she said, her eyes momentarily distant as she took the fact of it in.

"But we do have a delivery for you," Nigel put in.

Sarah couldn't stop herself from turning to him. "Shut the fuck up, Nigel."

"It was a machine to stop... this," Nigel insisted with a wave of his arms.

Smith's eyes went wide, but again she controlled her emotions well. "We had one of those and it didn't save us."

Sarah had not been expecting that. "You know who did this?"

"We suspect the Koru, but do not know for sure."

A chill went through Sarah, followed by a sense of inevitability. It was like being inexorably pulled back into the same bloody situation. *This*, and the sense of personal loss that came with it, was why she hadn't wanted to come back to the McMurdo Rift.

Smith glanced around, looking past Sarah and Nigel like she expected someone else to be with them. "Is Mark Franklin with you?"

TWENTY

The number of survivors that Franklin and Gus had collected from the rear passenger cabins had been surprisingly few. By the time they reached the closest foyer where people were trying to get onto life pods, the area was already quite busy, and Franklin could see from an indicator that several life pods at that location had already launched. Some members of the engineering crew—the few that had escaped the mess back there—were trying to organise the crush of people who were pushing to get onto the life pods while the ship continued to shudder, and he could hear occasional distant noises.

Sometimes the noises were an explosion. Other times, they were various bangs, creaks and other sounds that defied classification. None of them were reassuring, except perhaps the thump of a life pod launching, which was accompanied by one of the illuminated numbers on the wall turning from green to red. He had never been on a ship this big while it was coming apart. Well, apart from the Koru one he had destroyed in the war a decade ago, but he'd been fully engaged with fleeing that one in his own little fighter craft at the time, rather than—as was the case now—searching for survivors with his only protection a vacuum suit. If the ceiling caved in or a nearby section of ship ripped away, the vacuum suit would not be as much protection as he would like. Still, *at least* he had it. The passengers and crew did not.

Glancing around the gathered survivors in this evacuation area, Franklin wondered how many of them were even accessible. It was a triple or quadruple-width corridor that funnelled down towards the two curving entrance corridors to the life pods, a cramped space for so many beaten up and traumatised survivors. He scanned the faces, looking for a familiar one. "I'm going to have to go to the bar," he said.

"Now is not the time."

Franklin could hear the grim humour in his friend's voice. "There's always time for a drink, Gus, especially when it might be your last. But that's not the reason I need to get to the bar." Gus turned to face him, so the two friends were looking each other in the eye, just as one of the overhead lights flickered, letting out a murmur of disquiet among the people pressing towards the life pods, and there was a slight surge in reaction to it. "Chloe," Franklin said, craning his neck around the area one last time, "I can't see Chloe here."

"Come on, now," said a man in a company uniformed, flanked by two burly men in engineering suits. "There's room for everyone, but it's children and their parents' first. Then the elderly."

"Franklin..." Gus said. And Franklin didn't blame him for the meaning behind that one word. He understood that many of the people travelling on the *Majestic* were already dead and that time was very much against them. The ship might hold together, but the chances that the environmental system would do so before proper aid could get to them... well, that was a different matter. Chloe was probably already dead either way.

"I'll never be able to look Arnold in the face again if I don't try, Gus. You should stay, get on a life pod. We've done more than enough already, and Chloe is not your responsibility."

Gus shoved Franklin hard, causing him to stumble a few steps back down the evacuation area. "You're such a dick, you know," Gus said, and he sounded offended this time. "You know I'm going wherever you are. Plus, I like the shy little squirt. So let's just get fucking moving, eh?"

In ship terms, they were not far from the little cocktail lounge Franklin had briefly thought of as home, even while he had missed his own cocktail bar at the same time. But, on the *Majestic*, as the ship seemed to shudder and jerk every few seconds, running down the maze of corridors still seemed to take an eternity. Franklin half expected to turn a corner and find a sizeable chunk of the ship just missing, but soon they were running in through the doors of the cocktail bar. The engraved glass in the doors was, surreally, still intact, although everything else was a complete mess.

Nothing had coped well with the deadly spin that the *Majestic* had gone into for the ten or fifteen minutes—maybe longer—it had taken for Franklin and Gus to get back into the ship and stop it. As with all the glasses and the bottles of alcohol, the machine that the now-dead Torres and Franklin had put together for detecting the stealth ships was now in many pieces all over the cocktail lounge, but the place was otherwise empty, not even a fallen patron. "Who's that?" came a familiar voice from the behind a door at the far end.

Franklin dashed up to it. "Chloe?"

"Franklin! I'm stuck. I ran in here when the ship started spinning, figuring the small room would prove safer, but some of the shelving came loose and broke the circuit. I've tried the emergency release, but I can't get out."

Franklin tried the handle from his side again, pushing down on it hard, but it didn't even want to move an inch. "Is Smith in there with you?"

"She left for the bridge as soon as she knew the stealth ship was coming our way."

"Oh, Chloe," Franklin said, thinking about how terrified the poor girl must have been on her own. "We're here now."

"Stand clear!" Gus bellowed and pulled Franklin to the side before he stepped forward. "You clear?" he checked through the door.

"As I can be."

Gus did the thing he likes to do with his boot, launching the underside of it hard into the door close to the handle, but nothing happened, except for Gus staggering backwards, clutching at his knee. "What the...?"

"The door with the stock behind it is always well made," Franklin said.

"What do we do?" Chloe called from the other side of the door. Franklin could hear a shrill edge of panic there.

"Hang on, I've got an idea." He turned back to the rest of the cocktail lounge, in which, about an hour ago, they had gathered around the detecting machine. Franklin glanced across the wreckage, much of which was the disassembled parts of the detector. After a moment, he spotted it, one of the many pieces of equipment that he had attempted to liberate from the stores of the *Majestic* before the ship's captain found out and let him carry on with her blessing, anyway. He sighed at that thought. Captain Smith was a good sort and hadn't deserved to have this happen to her ship. Then again, who did?

"What's that?" Gus asked as Franklin returned with a small, brushed metal cylinder in his hand.

"Man, you just lift weights and look buff for a living, don't you?" Franklin said. "Weren't you watching me and Torres use this, like, shit loads over the last day or so?"

"No," Gus shot back. "I was too busy being fitter and better looking than you."

Franklin pushed a button on the side of the device and an intense red beam shot out and started to burn its way into the surface of the door around the area of the lock.

"Oh, compressed energy cutter," Gus said. "I actually knew that one."

"Might want to get to the side a little bit in there," Franklin shouted through the door. "Nasty beam about to come through."

When the door finally gave up the ghost and slid open, Chloe launched herself out of the room and threw her arms around Franklin's neck. Franklin felt a wave of relief flooding through him and, although he was not much of a hugger, put his arms around her. Not only because she was Arnold's niece. He had become quite fond of her over the last week or so, almost like she was his own niece. "We are not out of this yet," he said, just as the dying hulk of the *Majestic* obliged by giving out a brief but violent shudder, accompanied by loud creaking sounds that sounded like metal trying to tear itself apart. "There's an evacuation pod site close to here. Let's get you there."

Leaving the bar for the last time, all they had to do was retrace their steps, although Franklin feared that the crowd waiting to get onto the life pods might have grown, or that not all the pods would be working. *One problem at a time, thought Franklin. One problem at a time.* They could try to find another site, but there was no guarantee they could get to one. Better to go to the site that they knew was in use.

Chloe quickly got ahead of them, the slight young woman being nimbler than the two bigger men lumbering along in their all-encompassing suits and heavy boots as the ship rolled and lurched around them.

They came to a long corridor that Franklin recognised, and he knew it was only a couple of quick turns to get to the life pods. Chloe stopped further along the corridor, realising how far ahead she had got of the two older men. She turned around, somehow managing a small grin, despite the terrifying situation. It was a grin like sunshine breaking through cloud. "Come on, you two," she called.

The corridor rocked violently and the floor between them rose up so that were suddenly on an incline. For a moment, Franklin lost sight of Chloe, then the other half of the corridor was torn away from them. Like she was being sucked up by some invisible tube, Chloe went with it, tumbling away from them and into the deadly darkness of space.

TWENTY-ONE

Sarah was wondering whether she was still the best pilot on the *Mutt's Nuts* as Engee backed the rust brown ship into the *Majestic's* forward-most bay. The environmental systems seemed to have held better here than in much of the ship, although there was still a mess of cargo crates and support equipment spread across the floor, which Sarah had put the survivors to work moving out of the way. It was useful to keep the terrified and shell-shocked passengers and crew busy for those agonising few minutes as the *Nuts* made its way in. It had not been the plan at all, but their route to the nearest escape foyer had been destroyed, and the idea of making it to another one while the ship continued to disintegrate around them was absurd. Captain Smith had joined in the efforts, directing crew and passengers alike, despite having the look of someone with shell shock herself, her face almost ghostly white. Sarah had decided that she was an impressive woman, but she had just lost her shiny, brand-new ship, and likely hundreds of passengers that she was responsible for were dead.

A part of Sarah had wanted to look for Mark and Gus, even though the last Captain Smith had known of them was that they were aboard a shuttle and not on the ship when it was hit. It was only that even finding out that they were here—right in the line of fire, as it were—and not safely aboard the *Olympic*, where they were supposed to be, was unsettling. And yet, knowing Mark Franklin, should it have been surprising?

Sarah, Nigel and the survivors had, of course, needed to keep moving while their luck held. The *Laughing Zebra* was working to collect life pods, all the while hoping that the ship that had attacked the *Majestic* did not return. The *Mutt's Nuts*, at least, had weaponry to defend itself, although that would not be happen from within the bay.

Engee touched the ship down in the space they had cleared for it and dropped the main cargo ramp, so that the survivors they had with them—numbering less than thirty—could get into the ship as quickly as possible.

"Everyone hang onto something," Sarah called out. After checking that people had done so, she called up to Engee. "Okay, we're good to go."

Once they were some way clear of the *Majestic*, Engee brought the ship around and Sarah, along with Nigel and Captain Smith, came up to the galley. Sarah moved to the screen on the opposite side from the seating and brought up the exterior display. She did so without thinking of the ship's captain behind her and looked back as soon as the image of the ruined ship appeared.

"It's okay," Captain Smith said. "We need to look for life pods and signs of anyone else we can rescue, I get it." Nonetheless, Sarah could see the pain on her features, which were handsome and dignified, pale as they still were. Sarah wondered about the interactions between the almost accidentally charming Mark Franklin and this impressive woman, then guiltily shook such thoughts from her head.

As they watched, a part of the ship around three quarters of the way back broke off. It snapped, a little like a stick, expelling thousands of tiny pieces of detritus—tiny, at least, from where they were watching—into space at once, and the rear section of the *Majestic* fell away from the rest. As Sarah watched, a flurry of life pods launched from a part of the rear section just behind the break on their side, as if in reaction to what had happened. The timing seemed fortuitous, because several seconds later that section of the side of the ship broke away, too. The spot where the life pods had launched from moments before fell away from the side of the *Majestic*, exposing the interior of the ship like some gruesome cutaway drawing.

"Hang on," Captain Smith said, pointing at the screen. "Can you zoom in a bit?"

Sarah moved back to the controls. "Where?"

"Right in the middle where the evacuation section just fell away."

Sarah did as requested. Not quite knowing how Captain Smith had spotted it, she saw two figures hanging there, dressed in space suits and clinging to tables in some sort of small refectory. "Oh my God," Sarah said. "How are they still hanging on?"

"Can we get into them?" Smith asked. "Without too much danger for the ship?"

"We've got a pretty outstanding pilot." Sarah turned to make her way back past the crew quarters and to the cockpit, where Engee was.

"I was about to contact you," Engee said as Sarah walked in.

"You've seen them too? I'll bet it's Mark and Gus."

Engee's head snapped around at that. "I have just been on comms with the *Laughing Zebra.* They told me about a shuttle that went back into the ship when it was spinning."

Sarah nodded and sighed, perhaps coming across as mildly frustrated, although her stomach was churning. "That will be them. You think we can get close enough to help them?"

Engee grinned. "I am feeling more and more like the arrogant fly-boy."

"Well, that wasn't quite what I asked. But I'll take it. We'll need to get all the survivors out of the bay and into the galley and crew section. It's a sad thing, but they'll all fit. Get closer, but then wait for me to call up."

Sarah collected Captain Smith on her way, glad to give the *Majestic's* commander something else to keep her busy. Smith, along with a couple of her crew members, shepherded everyone else out of the *Mutt's Nuts'* bay as Sarah put the helmet on the EVA suit she was still wearing, then watched as the light next to the top airlock went green.

"Okay, I'm about to depressurize," she said to Engee. "Back us in nice and slow."

Sarah resisted the urge to open the back of the *Nuts* straight up and let the ship depressurize itself most of the way. In fact, rather than open the main door and expose the remodelled bay of her ship to the massive amount of detritus and, well, *crap* coming off the ex-cruise vessel, she moved to the personnel door that she had kept on the left-rear corner of her ship. It was the same bit of the ship through which her husband had left and never returned. She had thought of not having it, or moving it to the other side, yet something almost compulsive within Sarah could not let that be the case.

She attached herself to an EVA tether and leaned out as the door opened, gasping at the sight of the ruined ship laid bare. Powerful lights on the back of the *Nuts* lit up the structure, a terrible parody of a cross-section in some manual or one of those glass ant's nests. Except this was uneven and, in places, collapsed, and rather than displaying life or purpose, it showed only death and rapid decay.

Except for the two suited men she could see clinging to an exposed part of it. "Is that you, Mark?" She broadcast as widely as possible, although she kept the range short.

The answering voice was stressed and out of breath. "I couldn't decide whether or not that was the *Nuts*," Franklin said. "What the hell have you done to the back of my ship?

"Your ship?" Sarah exclaimed, tears of relief threatening to force their way out. "Do you and your mate want rescuing or not?"

"Quit pissing her off," Gus' voice said.

"Okay, I'll need to get you one at a time," she said, and glanced around at some of the debris flying about her. Much of it was dangerous to her, and there was enough that could do the *Mutt's Nuts* damage at speed. "You're going to have to push clear of the hulk and I'll EVA to you."

Gus went first, and Sarah tried to ignore the explosions and releases of debris still happening at almost regular intervals. The *SS Majestic* was a slowly expiring behemoth, and it was dying in dozens, if not hundreds, of places along its length at once. Gus pushed off a little too enthusiastically, and she had to fire her thrusters hard while Engee manoeuvred the ship behind her, using the tether to reel them back in to save her depleted thruster reserves.

"You still there, Mark?" she said as she stepped back into the doorway. He had been silent as she had recovered Gus and seen himself aboard the *Nuts*. Just then, she could see an individual connection request from his suit coming up on her visor display. She accepted it.

"You okay?" Sarah started to worry he was badly injured or something. It was a strange noise that came over the comms as his channel opened up to her. "What's the matter? Mark, are you hurt?"

"I couldn't save her."

Sarah realized, even across the several hundred kilometres that separated them, that what she could hear in her helmet was the sound of her ex-husband, or almost-husband, crying.

"What?" she said after a stunned moment. "Who couldn't you save?"

He didn't answer for a moment, instead launching himself from the wreck of the *Majestic* towards, and she pushed off herself, engaging the EVA thrusters after a couple of seconds.

"I couldn't save Chloe," he said as the two of them closed on each other. "Arnold's niece. She was just... ripped away from us."

TWENTY-TWO

The sun was setting over Proxima City, turning an even deeper red than usual, and Arnold Philby was finishing up the report for the council. He checked the clock on his desk. Damn it, he had a meeting in that new seafood restaurant by the harbour in half an hour, and he wasn't going to make it. He was about to signal his attaché to rearrange when the door chimed.

"Come in."

The door opened and his attaché, Keith, entered. Arnold was about to be impressed by the man's almost psychic level of efficiency when he caught sight of the solemn look on his face and felt chastised. "Yes, I'm aware of the time..." he began, then trailed off.

"It's not that, sir," Keith said, the man's face getting paler with every word." It's the SS *Majestic*."

Arnold stopped typing. "What about it?" At the same time as a sick feeling flooded his stomach, the rational part of his mind told him that surely there could not be any problem with the *Majestic*. It was new, the pride of the civilian fleet.

"Well, sir, we've just received word that it has been attacked, although the details at the moment are vague."

"Attacked by whom?" Arnold said. "Are there casualties?"

"We don't know yet. We've had a message from a freighter called the *Laughing Zebra*, which was in the area when it happened."

"Well, get back onto them and find out more!" Arnold yelled, infuriated by the bumbling awkwardness of a man he usually thought of as efficient.

"At once," Keith said, and Arnold almost felt guilty as the man scurried back and out of his office.

Arnold stood and walked to the window, looking out at the stars that were appearing in the sky as night arrived. He knew the McMurdo Rift was not visible with the naked eye from Proxima, even if he had been well away from the city on the darkest, clearest night.

What had he done? He had put Chloe on that ship. Hell, he should have been on board himself. Yet worrying and fearing the worst achieved nothing. The military had disabused him of those useless habits long ago. Still, if those Koru bastards had harmed one hair on his niece's head, he would hunt them endlessly and make each and every one pay. He had asked "who" had made the attack, but he knew in his heart who it had to be.

Arnold walked back over to the desk and pulled up the latest military intelligence reports on the McMurdo Rift. Nothing about the *Majestic*, of course, but there was a note about a higher level of ship disappearances than usual. Just a line, not even a theory what might have been the cause.

His mind went to what responses might be possible if this was proved to be a Koru action. He found himself wanting to launch an all-out attack, but those council fools would be much more cautious. Caution lost a person the initiative.

He thought for a moment about the possibility of sending the fleet straight to Home Nest. A fast enough first strike would be feasible and, as long as they could knock out the command-and-control infrastructure, it might work. Once the UTC had hold of the most populated Koru planet, superior military assets the Koru had hidden elsewhere—because there were no "motherships" around Home Nest, their intelligence could tell that much—would count for a lot less. The biggest mistake would be leaving it too late and then meeting unconquerable resistance.

Yes, decisive action would work, the kind Earth had always been famed for. They said a lot about Old Earth, but no one ever accused her of dilly dallying.

Poor Chloe. His stomach, his chest, lurched inside. Yes, she had been working aboard the SS *Majestic*, but it was also supposed to be the trip of a lifetime, and he had even hoped to share it with her.

But he couldn't let those thoughts get a hold of him, dammit. No wallowing in fear and regret until he knew more.

The communication relay on Arnold's desk chimed, and he walked over to it. He tapped on the controls and found a new transmission had come in.

"SS *Majestic* confirmed destroyed," Arnold read out to himself. "There have been some survivors, but the current estimate is that at least two-thirds of passengers and crew were lost." A moment later, while he still stared at it, there was another notification delivering a list of known survivors. He scanned it and, not finding the name he was looking for, he ran a search, sure he was missing her name in his panic. Still nothing. Two familiar names stood out, however.

"Fucking Franklin," he said. Of course Mark Franklin and the bloody fitness instructor had made it off. Franklin could have made a career out of escaping dying ships. In fact, he was often the one who had destroyed them. Arnold gripped the desk hard, knowing he was not being fair but, in part, not caring.

There was no 'Chloe Philby' on the list. Those Koru bastards had killed her. Grief came, sharp and pitiless, as he paced the room. He should have been there, and perhaps his would be another name missing from that list of survivors. Did this mean something? Was there a purpose to his being recalled to the military right now? Was he here to make a difference? He recalled the conversation with Spencer and Maxwell at his apartment. He had not wanted to hear their treasonous inferences, yet even then he had not entirely been able to deny the sense in them. If the council would not act, someone had to.

No. Don't fill yourself with that sort of self-importance, Philby. That way fanaticism lies, and the galaxy needs no more of that. All the same, once evidence came through that this was a Koru action, they would likely consult him on a plan for possible retaliation. The UTC Council would have to at least consider it, be seen to be weighing up all the options.

"They have to do to something this time," he said to himself. "Surely they must now act."

The door chimed and Keith, his attaché, entered at Arnold's response. "Rear Admiral, the council has asked to see you."

"Very well," he replied. That was quick, which might bode well.

"I'll have the car brought round the front, shall I?"

"Fine." Arnold picked up his uniform jacket from the back of the door once it was closed and did it up, then took the already familiar walk through the hallways. The west side of the building was floor-to-ceiling windows, offering an unbeatable view over the city, and giving the impression that everyone in the building was literally above all of it.

On a night like this, it usually looked spectacular, but Arnold barely even noticed it. He got in the elevator and rode in silence to the ground floor. Walking through the grand lobby and out of the security area, where he found his private vehicle idling in front of the building.

Its air-conditioned interior was cool and quiet as he slid through the well-planned streets. Like anywhere else, Proxima's capital had its shady and run-down areas, but so much of it was planned with the precision that foresight and space and a team of dedicated architects afforded. Earth, with its millennia of history, had been so ordered, yet it kept a character, a soul, which Proxima lacked.

The council was expecting a plan and, being a forward-thinking soul with a certain distrust of the Koru, he had begun to formulate one the moment he had arrived on Proxima. Well, in some ways, it had been rolling around in his head for years. It was not complicated, because the best military plans weren't. He would have them send the entire fleet to the rift, a show of force and the UTC's willingness to protect its citizens and its assets.

Of course, Arnold did not expect that they would go for something quite so bold. Yet, whatever he offered them, he needed it to have some element of decisiveness about it.

"Good evening, Rear Admiral, thank you for coming at such short notice." It was Councillor Hawthorne who greeted him, but they were all present. Not the grand setting of the chamber this time, although the meeting room that they had sent him to instead was not that much less ornate, if smaller.

"Pleasure," Arnold said. He wondered if any of them even knew of his own personal connection to what had happened to the *Majestic*. For the first time, he considered the idea that it might be something he should mention. Conflict of interest and so on.

Fuck that.

"If you would like to brief us," Hawthorne said.

Arnold took in the people in the room. He felt far less nervous than the last time he had faced them. "Ladies and gentlemen of the council, as you are no doubt aware we have just received confirmation that the UTC's latest starliner, the SS *Majestic*, has been destroyed. An early casualty assessment estimates two-thirds of the passengers and crew lost. It was running light on its first outing, but this could well add up to over a thousand dead. Unconfirmed reports from the scene suggest a stealth vessel of Koru origin."

The murmur of shock through those gathered there was at least a little satisfying. He waited for the doubting to start. He had used the word "unconfirmed," and regretted doing so, yet no one seemed to pick him up on that, not even Hawthorne.

"Considering the speed and thoroughness of the attacks, we ordered the other major passenger liner in the area, the SS *Olympic*, to withdraw and avoid that area altogether. Of course, we don't know the reach of the attackers, so it is a matter of how far, if any distance, is safe."

"Rear Admiral Philby, we understand you have prepared a brief for a response?" Hawthorne said. Far from the doubting voice he had been the last time Arnold had been in this position, he was now teeing him up.

"I have." Arnold lied. No well-researched brief. But he knew what needed to be done. "I believe it is necessary to make a definitive response to this injustice and I would push the council to move the closest UTC military vessels, which are all Explorer class, away from their exploratory missions and to the McMurdo Rift at once. Our main warships are too far away for now, but we need to hunt these supposed 'stealth ships' and eliminate the menace to civilian shipping in the area.

"Furthermore, I propose we move to target the Koru colonies and assets within the McMurdo Rift."

This finally brought some resistance from those present. "Are you suggesting we attack civilian targets?" one of the councillors asked, banging the table for effect. The top of his head was bald and a fuzz of grey hair wrapped itself around the man's head just below it, like some sort of laurel.

"We know the Koru have little if any distinction between civil and military," Arnold countered.

"That's not true," the councillor said, "they have an absolute distinction, all their societal roles are clearly defined."

Arnold narrowed his eyes, feeling his patience slip. "You have not fought the Koru, have you, sir?"

TWENTY-THREE

The *Mutt's Nuts* reverted to normal space and Sarah began to run the standard positional checks. "Locating the *Olympic*," she said.

The navigational screens flicked through the nearby star charts until the starliner's position was identified and locked in. "Laying course" she went on, noting the colours of the nebula, which seemed to change subtly depending upon where it was viewed from—one of the attractions of taking a cruise around the rift.

The sublight engines kicked in fully and they pursued the SS *Olympic*, which was, understandably, moving faster than usual and heading away from its regular route. All the same, it was not long before they found themselves coming up on it, highlighting to those in the cockpit—which included herself, Engee, Nigel and Smith—how vulnerable the *Olympic* was.

With clearance granted, they landed in one of the smaller bays towards the back of the ship. It wasn't where the *Mutt's Nuts* had ever landed before on the *Olympic*, and Sarah commented on this.

"Caution," Nigel said with his usual bleakness. "If we blow up or something, they want to make sure we're away from as many people and as much of the command structure as possible. "There will be confusion and worry about what has actually happened to the *Majestic*."

Smith shrugged next to him. "Or it could be the best place to deal with the..." her mouth seemed to catch on the last word for a moment, "survivors."

During their journey to find the *Olympic*, Sarah's mind had mostly been on one man who had refused to come out of the cargo bay, where most of the survivors were, as if he belonged there with them. Mark wouldn't even come up to the galley when she asked him, simply staying in the environment suit that she had picked him up in, minus only the helmet. She had never seen him like this.

As the controller signalled that the *Olympic*'s archaic bay was repressurised, a comms request came through to the cockpit. Seeing it was coming from Mark Franklin, she picked up her own comms unit to hear him privately. "Sarah?" he asked, the word almost timid, unsure.

"Mark?" All eyes in the cockpit fell upon her and she moved quickly past them, out into the crew corridor and towards her quarters. "Everything alright down there?" she added. "The cargo bay doors will be opening any moment. I don't know if the *Olympic* will be sending a welcoming committee or not. I get the sense everyone's a little jumpy. Understandable, I guess."

"My bar," he said. Sarah waited for a moment for him to the finish the thought.

"I'm sure it's still there," she answered when he didn't.

"Everyone who doesn't need medical attention," he went on. "They can stay there, at least until the *Olympic* finds somewhere better for them. I think everyone needs... to stay together."

"Okay." He still didn't seem like himself, Sarah felt. "Might recoup a little of your lost profits," she tried to joke.

"No one will pay for anything."

And his sense of humour wasn't back yet.

Sarah suspected that it was the busiest that Mark has seen his bar in months. Of course, he would not be getting the profits, but he did not look like he cared right then.

The bar was full of survivors from the *Majestic*, as the *Laughing Zebra* had met up with the *Olympic*, as well, and unloaded its survivors, as it was less well-placed to give proper medical aid or, well, any sort of genuine comfort to them. The bar had not been able to take all of them, but many had wandered in when they had heard that it was a gathering spot. A place both for misery and for the joy of survival, it seemed.

Geoff, Franklin's grey tabby bar cat, was a centre of attention, moving from table to table and providing a little help in his own way by relaxing the traumatised survivors.

Sarah watched Mark as he led occasional toasts to the name of the destroyed ship and to those who had died aboard her. Each time knocking back a drink himself. Now he was heading the way of their table, swaying a little.

"You messaged the authorities?" he asked Sarah as he sat unsteadily down between her and Engee on a booth seat, managing to bump into both of them. Nigel was also at the table, although he had been nursing the same drink since he had sat down and wore a sullen look. There was no sign of Gus anywhere. He had vanished since leaving the *Mutt's Nuts*.

"We did," she confirmed. "And the *Laughing Zebra* did; and, I daresay the *Olympic* has been communicating what they know."

"I need to tell him," Mark said, slurring a little.

"Tell what?" Sarah thought she knew, but sometimes one played dumb anyway. Maybe to avoid it, maybe to just let conversations play out by their longest natural course, like maybe they needed to... "To who?"

"Arnold," Mark said, a little impatiently. "I need to let him know that Chloe is dead. He should hear it from me."

Sarah regarded him for a moment then stood up. "Maybe we should head up to the bridge."

Mark looked quizzically up at her, his eyes foggy with confusion and with alcohol.

"Arnold's a Rear Admiral now and he's far away on Proxima. Regular, T-slate communications will take a while to reach him and you don't want to leave your old friend a message to tell him that his niece has died.

"The bridge will have a quantum comms link and, if it's coming from his old ship, the *Olympic*, it might just get the important Rear Admiral's attention too." *Although, if it was me, I think I would take the less courageous option of a message.*

Franklin's face seemed to lighten for a moment, then fell slightly again, almost as if following her thoughts. He drew in a deep breath. "We should," he said and stood up. There was a slight wobble that made Sarah wonder if it might not be better to wait a few hours at least and find Franklin some coffee. He did, at least, stay on his feet. "Good idea."

Franklin looked about the bar, as if only now realising where he was. "But, the bar..."

Sarah looked to the other two sitting at the table, especially her first mate. Sarah, Engee and Nigel had been keeping to themselves and, as the pilot of the ship that saved them, Engee was more than okay with all the survivors who had fled the *Majestic* and ended up in the bay of the *Mutt's Nuts*, despite her obvious heritage. The thing was that the word was starting to get around, and it was beginning to become general knowledge that the attack on the great starliner was being put down to koru actions. Leaving Engee in charge of the SS *Olympic* Cocktail Lounge would have been a questionable idea even before this. Heck, Sarah wasn't even sure that it wouldn't just be a better idea to get Engee back onto the ship for now, nice and safe.

She turned to Nigel. "Can you keep an eye on things here for thirty minutes?"

"Fuck that," Nigel said, beginning to get to his feet. "I need to find Smith and get her to sign the job off, like you should have done on the way back from the *Majestic*. Then I can get the fuck off this floating target at the first opportunity and never come back to the McMurdo Rift again."

Although Sarah did not exactly disagree with Nigel's sentiments, particularly the last part, it just wasn't the time. She leaned over him before he could stand up fully; it was probably the only time she would ever tower over the tall courier. "Don't fuck with me now, Nigel. NOT NOW!" She straightened a little. "I still want to get paid too, you know."

Nigel scoffed, even as he look cowed. "Gee, crazy much? I'll watch the stupid bar."

"Okay," Sarah said, a little taken aback by his quick capitulation and her own moment of rage, then she turned to her first mate. Well, her pilot, she was now reluctantly having to admit. Flying ships had never come that easily to Sarah, she just wasn't a natural at it, however much she wanted to be. Engee, on the other hand... "Come on, we'll see if we can find Gus on the way. If not, it might be a good idea for you to stay on the *Nuts* tonight."

Engee nodded her understanding and rose to join them.

Sarah resisted the urge to lay a hand on Franklin's arm as they walked out of the SS *Olympic* Cocktail Lounge. It wasn't that he needed steadying, although he was swaying slightly, but she wanted to show him support with what lay ahead: Telling his friend that the man's niece was dead, that he was right there when it happened. She shuddered at the thought of it and, of course—inevitably—her mind went to Vik and his death as they tried to escape the dying Koru shield cruiser.

The *Nuts* should remind her of Vik in all the wrong, sad ways, and perhaps anyone else would have found themselves drawn to a different ship—and different company, for that matter. Yet here she still was, putting what little she had into the ship's upgrades, and again pitched against the koru with Mark Franklin at her side.

There was a strange buzz in the corridors of the *Olympic* as they made their way towards the front of the ship. Sarah had half-expected people to be hidden away in their cabins, given the general state of emergency that the demise of the *Majestic* had brought with it. Yet people were abroad in the corridors and the public spaces. They just looked stunned... unsure what to do with themselves. At first, she eyed them as they approached, silently daring them to start trouble with Engee, but hardly anyone paid them much mind. And, if they did, it was to turn their head away and hurry past, eyes on the floor.

Passing the main medical bay—and on the *Olympic* this amounted to a small hospital, perhaps given the potential ailments of the main passenger demographic, which could best be described as "aging"—Sarah glanced in and saw a familiar figure. The tall, dark and slightly bulky—as well as very bald—figure of Gus was stood there, facing away from them. He was standing over someone who was lying on a bed, holding them in place as they moaned in pain. He wore medical gloves, she could see, streaked with blood.

"Gus!" Engee said, noticing him. They had not seen each other, not properly, since not long after the events surrounding the destruction of the Koru shield cruiser, and Sarah recalled what felt like a simmering attraction between the two, including a supposedly "innocent" episode where Engee had stayed at Gus' apartment after an evening of drinking. Right now, Engee's elegant alien face lit up and she took a step forward, but Sarah regrettably felt the need to put out an arm to stop her.

"Don't," she said, "he's busy."

Mark squinted at Gus, who still hadn't noticed them, looking almost as if he didn't recognise his friend. "I never knew he was medically trained." he sounded almost offended by this fact.

"Maybe it's just part of being a personal trainer," Sarah tried. She wasn't sure that she believed her own justification—he did appear heavily involved, working alongside the regular medical staff, who were distinguishable by their uniforms.

They moved on, the bridge not too far away now. Well, that answers the mystery of where Gus got to, she thought.

The *Olympic* was still being run by its first officer, the former sensor suite operator, Stanley. Promoted in the wake of a mutiny by the previous first officer during their adventures a few months before, Stanley was now acting captain until a replacement could be found for Arnold Philby. In the civilian fleet, so Mark informed Sarah, these things did not always happen at pace.

It was fortunate, however, as Stanley liked Mark Franklin and had been devoted enough to his former captain to stand with him during the mutiny. Stanley had already been aware of the possibility that Chloe, Arnold's niece, might have been among the casualties on the *Majestic*, and seemed almost relieved to Sarah's eyes when he found out that Mark was prepared to tell now "Rear Admiral" Philby the tragic news.

"I'll set you up in the captain's office... er, my office," Stanley said, beaming with an odd mixture of awkwardness, excitement and gravity at the three of them. He did not seem to mind Engee's presence in the least bit, although Sarah noticed a few hard looks in Engee's direction as they crossed the bridge to the office. She had thought to ask Mark if he maybe wanted to do this alone, was almost desperate to take Engee back to the *Nuts* and be away from everything, but the moment never seemed right and, before she knew it, the three of them were stood behind Acting Captain Stanley as he attempted the live link with the fleet headquarters in Proxima.

The moments ticked away as he attempted to establish the connection. "Weird," he mused eventually. "Seems that Fleet isn't answering. Busy day, I guess."

Sarah could hear the doubt in his voice, but it was Mark who spoke. "Fleet always answers," he said, and Sarah felt a sense of dread in the way he said it. "Even if it isn't a person, they answer."

Stanley met his eye but didn't say anything for several moments; it was Mark who spoke again, now appearing to be much more sober than he had been. "Maybe try someone else on Proxima. The Civilian Fleet Headquarters, maybe?"

"I had been thinking that," Stanley admitted. "But I didn't want to seem, you know, alarmist, just because Fleet isn't answering."

"Considering what's been going on," Sarah put in, "they'll probably understand either way. When did you last hear from them?"

"We contacted them when you arrived, just a message sent by the quantum system, and we got a reply back quite quickly."

Stanley put a call into Civilian HQ. A minute later, he cut the unanswered connection and all four in the room looked at each other. "It will be very busy," Engee offered to the silence, "maybe they are all… how you say, jammed up?"

Mark shook his head. "It can't happen. The very architecture of a quantum system means that you always make a connection with the other end; assuming it's on, that is."

"Fuck it," Stanley said and brought up another connection request, this time putting in a long, thirty-two-digit code seemingly from memory, rather than referring to an address book.

"Who are you calling?" Mark asked.

"Old school friend. Bit of a crazy. Lives out in the jungle and keeps an unregistered quantum transmitter that he runs backdoor through a commercial satellite. He's been doing it for six years and it was still up a couple of months ago. If I can't get some sort of ping off him… Well, end of the fucking universe, isn't it?"

The four of them watched the connection, no one even breathing.

TWENTY-FOUR

Arnold paced the office whilst Maxwell sat on the couch in the corner, seemingly relaxed.

"You are sure he is coming?" Arnold asked.

"He assured me he was on his way. Although we are maintaining comms silence for now, as I'm sure you'll appreciate."

Arnold did not know how the man managed to stay so calm while they prepared to commit treason. It was infuriating. Things had moved fast since the council meeting—one in which the councillors had seemed more receptive to the reality of the Koru threat than he had expected. Yet they had stopped short of being prepared to do what was needed and the UTC was clearly running out of time.

Still, when Maxwell and Spencer had been waiting for him outside of the chamber, he could never in a million years have predicted how quickly their frustrated conversation had turned to rebellion. Although maybe he should have.

"The UTC lacks resolve," Spencer had said, "it lacks backbone. We all know the UTC is only in power because of the Koru intervention in the war, and it seems evident to me—and long has—that their intervention was meant to lead to exactly this sort of dithering, indecision and reluctance to act against the UTC's erstwhile allies when the time came."

And then Admiral Maxwell had added the exact words that Arnold needed to hear. "If Earth was still in charge of the empire, then there would not be any of this softly-softly approach. We would project strength."

He was not a fool, however, the timing of his appointment as a Rear Admiral was no mere coincidence. They had been planning this and they needed him here for it. Maxwell, Spencer and whatever other allies they had needed someone of Old Earth's military, someone who had been prominent in the last battle as the Koru mothership had closed in on Earth. A man who had faced the terrible threat that the Koru could present the human race before. That was why they needed Arnold Philby, why he had first been approached to act on their behalf while still captain of the SS *Olympic*. Why he was stood where he was right now.

The thing was that he did not much care. A person was only being played if they let themselves be played. Rear Admiral Arnold Philby, nervous though he might be, had his eyes wide open. It had been so even before those alien bastards had killed his beloved niece. But now he had a hard, immediate reason to make the Koru pay, and gaining control of the UTC was a necessary means to an end. These years languishing in civilian obscurity had made him hungry for this.

"Good evening, gentleman." Spencer now greeted them as the door slid open and the general slipped in. Perhaps by habit, Arnold stood slightly to attention before he could check himself, while Maxwell stood up in a more leisurely fashion.

"Evening," Maxwell replied, like they were meeting up for after-work drinks.

"So, are we going to do this?" Spencer asked, looking back and forth between the two of them.

Maxwell turned to Arnold, his dark face lined and serious beneath the silver-spattered beard, despite the hint of a smile that played at the corners of his mouth. "That depends on you, Philby. What say you?"

Arnold did not want to be coy. This was not the time for modesty, yet he knew that—despite his recently acquired rank—these two men had far more power and influence on Proxima and within the military than he did, and he found himself wondering why his opinion appeared to matter so. Of course, as was the case with these things, they might be considering the need to shoot him dead if he wasn't with them. The coming minutes and hours would be crucial, they had to be sure he would not betray them, he supposed.

"I'm with you."

Maxwell clapped him on the shoulder "I never doubted it."

"And now I can be appraised of the plan?" Arnold looked to Spencer.

Spencer stepped past him and to the window, looking right to where several armoured vehicles were hovering down the street. "The plan is already happening."

"So when you said this depended on me?" Arnold said to Maxwell. "Not that I expected it would. I barely have my feet under the table."

It was Spencer who answered. "The tanks are only the first part of any coup. There has to be an 'after,' and that is where you come in." He gently put a hand on Arnold's shoulder and turned him around towards the door. "Now, come on, or we will be late for the party."

There was an armoured car waiting for them at the front of the building, which had been eerily quiet as they passed back through it. Almost as if all the other staff had been sent away. Arnold decided not to linger on that thought. The vehicle was like a cross between a limousine and a tank—sleek, black, long, with tinted windows, yet also heavy, menacing... buff.

Despite being quite impressive from the outside, the armoured car was cramped on the inside, and the three of them were squashed together on the forward-facing rear seat, as the area where the backwards-facing seat would have been was filled with a tactical suite. Arnold wasn't even aware the military had these sort of crossovers between executive transport and mobile operations centre.

"Where are we going?" Arnold asked.

"The barracks on the edge of town," Spencer said. "It's usually used for the reservists. They will be providing the equipment that we will be needing tonight,"

Arnold looked at Maxwell. "Is it just the army?"

"Oh no, old boy. Army, Fleet, Marines. We've been working on this for some time. It wouldn't work otherwise."

The armoured car joined the convoy making its way through the city streets. Civilian traffic, quite wisely, stopped to make way for them.

"And it's not just about forces," Spencer put in. "Get your slate out."

Arnold did so and found that it had no connection.

"We've taken the network down," Maxwell told him, "even the quantum comms. No non-military communications on Proxima and nothing coming in or out of the system until we've achieved our goal.

"And there is a planetary blockade in effect as well."

"You've been ready to go for some time," Arnold pointed out, feeling more and more like he had arrived late to the party. As soon as he had realised back on the *Olympic* that he was dealing with Admiral Maxwell, Arnold had known that he was involved in something important, something big, and he hadn't been so naive as to think that his re-enlistment wouldn't come with the possibility that he would have to act politically at some point. That he would have to take risks.

All the same, he had not been expecting his allies to be ready to mount a coup during his first few weeks in the job. Until today, he probably would not even have wanted to entertain the thought. No doubt, the Koru action—culminating in the destruction of the *Majestic*—had forced the issue, but the speed with which the two senior military men had launched this meant that, surely, it was always going to happen sooner rather than later. That thought sent a shiver slicing between his shoulder blades.

Arnold felt Maxwell looking sideways at him and he looked over, met the other man's sideways look. "It looks like everything has worked exactly as planned. We have the means to do this however we want to do it. We could launch a precision strike on the council chamber from orbit if we wished." He caught Arnold's sharp look. "We won't, obviously. I just want you to understand the position we hold here. They have no choice but to stand aside."

All too soon, the council chamber was looming up before them, its arrogant Greco-Roman architecture reminiscent of the hubris of Earth as it had been. Power never really changes, Arnold thought to himself. No matter where you find it, it always looks pretty much the same. Did he really want to do this? Did he really want to commit treason, to be part of a coup? How willing were these men sitting to either side of him to use the deadly means at their disposal? Maxwell had been too quick for Arnold's liking to point out the capability they had. In Arnold's experience, once people started shooting, they found it very hard to stop again.

The news of the *Majestic* had hit him hard and, without any news of Chloe's fate, he had felt powerless and impotent, all too ready to demand that something be done about the Koru menace. But, right now, it was not the Koru they were moving against. And his niece, Chloe. Well, with all outside communications blocked, who knew when he would actually find out what had happened to her?

Spencer, glancing at the tactical display in front of them, spoke. "My man inside says that they still don't know we're coming. We should be in time to catch the chamber defences completely by surprise."

Arnold liked a tactical display as much as the next man, although sometimes there was no substitute for using your own eyes. "They may not be ready for us inside," he said, "but the outside is a different matter." The other two men followed his eye line beyond the impact and energy-refracting glass of the vehicle's windscreen to where a mixture of city police and council security were waiting for them before the wide steps that led up towards the building. There were dozens of them— maybe fifty or more— with several armoured vehicles. Nothing much compared to what was backing Arnold and his band, but enough to make this far from a bloodless coup.

"Stop!" Spencer told the driver, before turning to Arnold and Maxwell. "Not to worry." Spencer climbed out of the car and walked up to the ranking member of council security, an army guardsman in essence, although independent of any other military branch. These were the only part of the military that the two high-ranking officers, for all their importance, would not have been able to reach or influence across the months or even years that they had been preparing for this.

Even from behind, Arnold could tell that Spencer was all authoritative smiles as he approached, while the other man's face remained professional and as hard as stone. Their discourse, unheard from in the car, quickly became animated, while everyone behind the ranking guardsman was looking twitchy and nervous.

Then, in one of those moments that happened alarmingly quick while, at the same time, seeming to stretch on for a horrible length of time, the guardsman raised his weapon and shot Spencer in the chest.

TWENTY-FIVE

Leaving the bridge and with no contact still established with Proxima, it seemed to Franklin as if, in the course of only about a day, everything was coming apart. He liked to think that he wasn't prone to overreactions and unnecessary drama, yet the destruction of the *Majestic*—seeing Chloe taken away right in front of his eyes—and now the unprecedented breakdown of communications between the *Olympic* and Proxima... Well, he was starting to feel a little bit nervous. It was all very... apocalyptic.

He should not have drunk so much back at the bar, he realised. Ever since Franklin had owned his own bar, he had been less prone to getting drunk. In fact, come to think of it, he couldn't even think of the last time he had been properly wasted, although he had got pretty close to it earlier on. The walk to the bridge and the problems communicating with Proxima had sobered him up a little, yet he still couldn't think as clearly as he would like.

Stanley, the acting captain, had shown the presence of mind to establish that quantum communication was possible with other systems, meaning that it was—as far as they could tell—only Proxima that was down. No one could get a hold of them.

The first thought Franklin had was that, as with the *Majestic*, some sort of koru action was to blame.

"But that does not make much sense if Proxima's communications are the only ones down," he explained to Sarah and Engee as they left the bridge. "Yes, the planet is humanity's capital and seat of government, that's true, but capturing it doesn't stop us from fighting back against an attack. If they can scramble Proxima's communications, why can't they do so more widely and effectively? Why wouldn't they?"

"And how the hell would they even strike there first?" Sarah, who had once lived on Proxima, interjected. "They shut their embassy there years ago and have no other significant presence on the planet."

Franklin remembered that Sarah's deceased husband, Vik, had worked within the government on Proxima when the embassy was abandoned, and it was this unexplained event that had sent him on a path towards investigating the Koru. A path that had eventually brought him and Sarah into Franklin's life. "There is no Koru territory anywhere near there," he agreed. "It would be impossible for them to take Proxima without taking other systems on the way. Or, at least, attracting a hell of a lot of attention as they passed through."

"What about this stealth technology?" Engee put in.

"I guess it makes something like that more possible," Franklin allowed, "but then why are they blowing up civilian ships light-years away in the McMurdo Rift at the same time?"

"A distraction?" Sarah tried.

"On the same day?"

Sarah shrugged. "You're right, too close together."

"You would want to pull the fleet away first, surely. Destroy the *Majestic* a few days before any attack as bait for the fleet."

Sarah stopped suddenly and turned to Franklin, her eyes glassy and serious. "I want to leave."

"You want to what?"

"I'm not one-hundred percent agreeing with Nigel about the *Olympic* being a death trap," she explained, "but this ship isn't my home, the *Mutt's Nuts* is. And, whatever is happening, I want to be on it."

Franklin could see that he wasn't the only one panicking about what was all of this meant. Yet the *Olympic* was his home and, he was a little surprised, he felt a sense of duty to it. Quite what duty the owner of the ship's cocktail lounge could perform was probably prone to debate, but he wasn't ready to abandon the old girl, he realised. At the same time, there was also something horrible about the thought of Sarah flying away from him right now.

"Look," he began, trying to find a way to convince Sarah and Engee to stay, at least until they knew some more, but he didn't get to finish the rest of his thought.

"Oi, what's that fucking Koru doing on here?" a voice shouted from just ahead of them.

Franklin expected to look up and see some disgruntled passenger, or perhaps a survivor from the *Majestic*; instead, he recognised the uniform of the SS *Olympic's* security team, even if he didn't recognise its wearer. Some of the security team had been replaced following the insurrection led by the former XO, and this had to be one of the new ones. "She's with us," Franklin explained, putting a hand up. "She's cool and she had nothing to do with what happened on the *Majestic*. In fact, she helped save lives there."

"Fuck that," the security team member said, and Franklin noted that he had two companions loitering a little further down the corridor. Again, he didn't recognise them. At least not well enough to remember their names. "All Koru will need to go into holding until we can determine they're not a threat."

"Is that an order from Acting Captain Stanley?" Franklin said, fully knowing that it wasn't the sort of order that Stanley would have given.

The security team member—Hopkins, Franklin could see from the badge – narrowed his eyes at Franklin. "I recognise you, are you the bar owner?"

"That's right."

"Well, what you're not is an officer or a member of the security staff. Now, step aside, she's coming with us."

Franklin felt rather than saw Sarah step in front of Engee just behind him. "No, she is not," Sarah said.

Hopkins raised his ballistic concussion gun for effect and the other two team members walked up behind him, their own non-lethal weapons drawn.

"Call Stanley," Franklin said, still hoping to de-escalate the situation. "We've just come from the bridge."

The other two concussion weapons were raised as well. "This is your final warning," Hopkins said flatly. "Stand aside the two of you, let us take the Koru into custody.

Franklin really wanted to hit the idiots, but there was no way this came out well. Most likely, he, Sarah and Engee would be unconscious on the ground in a few moments' time.

"Attention!" called a sharp, female voice from somewhere behind the three security staff. All three of them reacted by turning to some degree, although the one at the back spun too far without lowering her weapon, and she found herself pointing it at a captain. "Lower your weapon!" roared Captain Smith in a tone that even made Franklin snap to attention a little bit.

All three security staff appeared to point their weapons groundwards and the *Majestic's* captain glared at the one who had briefly pointed her weapon Smith's way. "How dare you point your weapon at me."

Although the captain's stripe was clearly visible on her epaulet, Hopkins had evidently not been part of the welcoming committee for Smith when she had briefly visited the *Olympic* before. "You're not the ship's captain," he said, a clearly suspicious and arguably insubordinate tone present in his voice.

This did not seem to faze Captain Smith in the slightest. For the first time, Franklin noticed that she was dragging something behind her, some sort of grey, metallic case on wheels. "You're a sharp one, you," Captain Smith replied, although if there was any humour in her voice, it was humour with an undercurrent of threat. "Does that make me any less your superior?"

Even though Hopkins was facing away from Franklin, it was plain enough to see his shoulders slump a little. All the same, he evidently wasn't going to let his problem with the Koru in the corridor lie. "You were the captain of the *Majestic*, I guess?" It was a simply asked question with no apparent malice in it, although there was no sympathy there, either. He thumbed over his shoulder. "We were about to take this Koru into custody for the protection of *Olympic*. We did not want the same thing happening here."

Smith stepped up towards Hopkins, the other two security staff moved to the side of the corridor to make room for her, even though it wasn't necessary. Smith's face was grim, and she had an almost regal air about her in that moment, Franklin thought, despite her uniform and her marked face showing the trials that she had been through that day. "This Koru is a hero. Without her expert flying, many of the survivors from the *Majestic* probably would not have made it. Including me."

She took a long breath, which sounded almost like a sigh. "There is no official version of what happened to the *Majestic* yet, and we are not at war with the Koru." She raised a finger only a few centimetres from his face. "You will not hassle this Koru or any other aboard this ship without very good reason. Do you hear me?"

Hopkins nodded and Franklin could have sworn he heard a gulp the same time. Smith patiently waited and watched the security team head back down the corridor before she turned to Franklin, Sarah and Engee.

"Thank you, Captain," Engee said.

"Not all," Smith replied. "I am still deeply in your debt. But this is not why I was coming to find you."

"You were coming to find us?" Sarah echoed.

"I tried your ship, then I saw Mr Franklin's friend Gustav as he left the medical centre. Finally, I asked at the bar, where that tall fellow you were with on the *Mutt's Nuts* appeared to be emptying all of your spirits from behind the bar into large bowl."

It was an effort of will for Franklin to hold his tongue; he knew it had been a bad idea to leave that Nigel fellow in charge of his bar. "Why did you need to find us?" he asked instead, eyeing the case-like object that Captain Smith was pulling behind her.

"That's the package," Sarah said. "That's the Koru stealth ship detector we delivered to you."

"It is," Captain Smith agreed. "I had the idea that it might be useful for it to be fitted to the *Olympic* in some way but realised that I didn't have the faintest clue how." She looked at Franklin. "I thought you might be able to help."

TWENTY-SIX

So much for the bloodless fucking coup. Perhaps there was some small poetic justice in the fact that the first loss had been on their own side. Although an ally, Arnold had not yet found the time to decide whether or not he liked General Spencer. All the same, so many years removed from war, the man's death was shocking.

Spencer had seemed so calm when he had got out of the car, so self-assured. Why shouldn't he be? He was a general. Was being the operative word, as now his body was sprawled in the road, his neat uniform charred and still smoking. And, worse than that, everyone else was starting to open up.

A tank had responded almost immediately with an incendiary round, putting a crater in the steps that led up to the pantheon-like council chambers. Several of the guardsmen had been blown to pieces with those steps, and the rest scattered, taking cover behind ornate stone pillars as compressed energy beams came their way.

Arnold looked at Maxwell, his own shock even more deeply etched on the older man's face. In Arnold's brief experience, the two high-ranking officers had seemed more than mere co-conspirators, they had seemed like friends. "Sir," the driver said to Admiral Maxwell, "we need to get you both safe." It was a statement, but he was obviously looking for an order so that he could drive the vehicle out of harm's way.

Given what had happened to Spencer, it seemed prudent, yet the lightly armed defenders of the council building appeared horribly outmatched and, unless they retreated into the building, their cover was scant. Spencer, Maxwell and—by association—Arnold were the official face of this coup. One was dead and, if the other two were seen fleeing the scene to save their own lives... well, that was how coups quickly came to nothing, how everyone involved just sort of lost their nerve and ended up on trial for treason.

Maxwell was slow to respond, no doubt still stunned by the death of his friend, so Arnold reached out a hand and was about to speak up and prevent the driver from acting on his own initiative when something hit the front of the car. The windscreen imploded and the driver was killed instantly. Arnold felt as much as saw a compressed energy beam cutting its way through the vehicle and instinctively he closed his eyes, waiting for death.

Death did not come and, when he opened his eyes, he looked through the part of the car that simply wasn't there anymore and spotted an emplacement-sized weapon that had been wheeled into place in the doorway that led into the council chambers building. Glancing down again, Arnold could see the melted insides of the armoured car still glowing faintly less than ten centimetres from his leg.

The council chambers kept heavier defensive weaponry than he would have ever expected on hand. It was time to move if they wanted to live. The near brush with his own death had finally brought Admiral Maxwell back to the moment, and he pulled open a compartment in front of him that held several weapons. Hurriedly handing Arnold a rifle, each of them exited the vehicle on their own side.

Arnold wasn't sure of the wisdom of using the remains of the armoured car as cover, but he was a long way from anything else, so he spun to his left, keeping close to the side of the car, and quickly got behind it. Being ambidextrous to a point—he had always written and used devices left-handed, yet played sports and had initially learned to shoot right-handed—it wasn't as uncomfortable for him as it might have been for someone else to raise the rifle to his left shoulder and make the most of the vehicle's cover as he returned fire. His first shot caught a city policeman in the chest and knocked him a meter backwards, steam rising from the point of impact.

Arnold looked at the weapon for a shocked moment. It hadn't fired the expected compressed energy beam, instead shooting off what he knew to be an elongated package of superheated plasma. These kind of weapons were relatively new and very expensive, although perhaps he shouldn't have been surprised that this was what the leaders of the coup were packing. There were various types of armour that could reduce the effect of or even stop a compressed energy weapon, especially the lower-rated pistols. Superheated plasma would burn straight through anything like that, although he knew that his shots would be more limited than on compressed energy or even similar-sized ballistic weapons. Looking at the projected sight, he had nineteen shots left.

Somewhere, in the back of his mind, Arnold was horrified by what he had just done. It wasn't even a soldier lying dead on those steps. A regular member of the defence team for the council chambers would have been bad enough, but a member of the Proxima City Police Force was a keeper of the peace, there to protect and serve the citizens, to investigate crime and not die at the hands of someone like him. Yet his horror remained at the back of his mind, because in the moment he had sprung from the wrecked car, the soldier from all those years ago had returned. The same young man who had gone through basic training and fought in the Revolutionary War. And that man, older though he was now, still knew how to kill. You killed by blocking everything else out.

And, somewhere beyond that, there was his sure knowledge that they were fighting for the survival of humanity here. That the right people had to be in charge to face the coming Koru threat.

And, of course, there was Chloe. His innocent niece, who was likely dead at the hands of those alien monsters.

The huge compressed energy weapon fired again, but this time over the top of the armoured car, having evidently decided that it could not waste its sporadic powerful bursts on them any longer. It hit a tank, not targeting the weapon where the tank was most heavily armoured, but instead cleverly hitting the side and affecting the antigravity system, so that the tank listed and landed hard on its left side. The rest of the antigravity system failed to register what happened quickly enough and tried to compensate, instead sending the tank skidding sideways to knock over several soldiers, crushing some of them beneath it.

Arnold gritted his teeth. Somebody needed to deal with that damned gun.

a moment later he was on his feet and looking through the high-quality friend or foe system on weapon's projecting sight. He fired one, two shots in quick succession and, although he was nowhere near hitting his intended targets, which were far away while he himself was shooting on the move, the explosions of plasma into the door next to them was enough to make them duck down for a second. Plasma was a nasty, imprecise weapon, but it was great for suppressing the enemy, Arnold was deciding.

Arnold's gallant action had seemed like a good idea until he now realised that he was out in the open, a close and tempting target for those taking cover in front of the building. He kept running, although the only cover he could head for was the same cover being used by all those defenders who would just love to kill him.

"Philby!" he heard Maxwell belatedly call from somewhere behind him, but his blood was up and the red mist down, adrenaline fighting and winning over the fear to keep him moving and shooting.

There was another explosion, an incendiary round hitting the front of the building again, and the percussive force of it sent Arnold off balance enough that he tripped and found himself rolling on the pavement right in front of the building. His shoulders hunched up while his eyes faced the ground, a tingling feeling down his neck anticipating the harsh beams that would cut into him a moment before he died. But nothing happened.

Looking up, Arnold saw the door at the front of the building was completely missing, along with a section of the building itself. Incidentally, that meant that there was no more large compressed energy weapon, the gun and its operating crew nowhere to be seen, as the tank round had blown all of them to pieces. More than that, the already scant defenders at the front of the building seemed to have had enough and now held their hands in the air.

Arnold walked into the council chambers at the front of an armed host. He had not made a conscious choice to be the one in front, but Maxwell now seemed to be hanging back and Arnold was driven by a fierce, angry desire to get this done and over with. "Councillors, we thank you for your service but it is no longer required."

Hawthorne looked at Arnold, clearly shocked, almost as if they had interrupted them mid-session, with no knowledge in the chamber of the firefight that had been raging outside and, to some extent, in the building itself since they had entered it.

"What do you mean, Philby?" Hawthorne said, and Arnold could feel as much as hear the disdain emanating from the older man.

"This council has failed its people and needs to be dissolved with immediate effect," Arnold said. The words felt like they were flowing out of him now. Somewhere—a little closer to his shoulder than a few moments before—Admiral Maxwell spoke to him. "Couldn't have said it better myself." He sounded almost proud.

Hawthorne walked out from behind the large, round table and approached them on his own. As much as Arnold had disliked the man from almost the moment he met him, he had to respect his nerve, facing off against a host of soldiers. Or, perhaps he was just too stupidly arrogant to be scared.

"Let me get this straight; you intend to remove the civilian government and replace it with what? Yourselves?"

"For now," Maxwell said. "This is a time when we must have the leadership that we need."

"Not while I live!" Hawthorne cried, his short exclamation reaching its own crescendo as a red beam lanced out through his clothing where he had been concealing a pistol in the pocket of his robe. It struck Maxwell in the chest, scoring a nasty line up towards his throat.

Arnold reacted quickest, instinctively pulling his own sidearm and shooting Hawthorne right between the eyes. Back on the table, several cries of alarm arose from the assembled members as they saw their esteemed leader fall to the marbled floor, dead before he hit it.

Arnold rushed over to Maxwell, who was still breathing but clearly in great pain and badly wounded. He tried to speak, but his first effort was more of a gargle and he winced, his hand weakly reaching towards where the angry scorch marks ended around his Adam's apple. Fingers beckoned Arnold closer.

"It's up to you now," he hissed.

Arnold drew back very slightly and gave the admiral a puzzled look. "Me?"

"Spencer and I, we saw greatness in you. Without us, it is up to you to see this through now."

"Absurd," Arnold said. "You rest up and you'll recover." He glanced up to where a medic was rushing over. "You are the leader we need. I'm a soldier."

"Too late... for me," Maxwell said, weakly trying to fight off the medic as he muscled in. "Lead us against the Koru. Make... make the council cede power now, or all... is... lost."

Admiral Maxwell's arm fell slack, his eyes rolling back in his head.

Arnold stood up and looked down at Maxwell as the medic tried fruitlessly to revive him. His salt-and-pepper hair, as ever, was stark and distinctive against his dark skin. Arnold had not made in mind up about Spencer, but he had liked Maxwell, even before he had come to Proxima. He had felt respect for the man. In fact, in some ways, he had never gotten over being starstruck in his presence, even when he thought that Maxwell might have been asking too much of him.

Arnold turned from the admiral's body and walked over towards the iconic round table on his own, brushed his fingers against the ancient wood that had come all the way from Earth to sit there. Eleven pairs of eyes watched his fingers intently and, eventually, Arnold's eyes found Councillor Angela Reid, the deputy to the now dead Hawthorne. In his mind's eye, however, he was picturing the face of his now-dead niece.

When Arnold eventually spoke, his words were slow and deliberate, his voice unsettlingly cold even to his own ears. "I don't need you to sign over authority to me, but it will be a lot easier if you do."

"We won't do it," Councillor Reid answered. Looking around the rest of the councillors, Arnold wasn't so sure that they appreciated the "we" in that statement. For her part, the fifty-something Councillor Reid—her chestnut hair short and businesslike, her slightly angular chin jutting out defiantly—looked to have a little more resolve.

Arnold sighed and turned back to the soldiers. He was cold inside. Calm. Eerily self-assured. "Fine, put them all against the wall." *Make the council cede power now, or all is lost.*

There were shrieks of protests from most of the other councillors, although when Arnold turned back to Councillor Reid, her look was more one of shock—perhaps disbelief—than fear. It was the look of someone who couldn't really believe this was happening. "Leave her," Arnold said, holding out a hand to stop one of the soldiers from taking Reid to join the others. "She can watch them die, one by one."

The councillors were lined up against the chamber wall near to the opposite entrance. "Who's first?" Arnold said, pointing a finger to a woman of East Asian descent. "Councillor Lin is it?" The woman barely had time to fearfully nod before Arnold called out, "Ready! Aim!"

"Okay, okay!" Reid interrupted shrilly. "I'll sign whatever you need me to sign."

"Oh, no," Arnold said. "You will do better than that."

He turned to the leader of the unit of soldiers that had come in with them. "Soon as the broadcast studios are ready, I want Councillor Reid with me to help me with an announcement."

Over by the wall, a couple of the slightly relieved-looking councillors started to edge away from it. Arnold turned back to them sharply "And where do you think you are going? You will all remain against this wall until Councillor Reid has done what she has promised to do."

Chloe, Spencer, Maxwell. None of them were going to have died in vain.

TWENTY-SEVEN

"Don't get me wrong," the acting captain of the *Olympic* said when Franklin finally emerged from underneath one of the consoles on the bridge and nodded that the Koru stealth ship detector should be working, "but I can't help but feel guilty about you fixing that thing on this ship. We are right now flying as quickly as we can for safety, while I'm sure there are still many ships in the McMurdo Rift that could do with seeing that stealth ship coming."

"And assuming it's only the one stealth ship," Sarah said, nodding in agreement.

Franklin eyed Stanley, who he knew better than many of the officers on the *Olympic*, and thought he understood the subtext beneath the man's words. "You're doing the right thing," he told him. "We just need to get everybody to safety and not put the *Olympic* in harm's way by going hunting for this Koru ship."

Franklin ignored Sarah's raised eyebrow as he turned back to signal where he had patched the bulky machine into the connections for the *Olympic's* sensor array. "That was easy," he said, "I just had to patch it into an adjacent port. Now, let's turn it on, because I've got a feeling this is going to be a lot better than the one I made."

Smith smiled sadly at him, and Sarah squeezed his shoulder supportively but, as expected, he wasn't wrong, and the machine immediately came up with a projection of its effective area, which stretched nearly to the extent of the *Olympic's* sensors themselves. "Shit," Franklin breathed. When he spoke again, an involuntary bitter note had made its way into his voice. "If the *Majestic* had had this in time, then we might have been able to get us and the Zebra out of the stealth ship's way before it ever had time to shoot at anybody."

A moment too late, he realised what he had said and turned to Sarah and Engee. "Sorry, I didn't mean..."

Sarah held up a hand. "It's okay." Although it clearly wasn't okay; the pair of them looked mortified. Franklin felt like an asshole. Smith just kept looking at the display.

A sort of pulse emanated from the middle of the 3-D projection every couple of seconds, showing the regular search by the sensors for the tell-tale phase field particles that would clue them into the presence of the stealth ship. Franklin fiddled with the buttons, managing to overlay all the other sensor data from the *Olympic's* main array, including the position of other ships. The closest to them, perhaps halfway out from the *Olympic* to the maximum distance of the detector's range, was a ship named the *Ellen Austin*. For some reason, the name pricked at the edge of Franklin's mind as one he should maybe be familiar with, but it wouldn't come to him. A second ship—perhaps smaller, although the accuracy of such things on the detector's projection was not as good as it would be on the main sensor station—was some way from the *Ellen Austin* and, peculiarly, was not showing up any ID. Although not exactly common, this was not unheard of either. Not every transponder worked, especially on older ships, and some ships that were up to things that they shouldn't be just blatantly got away with switching their transponders off in the rift. There was rarely anyone around who cared. No one to police it.

Sarah noticed it. "What's that?"

Smith had noticed it too. "Smugglers, probably."

"But look," Engee said. "Not every pulse is picking it up."

She was right; the occasional pulse seemed to miss it. Stanley, who had once been the sensor operator for the ship, rubbed his chin thoughtfully and moved away to the main sensor station. "Yeah, it's probably real small," he called out. "That's some way out from the *Olympic*; so, if it's small enough, then a narrow cross-section could cause it to only be picked up intermittently."

Franklin didn't like it. "Or, it could be a ship that's designed to give a minimal cross-section," he said. Across the way, Gus came onto the bridge. "Look, it's following the *Ellen Austin*," Franklin added.

"Or, it's heading to the same destination," Stanley suggested. But, catching something in Franklin's expression, he added, "But we could try and contact them, and the *Ellen Austin* too. I doubt either will have quantum comms and they are too far for real-time, but we could message."

"Hey," Gus said, arriving to stand behind Sarah and Engee, a mountainous presence looming over them. He had washed and changed his clothes since helping out at the medical bay. he looked more like himself again. "I just went by your bar, Franklin, it's chaos in there."

Franklin shuddered, but then nodded to Stanley as he tried to stay on topic. "Might be an idea to do that."

"*Ellen Austin*," Gus said, peering over at the projection and the label of the ship they were all staring at, "sister ship to the *Carol Dearing*."

Franklin knew that name, as well. Why did he know that name?

"Very helpful, Gustav," Captain Smith said in a way that made it sound like she was placating a nosy child. "Could that be the *Carol Dearing* behind it, then?"

"The *Ellen Austin* reported the *Carol Dearing* as missing a few weeks ago," Gus told her, then shrugged. "Could be worth asking them."

"McMurdo Triangle," Franklin said suddenly and a little too loudly. "That's one of your McMurdo Triangle ships!"

"Or 'victim of the killer stealth ship' ships," Gus said, sounding a little disappointed that there might not be a sufficiently mystical and mysterious explanation for the ship disappearances after all. He signalled the projection. "Or maybe not even that in this case. Which would be a happy outcome, I guess."

As Gus signalled towards the two ships that they were all looking at in the projected image, something strange happened, almost as if Gus had done it with his casual gesture. The pale blue image of the transponder-less ship suddenly glowed violet. For a moment, Gus looked at the end of his fingers then pointed at the projection again. It pulsed a bright violet with the next sweep of the sensors again.

"Magic," Gus breathed, looking in awe at the end of his own fingers.

"Not magic," Franklin said. "Phasefield particles."

"Them too."

"Phasefield particles?" Smith repeated.

"The ones that the stealth ship gives off?" Engee added.

"Yes," Franklin confirmed. "Exactly that."

"It's trying to finish the job," Gus said. "The one it started with the *Carol Dearing*."

"Maybe," Franklin agreed.

"We need to warn them," Stanley said, taking a step towards his comms officer.

"We need to help them," Captain Smith said.

Franklin caught a deep yearning in the way she said, the need to right a particular wrong, but he shook his head. "We can't risk all the people on this ship to do that."

"And if we fly the *Nuts* after them, we'll be flying in blind," Sarah added. As much as she appeared to be pointing out a negative, Franklin thought he heard something else there. Sarah wanted to go after the stealth ship. So did he, but he was tired of getting people killed when he was trying to save the day.

"Hmm," Stanley mused. "Not necessarily. Not, um... entirely."

It was maybe a sad indictment of Franklin's instinct for self-preservation that Stanley already had him convinced.

TWENTY-EIGHT

GH-456 took his seat in the cockpit and looked out of the main viewer. There were two ships in the system. One had just arrived and was heading towards the other one, which had been there a while. He ran the ship's profile against the onboard database, even though he already knew the answer.

The new arrival had been helping with the rescue at the *Majestic*, the large passenger liner that they had hit. That strike had been the triumph of their mission, the *Majestic* having wandered conveniently into their path as they had tailed a much smaller prize. Almost too convenient. It had been sorely tempting to head back in and hit the rescuers, along with the other ship that they had initially been tailing, all sat there like the plains beasts of Home Nest, waiting to be hunted.

Yet the rescuers had sported weaponry and, anyway, their ammunition was running low. The mission was to scare the humans away but not to be seen, and never identified or taken alive. There would be one more juicy target out there, he had known it, and that juicy target, the one they now tailed, had already escaped them once when they had destroyed its companion vessel, the *Carol Dearing*.

GH-456 had not known that the *Ellen Austin* had survived until they had started tailing it. Then something else had occurred to him and he had double-checked it with his navigation officer, never one to be easily accepting of coincidence.

"Yes," the navigation officer had confirmed, "we are very close to where we hit the *Carol Dearing*."

Well, that had been a mystery. Why, weeks later, would a ship be scouring the same area where their companions had disappeared? Were they looking for them? It had not occurred to GH-456 that they would not have known that their companions were dead. Yet, would not most have flown hard for safety if they had? The crew of the *Ellen Austin* were either oblivious or they were crazy.

"Do we prepare for an attack run, Captain?" the pilot, KH-901, asked him. "The other ship is armed."

GH-456 stared at the enhanced view of the *Ellen Austin* on his screen. "Run a radiation scan on the *Ellen Austin*."

"Sir?"

"I want to know what they're doing here."

"Sir?" KH-901 repeated, clearly not in agreement with his captain, although TS-187 moved to obey.

The pilot was right, they did not have long to make their decision, vital moments slipping away from them, but he was not in charge of the ship. "Are you having a problem with your hearing?" he snarled at the pilot. It had been a good mission where they had all got on very well in the ship's cramped quarters. Brothers in arms. But he had always known that there might have to be a time when he needed to remind one or more of them of the command structure.

"No Sir," KH-901 replied smartly. Good.

"You're right, Sir," TS-187 beamed—a suck-up, that one, and capable, he might yet go far—"a long range, low-level radiation sweep is coming from the ship. They are looking for something."

"Their friends?" GH-456 wondered, speaking his thoughts when he had meant to keep them to himself.

"Maybe," TS-187 agreed.

"Do we prepare, Captain?" KH-901 said, respectful but insistent.

"Do it!" GH-456 ordered, feeling the will to do so from among his crew and his own desire not to leave any possible loose ends. "There are two ships here and we have four torpedoes left. One last run for glory."

A quiet round of cheers went around the small bridge of the ship. Despite the inability of sound to travel through a vacuum, silence and stealth, that was who they were, how they did things. A mindset.

"On-field," GH-456 said. "We hit the armed ship first, then the *Ellen Austin*. Four more torpedoes, men. Let's make them count, then we can return as heroes."

The bridge lights dimmed and various screens went dark as all the available sensor data was lost at the moment that they, in essence, began to exist mostly in an alternate dimension.

Ben pushed the curtain aside that divided the cockpit from the rest of the ship. The dangling chimes rang out as they were disturbed by his movements. The SS *Ellen Austin* had cost most of his and his wife's savings and it had always been a "fixer-upper" of a ship, one part dodgy patch jobs, one part positive thinking and as many homely touches as it took to believe that the ship was too much "theirs" to ever let them down.

It had let them come here to the McMurdo Rift to finally investigate the truth of the McMurdo Triangle. The culmination of a life's ambition. They were missing half a year of their young son's life for this, now in the care of Mandy's parents who had last looked at him like the whole thing was his fault, like he had been dragging their daughter to the far reaches of the UTC on a dangerous flight of fancy.

It *was* dangerous, and maybe the jury was still out on whether the whole damned thing was a flight of fancy, but Mandy had always as been as keen as he had. Maybe more so.

They were close to something. He had realised this even before the SS *Carol Dearing* had gone missing, although now the disappearance of Nelson, Kristin and Loki—along with their ship—hung like a cloud over all of it. They had been his and Mandy's close friends. Just as committed to their theory of the McMurdo Triangle. The continued presence of *Ellen Austin* in the McMurdo Rift had come under some debate when it became clear that the *Carol Dearing* had just vanished on them—there one moment and gone the next. It was ironic, of course, that a ship that had come to test a theory on the existence and nature of the "McMurdo Triangle" should appear to become a victim of it—this had not been lost on any of them—but, at heart, they were all scientists. Rational, methodical thinkers. But also opportunists.

And the disappearance of the *Carol Dearing* had provided an opportunity.

Yes, of course they were searching for their friends, hopeful that they might yet find them alive, even if not precisely believing it. But, if their sister ship was gone, then they were damn well going to find out why and how. They were going to find the vast power at the heart of the McMurdo Triangle,wornholemhole that they were sure existed here, which had likely taken the *Carol Dearing.* Although, how it had done so without them ever detecting it was a different matter.

They had reported the disappearance of their friends to the "authorities"—which was a loosely applied term out here on the edge of things. The official theories were catastrophic drive malfunction or pirates. The *Ellen Austin* had turned right around and returned to the last known point where the *Carol Dearing* had been, but had found any signs of what might have happened to their friends. Wreckage, of course, was a needle in a haystack in the vastness of space, even if you had a reasonable idea of where to look. It could not be ruled out. But neither, Ben knew, could a wormhole.

An alarm began to sound as Ben closed the curtain behind him, and his wife reached up and silenced it, bringing up the relevant data.

"It's a hit," she said without turning around.

"Can we tell what?" he asked.

"Consistent with wreckage," Mandy answered glumly, "but we'll have to go and fetch it to be sure."

Ben stood behind her, a breath escaping him which, it seemed, he had been holding onto since they discovered the *Carol Dearing* was missing. "So they're dead then."

"We don't know it's them," Mandy stressed.

She didn't sound like she believed her own words, but Ben still felt the need to point out the obvious. "This is pretty much exactly where we jumped from before we lost them."

"That's that then," came a voice behind Ben. It was Tariq, the third member and a former star student of

Ben's. Before all of them had joined the crazies—the fringe theorists who threw away promising careers chasing ghosts and legends.

"We don't know why—" Ben began.

"The fucking engine probably blew up when they tried to jump to lightspeed," Tariq cut in. "The odds always were that either their shitty death trap or ours would give up the ghost at some point."

Ben didn't have the words for him, could hear the despair. Months of searching and all they had to show for it were some dead friends.

"We examine the wreckage," Mandy said sternly, standing up and turning to them. Technically, Ben was the expedition leader, being the respected academic and all, but his wife's voice could always carry more authority. "Because that's what we do. We're scientists, we look for answers, we do not assume them." She sagged a little once she had finished, as if the words had taken a great effort. "And then we go home."

TWENTY-NINE

"They're in, er... stealth mode," Sarah heard Stanley's voice say through the comms system of the *Mutt's Nuts*. Despite the fact that the SS *Olympic* was currently several light years away from them, Stanley's voice was coming through in real time. The *Olympic* had slowed significantly in its flight from the McMurdo Rift in order to stay within a certain range of the *Nuts* as Sarah's courier ship raced to meet the *Ellen Austin* before its unseen pursuer caught up with it.

"Stealth mode?" Franklin scoffed from the pilot's seat of the *Mutt's Nuts*.

"I... we didn't agree on a term."

"Leave the man alone," Sarah chided from next to Franklin. Engee was behind them in the secondary weapons and sensor station. Once again, Sarah was relegated to a bit-role on her own ship, yet she didn't mind. The only pilot she knew who was better than Engee was Franklin, and Engee was a whizz on both the offensive and defensive weapon systems. Sarah was basically just there to pick up any slack.

"Where are they?" Engee asked. "Can we start shooting?"

"Easy killer," Franklin said. If Engee had any compunction about shooting at her own people, she certainly wasn't showing it. Then again, it was likely to be a "them or us" situation. It made Franklin think, not for the first time, that "our people" were not necessarily those tied to us by race or by blood.

"It looks like they're coming for you, anyway," Stanley said. His voice was coming through on a "short" range quantum communicator—which was still a very long way away—a birthday gift, apparently from his friend with the illegal set-up back on Proxima. They were not sure whether the equipment was legal or not, which was why Stanley had kept it hidden away in his quarters and never told another soul about it until now. It had needed to be hurriedly wired into the *Nuts*' power core to give it the juice it needed, and then patched into the general comms system. No one really knew its range—which had been an incredible risk for everyone getting onto the *Mutt's Nuts* to try and save the *Ellen Austin*, including Gus and Captain Smith, kitted up for a boarding action if that became necessary—but it was working so far and the *Olympic* was still well out of harm's way. So here they were.

"Oh... good," Sarah said a little unconvincingly.

Stanley called through a course correction. "Meet them head on," he encouraged. "If torpedoes are their main armament, then that will make it difficult for them. I'll tell you when they're in range of your weapons."

"Great," Franklin grumbled as he made the adjustment. "This feels like playing chicken in the dark."

The *Mutt's Nuts* continued to slice through empty space, nothing on their own sensor display, seemingly empty space in front of them.

"Okay," Stanley said, after calling another small course adjustment, "give it five more seconds and start firing."

"Can we hit them if they are in another dimension?" Engee called out.

"Maybe not," Franklin told her, "but the tear between dimensions is unstable. We may not even have to hit the ship to collapse it."

"Or that may be completely fucking wrong," Sarah complained.

"It might," Stanley agreed. "But you need to start firing. NOW!"

"Time until off-field?" GH-456 asked his pilot.

"Ten seconds," KH-901 rattled off hurriedly. "Assuming that they've held course we will be close on their port side. One-hundred and twenty-four units, no more."

"Ready sweep and targeting," he told TS-187. They would be much closer than usual, but it was necessary to hit the first vessel quickly and then fire immediately on the second vessel, the *Ellen Austin*. They could not afford to take any fire if the second salvo was to be launched fast enough, lest the *Ellen Austin* fled again. This time, they would be staying to watch its destruction, then they could finally return home victorious.

"Three, two..." the pilot counted, but he never reached one as there was a suddenly flaring of all the dimly lit internal lights, accompanied by a violent shaking that tossed GH-456 about in his seat and caused one of the crew to hit his head on the console in front of him.

"What was that?" GH-456 demanded; although it was the essential nature of being "on-field" that they had very little ability to tell what anything was. A moment later, before any of the crew could even take a guess, the ship slipped back into the regular universe. Although, this time it was not so much a "slipping" as a "tearing," and the supposedly metaphorical gap through which they returned seemed suddenly too small. A terrible noise like metal or rock scraping along the exterior of the ship filled the space and the roof right above GH-456 momentarily seemed to buckle. He cringed a little, waiting for it to give entirely and for the terrible vacuum of space to take him, but then they were through, and the artificial viewport was flaring to light.

"Watch out!" TS-187 cried. "They're coming right for us!"

Acting Captain Stanley's directions had been accurate, almost too much so. For a moment, Franklin found himself looking at an emerging ship that was coming straight for them. They were closing so fast that there was empty space in front of them one moment and a ship almost in their face the next.

His hands jinked on the controls a little belatedly because the other ship was already past them, going by a little high and to the right. They were astonishingly close in the vastness of space, yet not as near as he had thought in that fraction of a second between it appearing and passing them. The ship was small, he could tell that. Much smaller than the *Nuts*, it was narrow and long and covered in a material that was oddly reflective for a "stealth" ship.

And then it was gone again.

"I've got them, I've got them," Sarah said. "Come around, Ma-."

But Franklin was already doing that, and Sarah's instruction was cut short as the sudden g-force overwhelmed the environmental system's ability to compensate.

"You are strapped in, aren't you?" Franklin communicated to Gus and Smith, who were down in the cargo section, armed and ready to go if needed. Franklin was kind of hoping they weren't, as he had seen Gus shoot. In fact, thinking about it, it would probably have been more effective to give him a sword.

"Are they turning?" Franklin gasped.

"Not quickly enough," Sarah told him, we'll be on their back at any moment.

"I am readying weapons," Engee said.

"Do we want to kill them?" Franklin said. He did want to kill them, for the lives they had taken, for the horror they had brought. For Chloe. But the ship that they were about to get behind represented their one known contact with a superior technology that the UTC could do with getting its hands on.

They had tried and failed to perfect this type of stealth technology during the war, and, just in case the military had not managed it since, it sure would be nice to get hold of this ship intact. Franklin's mind was going back to the shield-equipped vessel he had destroyed a few months back. The Koru had too many advantages over humanity if it did ever come to war.

"If it's them or us, or the *Ellen Austin*, for that matter," Sarah put in.

"But look how poorly they manoeuvre," Franklin said, "We can outfly them easily. Engee, if I can get you close enough, do you think you can manage a disabling hit on their engines."

"And if they get their stealth up again while we're pissing about?" Sarah's voice was shrill with a sort of panic.

"This can't all be for nothing," he shot back. Then, feeling a little guilty even as he said it, Franklin added, "What came of Vik's death, huh? What did we gain?"

"Fuck you!"

"Everything okay over there?" Stanley put in hopefully.

"I'm bringing us in behind the Koru ship," Franklin went on, knowing that they would have to deal with that later. "They're straightening out, but they haven't gone stealth again yet."

"But they are lining up on the *Ellen Austin*," Sarah pointed out.

"Greedy, greedy," Franklin muttered. It would be the death of them. Or hopefully the disabling of them, at least. They should have quit while they were ahead, slipped back into their out-of-phase mode and high-tailed it out of there. Then again, maybe they had already worked out that the *Nuts* could track them.

How was this possible? They had almost collided with the other ship, and GH-456 knew that the chances of that were infinitesimal, unless... unless they had been seen before they came off-field.

What ship was this that now appeared to be fighting with them? It did not broadcast its ID as many of the official UTC ships did, although he knew that it was the same one that had miraculously turned up to rescue those aboard their previous target, and now it had apparently attempted to ram them head-on. The ship had flashed by them just now, but GH-456 and his crew had gotten a better look at it—albeit from some distance away—during their previous encounter, and it did not appear to be anything other than a small but otherwise regular freighter. It was armed, but that was far from unusual in this region of relatively unregulated space.

Indeed, the semi-lawless nature of the McMurdo Rift had provided a part of the cover for what they had been doing. They had not come to start a war—even a cog in the great machine of the Koru military, as GH-456 was, knew that much. Instead, they had come to scare the UTC—and anyone else—away from the area, to make it easier for the Koru to operate in and around the rift.

"They are turning behind us," his helmsman informed him. "A greater rate of turn than we can manage."

Well, that was no great surprise. Everything about their ship's design revolved around stealth and speed; manoeuvrability had been sacrificed for those features.

"Shall we prepare to go on-field, Captain?"

That was what they would do under any other circumstances, what they had been taught to do, because targets you cannot see or track are much harder to hit, especially in the vast distances of space. Maybe it was still the best thing to do; even if their pursuers could see them, running on-field, mostly within another dimension, might still give them cover or protection from the enemy's weapons. It was the safest course of action.

On the other hand, they still had four torpedoes to use...

THIRTY

"How soon until they are on the *Ellen Austin*?" Franklin demanded.

"Twenty seconds at best," Sarah answered. Franklin could hear the shrug in her voice, but he appreciated her attempt at an answer. "Who knows what the range on their torpedoes is?"

"They can't turn for shit," he said, "but they're quick enough and fucking crazy, cos they've gotta know we'll be on them. Can we hail the *Ellen Austin*? We must be in real-time range, and they'll be able to see them coming on standard sensors by now, even a stealth ship."

"They do not look like they know that trouble is coming," Engee observed from behind him. The stealth ship was now coming at the *Ellen Austin* from behind and to the right, gaining on it quickly, as their target lumbered along slowly as if scanning or performing some other task.

"Wanna know something weird?" It was Gus, from down in the bay.

He didn't, not really. Not right bloody now as he worked to get the most out of the *Nuts* and get Engee's weapons within firing distance of the Koru vessel. "What?"

"We're almost exactly at the coordinates where the *Carol Dearing* disappeared."

Oh, that was awful; that was fucking tragic. That might well be why the *Ellen Austin* were going so slowly. They were looking for their vanished companion, with no idea what had actually become of them, and even less that the same Koru bastards who had blown the *Carol Dearing* to bits were now bearing down upon them too. No, he probably hadn't wanted to know that after all.

"SS *Ellen Austin*," Sarah said, "this is the *Mutt's Nuts*. Please come in. You are in imminent danger."

Long moments passed with no reply. Finally, they pulled into line behind the Koru ship and were gaining on it.

"*Ellen Austin*, come in. You are about to come under attack by a Koru vessel. The same vessel that destroyed your sister ship." There was continued silence over a slight background crackle.

"Either they're not listening or the Koru are jamming them," Franklin said. It was surely too late now. In fact, just as he had that thought, the bright plumes of two torpedoes lit up and sped towards the *Ellen Austin*.

"Engee?" he roared.

"We are still beyond maximum weapon range," Engee said. Usually matter-of-fact, the Koru almost sounded apologetic on this occasion.

"Let's just make our fucking point anyway, eh?" he suggested, fearful that the stealth ship would simply slide out of existence again and, for all he knew, beyond the reach of their weapons. Or maybe he was just angry—angry that they had lost, angry that they had been unable to prevent the loss of another ship and likely more deaths.

"The torpedoes missed, Captain," reported the weapons officer, stating the obvious.

GH-456 had seen that one for himself. Usually, they would have gone back on-field as soon as the torpedoes were launched— perhaps to then stop some distance away and check the results of their efforts, as they had done with the SS *Majestic*. There had not been much chance of that with the mysterious little freighter pursuing them, but he had been determined to know that at least one of their loose ends had been taken care of.

But then their torpedoes had done something which, as far as he was aware, they had never done before. Both had slowly veered to the right, pulling an almost gentle arc that took them past the *Ellen Austin* and on towards a distant point, where both suddenly exploded. Odd though it was—the ship might have been new technology not long past the experimental stage, but the torpedoes were a barely modified version of those that had been used successfully for many years— he could perhaps have accepted it on some level, have written it off as one of those things that happened in battle... A highly unlikely malfunction. He could have lived with that if it had only been one of them.

But both?

"Load both and fire again."

"But Si-"

"Am I captain, KH-901, or not?" he bellowed.

"The ship behind will be in-"

"One more word and I will be piloting us back myself!"

"Loaded Captain," the weapons officer called out.

"Fire!" They fired again, close now as the *Ellen Austin* was going much slower than they were. In fact, they may need to... "KH-901, begin turn."

"Captain." The pilot might be insubordinate, but he knew his job and understood that they did not want to be anywhere near the shock wave that would accompany the impact of the torpedoes into their target.

However, as he watched, the torpedoes seemed to turn with them, then even more sharply, again veering away from their target.

"What...?" was all GH-456 had time to say before a compressed energy beam sliced through the ship right next to his seat, instantly killing the pilot a little way in front of him. "On-field!" he called out. "We cannot be captured."

Franklin sprang out of the pilot's chair the moment he saw that the stealth ship was hit and slowing. "Take the helm," he said to Sarah. "I'm joining Gus and Smith."

"Take the helm of my own ship," she said sardonically, "how good of you."

"You need to get us close to that ship," Franklin said. "If we can get on board it. Take control."

"That sounds suicidal to me. Remember what happened on the shield cruiser once you had scuttled that? Everyone went down with the ship. I doubt that they'll hesitate to blow that stealth ship."

"Fine," Franklin huffed. "I'll get Gus and Smith to stay."

"And take on the whole ship on your own?"

Sarah saw Franklin's shoulder's drop in an almost childish gesture, like she was trying to take his toys away from him or was telling him that it was time to come in for dinner. *Honestly*, that man once he got the bit between his teeth. He seemed to think he was invulnerable, and so far the universe had been too soft with him on that point.

When he spoke, his tone was less demanding and more imploring. Sarah wasn't proud about the fact that it gave her a small measure of satisfaction. "Just... can get us as close as you can? Come in slow from the back because their weapons are forward firing. If they had anything that shot behind, they would have used it by now."

"In a minute," Sarah replied, her tone brooking no argument. "Let's look at the *Ellen Austin* first, see if we can get their attention."

Sarah manoeuvred the *Nuts* around in front of the other ship. Up close, the thing looked like a death trap. It was an extremely old small freighter, although close to twice the size of the *Mutt's Nuts*. The hull was visibly well-patched, with no effort to repaint it—far from unusual in old workhorse ships, but the sheer extent of the patching made it a toss-up as to whether or not the majority of the outside of the ship was original. Who knew how bad the inside must be? She was worried that they might not even have comms... Or life support.

The *Ellen Austin* was going slowly enough that—with probably the best bit of piloting she had ever performed, and with bloody Franklin having already left the bridge—Sarah was able to park the *Nuts* so that it was flying backwards in front of the ship, close enough that she could just make out the narrow slit of light at the front of the cockpit. Close enough that anyone looking out of it could not miss them.

As she flew, she constantly had to correct her path, as if some gravity or other unseen force was acting upon it. She remembered the tractor beam that had pulled them into the Koru shield cruiser, although this was only the tiniest fraction as strong as that. Or the *Mutt's Nuts* didn't fly well backwards, it could also be that.

Comms crackled to life and the distorted voice of a woman came over it. "Unknown vessel, this is the SS *Ellen Austin*, please identify."

Even over the poor-quality channel, Sarah could hear a certain confusion—maybe even nervousness—in the woman's voice. "SS *Ellen Austin*, this is *Mutt's Nuts*. You haven't been answering communications and you just nearly died."

"We are a research vessel, *Mutt's Nuts*. Some of the scans we run interrupt line of sight communication." The woman made her statement in the manner of someone who was used to explaining the fact, although Sarah wasn't sure of the legality of it because continually working comms were a legal requirement as she understood it. After a pause, the woman added, "Did you just say we nearly died?"

"Yes, a Koru ship with stealth capabilities has been praying on ships in the area. Somehow four of its torpedoes missed you. Just veered right off course."

"Oh, that's what those lights were."

Sarah rolled her eyes, feeling that even if the woman had been right in front of her that she might not have been able to stop herself from doing so. Still, maybe whatever research they we doing was very absorbing. And, she remembered, they may well have been looking for their missing friends. In fact, Sarah realised, she was going to have to bring up the *Carol Dearing*.

"Is that...?"

Sarah heard the hesitation, the edge of grief in the woman's voice. "We believe they were responsible for the destruction of the *Carol Dearing*, yes."

"Oh."

It was a slightly odd reply. Disappointed, yes, but not quite the horror and grief that she had been expecting.

"Were you looking for them here?"

"Yes. And... We hoped..."

"That they were lost or broken down?"

"Or..."

"That the McMurdo Triangle had them?" Sarah offered sadly, hoping that it didn't sound like she was making light of the situation.

"Actually, yes."

Franklin hurried out of the cockpit.

"Are we going in?" Smith asked, although she spoke with her captain's voice and somehow made the question sound almost like an order. Then she added, "I want to go in if you are."

"Too right," Franklin answered, descending the steps and grabbing a suit. He knew Smith's intentions, then, and was not surprised. She had a big score to settle. Maybe he should discourage his friend, though, who was often too keen to follow him into danger. "Gus, you want to sit thi—"

"No fucking way," the big man said, cutting him off, his eyes two white circles within the darkness of the helmet that he already had on.

"They could blow that ship at any point, and they'll probably outnumber us," Franklin warned. He indicated their suits, including the one he had quickly put on in the galley. "These are not military grade suits. If we get shot in a vacuum, then it's a shitty death for us."

"I'm coming," Gus said flatly, his deep baritone voice almost threatening.

"Thought so." *I did try, Sarah,* he thought, although he also knew he was reassured that the other two were both coming. He held out a compressed energy cutter to Gus. "Swap you?"

Smith looked doubtfully between them. Franklin with the cutter, Gus with a compressed energy rifle, the same as she had, both of them brought from the *Olympic*. They were Morningstars, a line of non-military rifles that were kept on the passenger liner so that it had something better than concussion weapons to defend itself with in the unlikely event of some sort of pirate or terrorist boarding action. A decent enough weapon. "I wouldn't take that swap, Gus."

Gus grinned, however, his white teeth flashing within the helmet in the semi-darkness of the bay as he handed the rifle over.

"You haven't seen this man wield a fencing sword," Franklin said in answer to her incredulous expression as he completed the swap. "Or shoot a gun, for that matter. He's far more dangerous with the cutter. Well, to the enemy, at least."

"Asshole," Gus said, but Franklin could hear the smile in his voice.

He finished putting on his suit with practiced quickness, sealing the helmet section as Sarah came on the comms. "We've caught up to the Koru ship," she said. "They look dead in space, but I've come at them from the back like you said. It would be a lot safer to just shoot them and go, you know."

"I know," Franklin didn't have to give any further justification to offer her. She was clever enough to understand what taking this ship might mean and she had made her protests, but he was doing this.

"I'm spinning us around," she went on, "but I'm not sure if you'll be able to board."

"Why not?"

"See for yourself. Are you all suited and secure?"

All three of them confirmed that they were, and Sarah depressurised the bay, then opened the cargo door rather than the crew door, revealing to all three of them at once the crippled stealth ship that had been responsible for so many deaths. Exactly how many, they would probably never know.

"Oh," Franklin said, seeing the problem. Only half the ship was visible.

"What happened?" Smith asked.

"I don't know," Franklin answered, "Maybe it has something to do with their phase-field generator, or whatever they used to go undetected. I never actually saw Earth's version in action, so I wouldn't know."

There was a plane which, this close up, could just about be made out as an area of shimmering pearlescence. The rear part of the ship stuck out of that plane. Yet, as far as they could tell from where they stood, nothing extended out of the other side of it. There was only regular space there, as if the rest of the ship was... somewhere else?

"We can still do it," Franklin said, although his voice sounded a little high-pitched and croaky to his own ears. "We should still be able to get into the rear of the ship. But I'll go alone if I have to. I'll understand if neither of you want a part of this."

"I worked in the med bay today," Gus answered, "and the captain here..."

Smith merely nodded in affirmation of Gus' unspoken words. Both of them had scores to settle on that ship, a sense of commitment that went beyond concerns for their own safety.

"Okay," Franklin said, forcing away a gulp, "for Chloe." The three of them crossed the short expanse of space to the rear of the stealth ship. It was thin, a fraction of the width of the *Mutt's Nuts*, and, judging by what they could see of it, a little shorter too. Small for all the trouble it had caused. For the lives it had taken.

There was an otherness to the vessel that gave it more presence than its size, though. Koru ships were rarely seen and always a little different to most of the ships he knew, but this ship was something else again. It started with the odd, reflective nature of the hull, which Franklin might have expected to be matt black on a ship that did not want to be detected, or at least some sort of dull gun metal grey, but was instead almost the shining silver of polished steel or aluminium, like some of the pictures of early jet aircraft he had seen, glinting in the sun. He wondered if this was a function of the way it came into and out of the "otherspace," the thin dimension were hid to be unseen.

Aside from the engine stack on the back, its shape was almost that of a cigar, which was similar to the prototype vessel he had narrowly avoided dying on during the war. The same one that had been utterly obliterated in a live test, along with all of its crew. As the three of them landed on the hull, he wondered about the integrity of the portal that the ship was sticking out of. Could it collapse at any moment?

They landed on the port side, close to the engines, which were dark, seared as they had been by the *Nuts'* heavy CEW beam, although he could feel some of the remaining residual heat coming through his suit. "Where shall I start cutting?" Gus asked, holding up the torch.

Franklin pointed to the outline of an obvious entry hatch just a few metres further along the hull. "Let's keep it simple. Who knows what we'll come into if we cut elsewhere."

"Won't they expect us that way?" Smith asked.

"I didn't say this would be easy," Franklin replied. "But we've got a little help. You there, Engee?"

"I have you on my view," Engee confirmed. "Point defence weapons are ready to fire on your command."

"Okay," Gus said, firing up the cutter , "let's do this."

THIRTY-ONE

GH-456 came around slowly. He was cold. As a people, the Koru preferred warm climates, it was true, yet he had always been different. Indeed, his first job in the navy had been on an ice freighter, delivering precious water supplies to all the varying installations and outposts of the sprawling Koru empire.

It was a terrible job; *Enku-Mar*, was what everyone called it, referring to the wild cats found in the polar reaches on Home Nest and their famously smelly droppings. Cold, shitty work. But he had loved it and had always volunteered for extra duty in the most dangerous part of the work— loading and unloading the ice. There had been something about working so close to the vast blocks of the stuff, something about the incessant cold of the bay and its surrounding sections— as likely made cold by proximity to the vacuum as anything else—that had suited him. His superiors had taken his willingness do such work as a sign of his commitment and self-sacrifice, qualities always prized in those of a military designation, and GH-456 had soon been fast-tracked into command.

That had been a long time ago now.

This cold was unpleasant, a feeling like a thousand tiny, icy spikes jabbing at his skin. Not painful, but uncomfortable, the same sort of discomfort when an unwanted insect is crawling across your skin. He forced his eyes open, which took an unexpected amount of effort. The body of KH-901 was in front of him, slumped forward against the control panel, an ugly line seared through his back, a few blobs of dark blood floating above him. No gravity, then.

TS-187—a little to the pilot's left—was unconscious, as were the other two crew members whose positions were forward of the captain, their skin the amber-tinged grey that seemed to reflect the almost always low-lit nature of their surroundings while on the ship. He could not see any wounds. Hopefully, they were merely unconscious, as he had been.

GH-456 tried to recall the moments before he passed out, feeling the cold now intensely on the back of his head and neck. *Parnuck*. That fearful sensation of someone or something behind you that make the muscles contract and the skin itch. He turned slowly, realising that there was a faint glow just behind him, and he found himself staring right into it, memory flooding back as he saw the shimmering surface almost within touching distance behind his chair.

They had tried to go on-field after taking the hit, hoping at least to remain untouchable in that other space, yet there had been an explosion from somewhere towards the rear of the ship—he had heard it and felt the forward jolt of motion—then there had been a blinding flash of light.

Moving into the other dimension, sitting just beyond the thinnest of veneers as they remained almost undetectable, was something that happened entirely outside of the ship, the barrier between the regular universe and the other place washing over its surface and reforming again behind it like an object moving through and into a bubble. They were not entirely hidden there, nor were they entirely safe or unreachable, as they kept open an all-important tether back to normal space, because the ship could not open a way back from the other side and continued always operating keep a narrow "thread" connected back to real space. All of the consequences if things ever stopped working while they were on-field. They were stuck; there was no way back.

But this... GH-456 looked again with a mixture of terror and wonder at the surface that looked like a luminescent pool on its side and completely filled the cross-section of the ship—and, he supposed, an eternity beyond it. This was unprecedented. This had not, as far as he knew, even been thought of. Had this happened because they had been hit as they attempted to go on-field, or was it something else? As far as GH-456 understood the physics of their ship and its drive, they should be vaporised right now. Atoms spread across space. And yet here they were.

Looking again at the unconscious figures around him, at the various controls, at his own hand, even, GH-456 realised that this half of the ship, at least, lay beyond the barrier behind him, some "other" place. Was the ship itself wedged between one existence and another? A finger in a *mitik* nest, stopping the nasty little insects from flowing out?

He shifted, carefully rose from his seat. The stealth strike ship was a cramped space. Although he could stand, walking through the ship always involved a lot of ducking, stooping and side-stepping to avoid bumping into things. GH-456 turned and looked at the barrier. He was fascinated by it, wanted to reach out and touch it, yet was equally terrified by its presence. *Why are you not dead?* his mind kept asking him over and over again, almost like it was put out by this turn of events. Easier to die than to try and comprehend this impossibility.

Morbid fascination pulled his hand forward. As he did so, it was almost as if the shimmering mass was singing to him. Was that singing, was that what it was? Or was it scre-

"Captain!" a voice hissed quietly from behind him.

GH-456 spun around, snatching his hand back in. TS-187 was looking up at him, blinking, although he was still sprawled against his console, floating just slightly above it because of the lack of gravity, but held in by a restraint. The captain moved over to his trusted sensor operator. "Slowly now," he said, although TS-187 had so far moved nothing other than his eyes and his mouth.

"Cold," he said, and GH-456 crouched down beside him.

"It will pass," he lied. "I will need you up soon so we can assess our situation, eh? See if we can get the ship going again."

"I can hear them," TS-187 wheezed, a little breath condensing in front of his lips. "They are coming."

"Hear who?" GH-456 asked. He looked around, wondering if the other ship that had been their undoing was still coming for them, if the sensor operator had glimpsed some vital information on his instruments.

TS-187's eyes fixed on the barrier that bisected the ship. "They are in there," he said.

GH-456 turned to see if he could wake the other two in the front section of the ship with him, reaching out for the weapons officer first. Shaking the man did nothing and, feeling the back of his neck, he realised that he was ice cold.

"Can you not hear them screaming?" TS-187 said, as the captain reached out to the other crew member, who was equally cold, equally dead. He now noticed, on the floor, one of the ship's engineers, or at least his shoulders, head and some of an arm, as he had been dissected by the barrier. There was, however, no blood. Looking up again at the shimmering light— at once unobtrusive and at the same time magnificent—GH-456 could hear the singing. Melodic at first, but the longer he heard it, the more he agreed with the sensor operator. It sounded like wild, distant screams coming closer, echoing through a thin but impossibly long chamber.

A compressed energy beam suddenly lanced through the middle of the opaque layer, coming close enough to slightly singe his uniform, although it didn't actually pierce him. "What the...?" he said, staring into the surface as if it had answers, and all the while the distant screaming drew just that little bit closer.

Franklin drew back in behind the bulkhead, his shot having missed its intended target. They had discovered that the surface of the ship had been almost paper thin and easy for Gus to cut through, so that they had been inside it in mere seconds, but this bulkhead, at least, looked a little thicker, and he hoped it would give some cover as the ship's crew returned fire.

Gus had put down two crew members at close quarters as they entered close to the rear of the ship in what appeared to be a cramped engineering section, even by the standards of the smaller Koru people. More crew members had found firing positions further along the small cylinder of the ship, and now they were at a stalemate, pinned down and with little cover if they advanced, as there was only really a narrow gangway down the middle of the ship.

"Engee," Franklin said into the comms, "you think you could put a shot or two in to discourage them? They have us pinned."

He could see where the strange, pearlescent plane bisected the "KorU-boat," as Gus was calling it, a little beyond where most of the defenders were hunkered down behind chairs and jutting bits of equipment and consoles.

Several quick beams from the point defence weapons cut into the ship at about a forty-five-degree angle. A relatively weak beam like the one used on the point defence weapons would usually take a second or so—in some cases maybe even more—to go through the thickness of a ship's hull—but the thin exterior of the Koru ship offered no resistance, as had been the case with the cutter. The shots didn't hit anybody, but they got the defenders' attention and both Franklin and Smith used the opportunity to rush forwards, stooped as they rushed to find a better angle on the Koru in their hiding place behind seats and equipment.

They each shot one of the defenders and Franklin targeted another who was running back towards the shimmering plane, holding out a hand in a "stop" gesture, hoping that he could stop the killing but without any air or linked communications to carry his words. The crew member fired his weapon as he ran. It was a random, inaccurate effort, surely meant to cover his retreat rather than hurt anybody. He got lucky, however, and Smith went down with a yelp that Franklin heard in his helmet, clutching at her right side. Instinctively, he shot at the fleeing Koru, catching him in the back as he fell through the barrier.

"I've got you," Gus said, hurrying over to Smith and producing a contracting patch that would seal the damage to the suit. "Maybe we should retreat. We tried but there could be anything waiting for us past that barrier. If going through it doesn't kill us."

Franklin walked up to the strange division in the middle of the ship; a foolhardy thing to do that made him vulnerable if compressed energy shots started lancing through it. What was it? Why was it here? Earth scientists had created a way through into a parallel dimension and had tested it in the vacuum of a facility, but never made it work in the "real world" conditions of space before the Koru entry into the revolutionary war changed everything. All resources had been moved into making and improving the weapons and technologies that already worked, although it ultimately did not prove to be enough.

Was this that gateway into an "other" space? Or had they stumbled into something else?

"Franklin!" Gus barked in the comms. "Did you hear me? We should go."

Franklin was captivated by it. Mesmerised, perhaps. He really, really wanted to touch it, to see what lay beyond it. And there was something else, quiet but clearly held inside his helmet. A sound like singing.

GH-456 saw his propulsion tech, EN-808, burst through the barrier and his fluid helmet automatically melted away, no longer held to its form by the vacuum, which the captain therefore now knew existed in the rear section of the ship.

"What is happening?" he asked. "Is the rest of the ship still intact back there?"

EN-808 looked around in apparent confusion for a moment, staring back at the shimmering plane behind him for a moment. "Singing?" he asked, falling into GH-456's arms and enabling the captain to see where he had been shot in the back. "And..."

"Screaming," GH-456 finished for him, "I know. But tell me, do the humans have control of the ship back there?"

EN-808 looked into his captain's eyes and nodded, while GH-456 lowered him into a seat as best he could, encouraging him to. "I'm sorry, Captain."

Koru military protocol dictated that he should reprimand EN-808 for fleeing in the face of the enemy, but there was little point in that now. "We need to scuttle the ship then."

"Engine... dead," TS-187 wheezed from behind where the captain stood. The sensor operator had managed to reach something akin to a sitting position, helped by the lack of gravity, but he did not look any better. In fact, he looked on the edge of death and the amber in his skin had taken on a more muted tone. Passing through the barrier with his skin exposed to it looked to have killed him as it had the others who had been in the front of the ship— save for the pilot, who had already been killed by fire from the enemy ship. All had been killed by it except for the captain, who had felt no more than a numbing, writhing coldness. It had not killed him, and he did not know why for sure, although he thought again of his time moving ice in the coldness of the vacuum.

GH-456 looked at the barrier, both awed by it and in fear of it. "Yes, the self-destruct needs the engines, or access to them at least," he agreed with TS-187. "But we can rerun and overload the field routine from here."

Neither of the mortally wounded crew members with him said a thing, although he fancied he could see agreement in their eyes.

GH-456 closed his own eyes. He could hear the voices more clearly now, coming from where the shimmering edge of reality bisected the ship. It was neither singing nor screaming, he now realised. This sound, whatever it was, was something else. Something unknown and terrible. It was inside his head, he realised, rather than heard by his ears. Yet no less real for that. "If this is a gateway between dimensions," he told them, "then we must close it. If it is something else…"

Same answer. And, either way, the humans could not be allowed to have their technology. Not at this time.

GH-456 turned back to the console. Unseen behind him, fingers appeared from the middle of the shimmering gateway.

Franklin pushed his hand into the shifting, pearlescent layer in front of him, a sight a little like a rippling, moonlit pool, he thought. He could feel the cold inside it through the material of his suit.

It was an exceptionally stupid thing to do. For one thing, he was probably about to get shot at any moment—but there was always a part of him that had to know, that needed to stick his nose in. And it was always the Koru technology, be it impossibly large mother ships, shield cruisers or stealth... er, KorU-boats. But this, he was realising, was something else.

Franklin knew it the moment he touched it. This was not barrier between dimensions that the stealth ship had been hiding behind. Or not *only* it. They had run into something else here. Something huge and terrible. Not in visible size, perhaps—seen from outside of the ship, it was less than twenty metres across. Yet it felt, as his hand slipped further inside of it, Franklin felt connected to a yawning vastness that existed within that thin barrier.

The desire, the pull to step into it was almost a physical one. The noise was filling his head now. Not coming from the comms speakers, he realised, but more clearly inside his head for every centimetre of his hand that slipped out of view. Suddenly, the shimmering vertical pool convulsed and seemed to shove him backwards onto the floor. He landed on his back. "You alright?" Gus asked, looking down at him.

Franklin scrambled to get to his feet again, noticing that the whole of the ship was vibrating. "We need to go."

"Uh-huh," Smith agreed, "we've been trying to tell you that, but you had to stick your hand in the cookie jar."

Franklin glanced at it as it continued to convulse. *That wasn't me, was it?*

"Guys," Sarah's voice came over the comms, "something weird's happening."

Another time, maybe Franklin would have complained that she needed to be more specific, but he could still feel the sensation of when he had touched the plane between realities, and yes, he could imagine that "weird" covered it. "We're coming. Be ready to burn it once we're aboard."

"So you're not taking the ship then?"

"Nope."

"Good. The more I'm looking at it, the more it's freaking me out."

"I am getting out of freak too," Engee's voice piped in from the *Nuts*.

Franklin stopped at the door, glancing back to the scene inside. The barrier convulsed and roiled. For a brief moment, it almost seemed to reach out for him, covering half the distance in an instant, streaming across the vibrating ceilings and the space between, images appearing for the briefest blink of an eye in the middle of it. Franklin felt like he was looking down a long tunnel, peering through a telescope and seeing a space many light years away. Whatever this was, it was more than a barrier between dimensions, but more like something that connected the spot where they were to distant parts of space.

Then, a fraction of a second later, the space in front of Franklin was empty, the barrier back in the middle of the ship again, bubbling and swirling angrily as if nothing else had happened. It seemed like the moment before was no more than a false memory, like something imagined in the corner of vision, even though he had been staring squarely at it.

Franklin followed the others through the hatch and was away quickly.

"Nearly there," Gus said encouragingly to Smith, bringing Franklin from his thoughts, which were lingering on his vision back in the ship. The open rear doors of the *Nuts* quickly grew big in front of them. There was a flash from behind, blindingly bright like that of a nuclear detonation and, as it faded, a sort of ripple went past, momentarily bending everything it washed over like the refraction of a rock in water lapping on a shore. Then they were in the bay of the *Nuts*, the doors closing behind them.

"Fuck me!" Gus whistled, panting and lying on his back. "You good, Captain?"

Franklin looked across to where Captain Smith was lying on her back, Gus on her other side. Franklin had landed hard and mostly on his face, and he shook his head trying to clear it, while willing his limbs back into movement. It was too dark to properly see her face inside her helmet,

"Captain," Franklin said when they heard no response from her. "Kate, are you good?"

THIRTY-TWO

As Gus walked into the cramped confines of the cockpit on the *Mutt's Nuts*, Engee noted how Gus' reassuringly big frame made the space feel even smaller.

"How's she doing?" Mark Franklin asked. Captain Smith was on a makeshift hospital bed in the galley.

"Still unresponsive," Gus replied. "The med bay on the *Olympic* will have better facilities, though, so maybe it can tell us more about why. She's not bad physically, considering that she was shot and then suffered a hard landing down in the bay. She's just—"

"Not there," Franklin finished.

Engee felt she understood this turn of phrase, as she was getting better at the comprehending the varying literal, not-quite literal and not at all literal human uses of speech. Mark Franklin was referring to Captain Smith's personality, her ability to communicate, which was considered as integral to Captain Smith's—and any human's—identity as their physical presence. If her own people made such a distinction, it was as these states related to "useful" or "not useful." Although, the Unbound, the rebel group that Engee once led, had toyed with ideas of individual consciousness, it had been hard to understand until she lived among humans.

"It's my fault," Franklin went on glumly, his eyes on his feet as he sat in the third seat—the main weapon station when it was needed for that. They were on the way back to meet up with the SS *Olympic*, so had no more expectation of danger from unseen stealth ship, unless there were more out there. They had the quantum communications device, however, and she assumed that the *Olympic* was continuing to run its scans with the official detector that she and Sarah—and Nigel, Engee supposed—had delivered to Captain Smith. "If I hadn't been messing about with that gateway or whatever it was," Franklin added, explaining the guilt he apparently felt over Captain Smith's condition.

"Rubbish," Sarah told Franklin, showing her support.

"Come on, man," Gus pitched in.

"It might be your fault," Engee observed, earning a sharp look from Sarah that she studiously ignored. "But there is no way of accurately calculating it."

Sarah spoke softly to her pilot. "That's not helpful, Engee."

"Why not? Guilt is a terrible emotion. If I am going to feel guilty, I want to be sure about it." She looked Franklin. "You should not feel guilty."

He looked up, managed a small smile.

"Unless you feel guilty for making them go on the stealth ship in the first place. That was without a doubt your fault. Ow!" Sarah had punched her in the arm. "What was the reason for the personal assault?"

"I wonder if the phenomena we encountered on the ship was the same thing that made their torpedoes miss?" Franklin wondered out loud. "I know that the *Majestic* was a bigger target and that the Koru stealth ship wasn't being chased at the time, but all three torpedoes struck home then. What were the chances that four would miss the *Ellen Austin*?"

"The *Ellen Austin* said that they and the *Carol Dearing* were investigating unusual gravitational anomalies in this part of the rift," Sarah said. "Including the possibilities of wormholes."

Engee scoffed. "Wormholes are only theoretical."

"I would have been right there with you, Engee," Franklin said. "But there was something very strange about that thing that was stuck through the middle of the Koru ship."

"Was it not a side effect of stealth technology?" Engee asked. "Something that went wrong, perhaps because we shot them as it was activated?"

"I thought so," he replied, "when I first saw it. But..."

Engee thought she saw something unfamiliar in Mark Franklin's face. It was a look that she associated with fear.

"Go on," Sarah said.

"It felt like being connected to a distant place. And there were... voices. But at the same time they weren't."

Gus put a hand on Franklin's shoulder. "Way to be cryptic, buddy."

Franklin shrugged. "If it was a gravitational anomaly, like a wormhole, would it not have pulled us inside if we were that close to it?"

"I remember how poorly the *Mutt's Nuts* handled," Sarah said. "When we spoke to the *Ellen Austin* and they told us what they were doing, I assumed it was something to do with the scans they were running. But it did feel like being pulled."

Franklin grinned. "You mean when you were flying backwards? That must have been something to see."

Engee saw the rosy points on Sarah's pale cheeks grow a little bigger for a moment. "What if the effect you saw was a combination of both things?" Engee asked Mark Franklin. "The stealth device malfunctioning and the presence of a wormhole nearby?" She sighed. "Although I am still having trouble with the idea of a wormhole at all."

Franklin shrugged. "A mystery, I guess. Like the one where the UTC had a full-on phase-field particle detector ready to go."

"The UTC?" Sarah said. "Even if the UTC built it, then I don't think they sent it."

"The people who hired us and hired Nigel were not official UTC," Engee added.

Gus grinned that silly but endearing grin of his. "Thicker and thi-"

He was interrupted by an alarm from the illegal quantum communication device that had been supplied by Captain Stanley's friend. All of them stared at it for a moment, thinking that his using it again could only mean one thing: danger.

"*Nuts?*" Sarah said.

"Hello, Sarah," came the familiar voice of the *Olympic's* acting captain, "It's Stanley. Are you all together?"

"Yes. All apart from Captain Smith, who is still unresponsive, I'm afraid."

All the eyes in the room looked at each other.

"Okay. I'm sending media through to you. I thought you might want to see this straight away."

"Go ahead," Sarah replied after a moment, with an undercurrent of: *So we're not about to get shot by another Koru stealth ship then?*

A picture popped up on the enhanced viewport, which gave the scene on it a grand, almost cinematic look.

The picture showed an official UTC background and a woman appeared in the ceremonial garb of the council on Proxima. She looked to be in her fifties at least, with short, dark hair. "Who is that?" Engee asked.

"Councillor Reid," Sarah said. "Deputy on the council. Which makes me wonder where Hawthorne, the council leader, is."

The woman had a slate in her hands, which she glanced down at as she began to read. "My name is Councillor Reid. I am acting head of the UTC Council. For the continued good and security of the United Terran Colonies, I am hereby, in sound mind and with the authority invested in me, dissolving the council by unanimous vote."

"What the...?" Sarah reacted out loud. "Why?"

"It has been deemed that, in the face of an increasing threat from the Koru Empire, the council is not capable of taking the required actions to defend its people.

"As such, I am ceding power to a military coalition until such time as the threats to our union can be dealt with and neutralised."

"Anyone else thinks she looks fucking terrified?" Gus said.

Engee agreed, Councillor Reid did not look pleased to be making her announcement.

"Coup," said Franklin "That's what's happening, there's been a bloody coup on Proxima, Shit, and poor Arnold's there."

A moment later, the camera panned out and a familiar man in uniform was sat beside the councillor. "My name is Rear Admiral Philby and it is my grave responsibility to speak to you all today, but also my great honour to lead you in the fight that must come."

"Hmm," Sarah said, turning back to Franklin. "What were you saying about Arnold?"

Mark Franklin and Gus had both left the *Mutt's Nuts* moments after arriving back on the SS *Olympic*. Gus had accompanied Captain Smith to the medical centre, while Mark Franklin had headed to the bridge to speak to the ship's acting captain, Stanley. Presumably, he would also be keen to get back to his bar and to his cat, Geoff.

Engee and Sarah had stayed on the *Mutt's Nuts*. There was much to do and to check after all the stresses the ship had been put through. And Sarah, Engee noticed, seemed quiet and—what she supposed to be—contemplative.

"It looks like there might be war," Sarah said after returning from a visual inspection the ship's exterior, while Engee had been running a diagnostics check on the environmental systems, "if Arnold Philby gets his way."

Engee was quiet for a moment as she considered her reply. "Is he grieving over the loss of his niece, Chloe? I heard Mark Franklin say that he thinks Rear Admiral Philby feels guilty, because he got her the job on the Majestic."

"This could be right," Sarah replied. "But I also think that he has unfinished business with the Koru, or at least their military forces. Are you worried about a war?"

"I am worried the UTC will lose very quickly," Engee replied. War worried her in many ways, yet the strongest feeling she had on the subject was a sense that humanity would be starting a war it could not win.

"I didn't mean that. I mean that things will become a lot more dangerous for any Koru if we are at war. There is always a place for you on my ship, Engee. But it might not end up being safe for you."

"It will not be safe for me on Home Nest, or anywhere else in the Koru domain. Although..."

Sarah nodded for her to continue.

"It may be time for me to... how do you say it? ...Look up old friends."

"The Unbound?"

Engee nodded. She enjoyed the human gesture. "If they still exist in any form. I do not know what was taken from my head by the machines of the intelligence services on Home Nest. For all that has come back to me since, I do not remember any details of my interrogations there. For all I know, I gave them up."

Engee shuddered a little before she went on. "I told myself that not contacting them was for their safety. That I was tainted and a danger to them. But it was also because I feared finding out that they were all gone, perhaps all dead or worse because of me."

Sarah took her hand in a reassuring gesture.

"But if war really is coming, now is the time to see if there are any of us left."

An alert from the bridge interrupted them and Sarah answered. "*Mutt's Nuts*."

"Mrs Shah?" came the familiar voice of the acting captain, although he was speaking in hushed tones. "We have an encoded message that has come through our quantum system for you."

"Oh," Sarah said. Yes, Engee thought, that is interesting.

"I know. I have moved to my office to send this through to you, and I am going to purge it from our records as soon as it is sent. The only quantum comms coming out of Proxima are essential transmissions, and they are all being routed through fleet. This... well, it is from Centauri system, but it is not official."

"Who sent it?"

"Don't know; don't want to know," he said, and sent the message through.

An elderly woman appeared on the view port. She had a regal bearing about her. Or perhaps just an air of entitlement. "Mrs Shah. My name is Dame Hatherleigh and, although you were not aware that you were working for me, your inventively named ship recently completed a contract on my behalf. Under difficult conditions, I believe.

"We were too late to save the *Majestic*, and this was our fault, not yours... Miscommunication about the urgency of the situation, not to mention squabbles over who was to carry it. I would like to clear up any confusion in this regard and place you under retainer, if you will accept, for possible future deliveries.

"We are in dark and dangerous times and what I am asking could prove to be dangerous work. The SS *Majestic* was sent to the McMurdo Rift for the express purpose of being destroyed at the hands of the Koru stealth ship. The faction that has now taken control of the government on Proxima knew it was there and they needed a pretext to send military forces to the region, with the intention of further escalating tensions towards conflict. Even I did not know that they would resort to a coup, however. At least, not this soon."

"I wonder if Arnold Philby knew that about the *Majestic*," Engee wondered out loud.

"Surely not," Sarah replied, although her voice was peculiarly strained, like she could not accept the other line of thinking. "The *Majestic* was already here before he left."

"You cannot reply to me, and it may be difficult for us to send a message again for some time," Dame Hatherleigh went on. "I will understand if you do not accept this, and I will be in contact when I can to get your answer. In the meantime, please tell no one about this message and delete it when you are done."

It seemed like the message was finished and Dame Hatherleigh stood still for a several seconds, then she looked upwards slightly, as if considering something. "I know you have an association with Mark Franklin. I am not sure which side of this debate he will fall, but if you think he can be trusted, then I leave that to you."

She stared hard into the camera. "We are few, but we are well-resourced and influential. And we will not allow the UTC to be run by a military junta hell-bent on a vengeful war. We must not allow that."

THIRTY-THREE

"Are we ready to go?" Tariq asked, sliding back the curtain that separated the sensor and monitoring area from the ship's cockpit. Once, all of it would have been a bridge and, despite all the modifications they had made to the ship since buying it, the partial walling-off of the flight section at the front had been an inexplicable and seemingly pointless change made before their purchase of the corroding hulk they currently called home. Their folly, it had turned out.

The mood had been muted since the *Mutt's Nuts* left. They had watched at a distance as the little freighter approached the stricken Koru ship. The *Ellen Austin* had thrown every sensor they could at the strange spectacle of the ship that seemed to have been stuck halfway between where they were and some other place. The data had been inconclusive as to whether it could be described as a "wormhole," but it had been the closest evidence they had found in all their months in the area.

So they had stayed and continued to monitor. No longer looking for their friends, of course. It seemed almost definite that the Koru ship had destroyed the *Carol Dearing,* but they could spare a few more hours to try and understand what they had seen for those minutes before the Koru ship destroyed itself.

"Yep," Ben said in answer to Tariq's question. No point in putting it off any longer. Except... "What you doing, honey?"

Mandy had turned the ship and was heading slightly away from the area where they had encountered the *Mutt's Nuts* and the strange Koru ship several hours before. When she didn't answer, Ben stepped up to her shoulder. "You alright?"

She had that fixed, concentrated look that she would sometimes get. "Something the *Mutt's Nuts* said earlier on just bothered me," she said at last.

"Uh-huh?" Even Ben, whose patience with his clever, capable, go-getter wife was usually boundless, wanted to get going, to put the fucking shit-hole rift behind them. To figure out how they were ever going to put their life together again.

"She said that the torpedoes, the four that missed us, just turned away. It didn't really register at the time, but she sort of made a point of it."

"Yeah," Ben agreed listlessly, "it was a gravitational anomaly."

Mandy half-turned back to him. "Think, Ben," she chided. "You're a clever man but you miss the obvious details." Harsh, but he was used to it. "The Koru ship would not have ended up where it was until after it shot at us. At best, they were on the edge of its area of effect. But, looking at where they came in from and where we would have been when they fired..."

"Come on, Mands," Tariq said. Ben never liked Tariq's not exactly abbreviated name for his wife. "There's nothing out there."

He was irritating but he was also correct. "The sweep still showed nothing as the continued on.

"Shut it, Tariq," Mandy said in a way polite, reasonable Ben never could have, even to a man he had spent months shut in the same giant metal box with. "We've been operating on the theory that a directed energy sweep will reveal them," Mandy went on, but what if they are only activated by an intense burst of energy, and what if the manner of their activation depends upon the level energy they receive?

"Assuming the Koru ship activated its stealth drive right with a large amount of power on the edge of the wormhole and it got a small effect."

Ben—clever but not always "quick"—picked up on where his wife was going with all this. "So, maybe the energy from the propulsion system of a torpedo creates enough of a gravitational effect closer to the centre of a wormhole to turn the path of the torpedo?"

"Yep," Mandy said. "But we were moving so slowly through that area earlier on that, even if our engines did have an effect, it was probably nowhere near enough for a big ship like this to actually feel it."

Tariq—on his day probably the sharpest mind in the ship—finally decided to contribute. "So, if I concentrate everything the Hawking Array puts out over a whole search area as close as I can to the point where the missiles supposedly turned away from us...?"

No one agreed with him, they didn't have to. Tariq was already moving back to the huge bank of sensor controls as they neared the point where they had been a couple of hours before. It didn't take long.

"Look!" Mandy called out, and the two men did as they were told. The sight in front of them, seen with their own eyes and without an enhanced view, was almost as colourful as the graphic display now showing over at the sensor station. Vaguely similar to the thing that the Koru ship had been wedged through, yet large and much more vibrant, its pearlescence shimmering with colour. "This is it, Ben, we've found a wormhole."

Ben sat down next to her. "Great, let's back up and get some readings."

She looked at him, then back and up at Tariq. "I can't," she said, gently shaking the controls for effect, "it's pulling us in. Like it should do, I guess."

Inside the ship, everything seemed to stretch for a moment, time almost suspended and every molecule of their being became vast and long and full of colour.

Then the *Ellen Austin* was gone.

Want to find out how Vik ended up on Enceladine?

Sign up for the newsletter at www.BradleyLejeune.com to download the short story "Withdrawal."

Afterword

We hope you enjoyed this book just as much as we enjoyed writing it.
We just wanted to take a moment to encourage you to review the book. Follow this link: The McMurdo Triangle to be directed to the book's Amazon product page to leave your review.

Each review helps other sci-fi fans discover new books to enjoy.

Acknowledgments

Martin would like to thank:

Shanon, writing under the pen name S.D. Huston for her continued support and for saving our bacon.
Alex, Chris, Boter, and Bethany, the best Betas in the land.
The Youtuber known as 'Shivering Cactus' who helped me with that planet on the front of the book.
and of course Mrs Lejeune and PtC.

Malcolm would like to thank:

As always, thank you for the love and support of my wife and children. My parents, for encouraging me to do what I loved, and Aunty Lyn for always taking an interest, even in that first terrible book all those years ago.
This book is dedicated to the memory of Stuart Bentham, AKA Uncle Roy. For a long time, the only other writer I knew.

About The Author

Bradley Lejeune is the ingeniously abbreviated combination of writers Malcolm Bradley and Martin Lejeune.

Malcolm has worked for eight years as a freelance ghostwriter, while Martin has a background in filmmaking and visual effects.
They figured that attempts to forcefully join their various talents with one another might result in some good books. Or crimes against nature... Only time will tell.

Martin loves graphic design, reading sci-fi, and he dreams of one day visiting Mars. When he can do it in a long weekend.

Malcolm is a total fantasy nerd with a leaning toward horror, who identifies a little too strongly with zombies. They met far too many years ago while working in a cinema together. Except that they talked about movies and never did any work.

Printed in Great Britain
by Amazon